A Brief, Fleeting, Almost Impossible Gift

By Karaya Vega

Sphinx Moth Press

karayavegawriter@gmail.com

sphinxmothpress@gmail.com

Paperback ISBN 978-1-7357832-3-9

Ebook ISBN 978-1-7357832-1-5

Chapter 1

When Dad sold one of the apps he'd been developing in his free time to the big tech company for ten million dollars, I knew my life would change, but not quite like it ended up changing. We moved to the big island of Hawaii, to this little neighborhood near the sea called—I kid you not—Hawaii Paradise Park, where the houses all overlook the jungle, and the sea is just a 15-minute walk from our front door, if you're walking fast. These days, I can't walk very fast, and the walk takes me more like 30-minutes on a good day, but I don't really want to think about that today...

When we first moved in, the house honestly gave me the creeps, not in a haunted house kind of way, but in the way a place feels when you know it's the last house you'll ever live in.

This is the last house my parents will ever live in. And this is the last home I will ever live in.

I know this because Dad said so himself after he bought it with cash while we were staying at the Four Seasons in Kailua-Kona. I thought the trip to Hawaii had been a vacation to celebrate the fact that Dad finally sold the app he had been working on, basically since I was born. I thought we'd spend a lot of time by the pool or the beach, eat a lot of fancy food, and maybe I'd get a massage or two with Mom to celebrate the fact that we weren't going to be poor anymore. I figured that by the end of the week, we'd fly back to Oregon, drive back to our little apartment in Gresham, and talk about maybe buying a bigger house closer to downtown Portland—maybe a place with a fenced-in yard near the rose garden, or a nice park.

What I hadn't anticipated was Mom and Dad coming back from what they told me was a date night to Volcano, with Mom holding a thick file folder of papers under her arm.

For a second I thought they might be getting a divorce. My parents didn't really fight, but you never know. I'd had a few friends who were blindsided.

But Dad got down on his knees, took my hands, and said, "Maya, we now own a house in Hawaii!"

While I wasn't particularly happy about the idea of moving, I never really liked winter. I knew I'd be able to keep up with my best friend, Tay, over Zoom. We were both going into our senior year and had already been drifting apart—her looking into Ivy League schools and scholarships—me daydreaming by the pool, wondering whether I'll ever be kissed.

The move happened faster than I anticipated. Mom and Dad broke their lease in Gresham the day after we came back, and sold or donated our furniture the week after. We gave all our winter clothes to the Salvation Army, and by the end of the month, I found myself standing at PDX, holding two large bags that contained what remained of all my earthly possessions.

"You can buy all the new clothes you want in Hawaii. You won't be needing any sweaters there, that's for sure. I'll give you your own credit card. You can go crazy," Dad said, seeing my hesitation when I put the last of my sweaters in the donate pile.

"Are there even malls on that island?" I asked. It was a legitimate question. The Big Island, was a rural island compared to other islands in the island chain of Hawaii. If O'ahu is the New York City of Hawaii, Big Island is so far upstate it might as well be Canada. When people think of Hawaii, they most often think of O'ahu, with the turquoise waters of Waikiki Beach, the hotels, and Diamond Head behind it. People think of O'ahu as being the biggest island, but even though O'ahu had a much larger population than the Big Island, the Big Island is a much bigger island in terms of square miles.

I knew O'ahu had malls. Big Island–I wasn't so sure about.

"I know there are shopping centers!" Dad quipped cheerfully.

"No, you don't," I whispered, under my breath.

Dad pretended not to hear.

The fact that Mom and Dad bought the house in Hawaii without getting my input had been the subject of all our recent fights. Mom and Dad claimed that they wanted it to be a surprise, but I know that they just didn't want to have to hear me whine about missing my senior year of high school or leaving Tay behind. That part bothered me less than not being able to get input on the house. At the end of senior year, I knew that Tay would be going to some fancy college in California or to some ancient college on the East Coast. Tay was in the running for valedictorian along with another twenty kids enrolled in basically every Honors and AP class our mediocre high school had to offer.

My grades, however, left something to be desired by most college admissions officers' standards, and I figured that my prospects would have likely been a community college closer to home. Moving to Hawaii with Mom and Dad just moved the timeline of our separation by a year and gave me a small win; I would get to go on a cool adventure a whole 12 months before Tay would even start hers.

What I wasn't happy about was that Mom and Dad basically chose to live in the shadow of a volcano in the middle of the jungle, when we could have moved to O'ahu, where there was at least some semblance of civilization in the form of malls, streetlights, and yes, I'm going to say it, hot surfer guys. It also didn't help that they chose to move us in the middle of the summer, before the school year started, which meant that I'd have to wait a whole two and a half months before school started, and I could make any friends.

"We'll fly Tay to visit for July. I'll talk to her mother," Mom said, cheerfully, but I knew that the chances of Tay's mom letting her fly to Hawaii were basically zero, especially given the fact that Tay was scheduled to spend all of July attending Columbia University's summer program studying Public Affairs and Sustainable Futures.

I resolved myself to spend the summer working on my tan, so that I could maybe try to get myself a boyfriend when school started. Even though I complained to Mom and Dad constantly about the move, I was secretly a little excited about the idea of getting a fresh start, especially in the guy department. I'd known most of the boys in my high school since we were basically Kindergarteners. I'd seen them pick their noses and poop their pants. There was no mystery there, no danger, and no vampire vibes (not that I'm into that sort of thing).

I imagined who I would become in Hawaii. Would the pale nerdy girl with shoulder-length auburn hair who liked to read thrillers late into the night transform into some tanned surfer mermaid with a toned belly? Unlikely. The idea of wearing a bikini still mortified me, and the actuality of wearing one, the one time I had left me hunched over with crossed legs on a lounge chair at the Four Seasons, checking to make sure that I didn't accidentally flash everyone by moving the wrong way. I imagined myself maybe getting dread locks. Maybe buying a bunch of those baggy, colorful pants, and shirts covered in Buddhas and Sanskrit that they sold at Thai and Indian shops. Maybe I'd join a drum circle or volunteer at an organic farm. Maybe I'd meet some cute hippie guy who made ceramic pottery at the farmer's market, and we'd live happily ever after.

With the whole Pacific between me and who I used to be, anything seemed possible.

And I was admittedly not just a little excited to live in Hawaii. I mean, it is *Hawaii,* after all. And, yes, the idea of getting free, or almost free, rein of Dad's newly minted no-limit credit card didn't sound too shabby either.

And yet, not long after we'd moved into the new house, not long after I'd unpacked the few summer clothes I'd chosen to keep for the move and hung up the framed photo Tay and I had taken at the rose garden last summer, a cloud of fatigue settled into my bones. It felt as if the house itself held exhaustion within it, as if the thick humid air of the jungle was some soporific that left me feeling tired even when I slept in way until noon. I'd collapse in my bed in the middle of the day, and nap for four hours straight, and then wake up, somehow still exhausted.

Mom thought I was depressed. She encouraged me to get out more and sometimes took it upon herself to wake me up herself and drive me into town—a protracted affair which took several hours, given how far away we were from *everything*.

"I've never felt tired like this," I confessed to my parents one afternoon, over my breakfast and their lunch, after Dad asked me if I'd really been sleeping up there that whole time.

"We're all still getting used to the time change," Dad chimed in my defense. It was true. Noon in Hawaii was more like 9 a.m. in Oregon time, but still, I was never really one to sleep in until the afternoon.

"Besides, it *is* summer. It's a good time to catch up on your rest. Big moves are stressful. Sleep is your body's way of healing and processing the change," Dad added.

Mom wasn't so sure. She was still worried I was depressed.

But when June slipped into July, and I still hadn't adjusted to the time change and found myself spending most of the afternoons and early evenings in bed, mom started to double down on the idea that I'd become depressed and needed to see someone about it.

"Maybe I should make an appointment so you can talk to someone. Moves like this can be hard on a teenager," she said one late afternoon, when I stumbled down to the dinner table, feeling dizzy as I made my way to the heaping plate of spaghetti mom had set down for me, but found myself unable to take a single bite.

I'd had a dark feeling deep in the pit of my stomach that the fatigue wasn't just due to the time change or depression.

"Talk to someone about what?" I asked. Somewhere between sitting down and contemplating the spaghetti, I'd lost the thread of the conversation.

"About the depression, Maya."

"I'm not depressed."

But back in bed, I couldn't help but feel like something was deeply wrong with me. I felt something dark seeping into my blood and bones and brain, something mean, angry, and toxic, something that felt far worse than depression. Something horrible seemed to be working its way through me, a stark contrast to the cloud-shrouded mountains, rainbow-covered waterfalls, and perpetually sunny days.

But maybe Mom was right. Maybe I was a little depressed. I missed Tay. Between her being so busy with her Columbia Summer program and the 6-hour time difference, we hardly had a chance to talk.

"You need to put yourself out there and make new friends," mom said casually one morning as she poured me a glass of orange juice for another noon breakfast. "I hear there's an actual labyrinth not far from here. It's a replica of the 13th-century labyrinth in Chartres Cathedral in France. But instead of stone like in Chartres, it's made from plants. I hear they hold weekly circle shares there. Maybe it might be a good way to meet new people? Do you want to go with me this week?"

"No thanks, Mom. If I wanted to walk a labyrinth, I'd just ask Dad to buy me a plane ticket to France and do the real thing."

I knew I was being mean, but between the exhaustion and the displacement, I felt something mean inside me open up, and found myself surprised when I didn't resist it.

Dad spent the afternoon hammering tiki torches into the perimeter of the backyard. I sat in the hammock Dad had hung on the back porch with a book on my lap. I didn't read. I just watched him work.

Ever since Dad made all that money, he's become a total cliché. He walks around now in corny Hawaiian shirts covered in pineapples. He's got himself a Fitbit and says he wants to train to run a marathon. He started following one of those rich billionaires who want to live forever and live off green smoothies. Any day now, he's going to walk into the house and tell Mom he bought himself a Harley. I can't think of anything more cliché than a bunch of tiki torches in our backyard, but I don't say a word. I just watched him hammer the posts into the volcanic soil and don't offer to help. Even if I wanted to help, I'm too exhausted to move from the hammock. To make matters worse, I'm getting eaten alive by mosquitoes.

That's when I get the thought that somehow brightens my mood.

Maybe I caught malaria or Lyme disease from a mosquito? It would explain the exhaustion I'm feeling. I read somewhere about this special kind of Lyme disease that's been going around, where if you get it, you get deathly allergic to meat. You can go into anaphylaxis and stop breathing if you so much as take a bite of a hamburger. I'm not too worried about that, though, because I'm a vegetarian and I don't plan on eating meat to see whether I've developed the allergy.

I got tired just watching Dad hammer the tiki torches into the ground, so I went up to bed and fell into a disturbed sleep where I dreamt of bird-sized mosquitoes eating me alive.

When I woke, it was dark, and the house was quiet, and the exhaustion sat heavily on my chest like a weighted blanket. I could usually hear Mom or Dad puttering around in the kitchen or hear the television on in the living room, but the quiet told me they'd either gone to town to get dinner or I'd woken up so late that everyone had already fallen asleep. Given my ridiculous sleeping patterns, I realized it was probably the latter.

Something about my room felt different, though.

A flickering on the walls. Fire? There's a fire outside. Even though my whole body felt like it had been weighed down with rocks, I threw my heavy, aching legs over the edge of the bed and made my way as quickly as I could to my window.

I couldn't smell smoke, so I figured it wasn't likely to be the whole neighborhood on fire.

Instead of the neighborhood on fire, I opened my curtain to a ring of tiki torches burning in the yard. The corny black metal poles with weird basket tops disappeared, replaced by twelve dancing flames that seemed to hover like a circle of will-o'-the-wisps—strange spirits holding a prayer circle in our back yard.

That's when I noticed something moving in the margins of our yard, right where the grass became jungle. At first, I thought it might be a pig—I'd heard Hawaii has a lot of wild pigs—but this thing was way bigger than a pig, more like a werewolf. But we're not in the Pacific Northwest. I know werewolves don't exist here. I found myself laughing at the thought, but then another movement near the edge of the jungle made me take a deep, trembling breath.

The shadow lurking at the edge of the light was not an animal.

It was not human either.

Whatever it was, it walked on two legs, and slouched into the darkness, carrying something heavy on its ill-formed back.

Chapter 2

I stare into the darkness, not moving, almost half-willing it to come back, half-not wanting it to come back, but nothing returns.

This is just great. Not only am I exhausted and probably have Lyme disease and that stupid allergy that makes meat deadly, but I'm also probably developing schizophrenia or some other mental health disorder that gives you hallucinations. I hear that some people with bipolar disorder get hallucinations. Maybe that's why I'm so exhausted all the time?

Maybe I have bipolar disorder, and I'm in the depressed phase of it? With bipolar disorder, you can go from being clinically depressed to being manic, a phase where you're so happy and energetic, it feels like you're on drugs. (I spent a whole evening on a Reddit thread where people posted all about the mania part in half-finished sentences.) If that's the case, I'm looking forward to the mania. I'm looking forward to losing all my inhibitions. One of the girls on the Reddit said that she lost her virginity to a guy who lived in a tent under a bridge at the park. I don't want to have sex with randos, but I'd settle for making out with a bunch of surfer guys, if I could find them. Another guy wrote about spending all his rent money on Labubus. I'd probably just end up in the one bookstore in town, spending a bunch of money on books, but even that sounds more exciting than my current, practically bedridden situation.

I've been Googling way too much all the possible causes of extreme exhaustion. I can rule out being pregnant. Unless I'm next in line to have an immaculate conception, pregnancy is impossible on account of my virginity.

A more realistic diagnosis is just a bad case of hypochondria, which I think might be, unfortunately, less treatable than the other conditions I could potentially have.

I know I should ask Mom to take me to the doctor, but the darkness working its way through me acts like a kind of force field.

The truth is, I don't want to know what's wrong with me.

It scares me.

I end up not having much of a choice, but it takes a while.

The next morning, when I stumble into the kitchen to eat breakfast, Mom says she's had enough of seeing me mope around the house. It's early afternoon already.

"We're going to walk to that Labyrinth. It's right down the street."

"Mom," I say in protest, but I know it's useless.

"It's either that or I'm booking you a session with a therapist."

"Okay. I'll go," I say warily.

The thought of seeing a therapist sounds about as exciting to me as the thought of sunbathing on a public beach in a bikini.

My legs feel heavy the whole long walk to the labyrinth, but once my body gets into motion, it seems to want to stay in motion, and I find myself feeling a little better. I don't want to admit it, but maybe Mom is right. Maybe I am a little depressed and homesick. Maybe I need to push myself to get out more, explore, try new things.

The labyrinth isn't as exciting or cool as Mom made it out to be. At first, it just looks like an empty field in the middle of the jungle, but when I notice that a little path has been cleared and that it winds and folds in on itself like the folds of a brain in anatomy books, I find that the rhythm of my feet changes the pace of my thoughts. The worry and anxiety settle a little into a buzzy peace. Every few steps, people have left offerings on the side of the path. Flowers. A heart with the word "angelic" written on it. Ti leaves folded into little green bundles line the path.

"Did you know that the Ti leaf was brought to Hawaii by Polynesian voyagers? It was, what they call a canoe plant. There were 23 canoe plants. Coconut, turmeric, bamboo, banana, even sugar cane. Most of the plants were used for food, but the Ti leaf plant was special. It was sacred. A symbol of divine power. It's used to ward off evil spirits."

The Ti plants grew on skinny stalks that blossomed into bouquets of long green leaves. Some of the leaves looked more yellow than green, and others tended toward purple.

At the center of the labyrinth, Mom and I paused and stood in silence. I would have stayed longer, but I started to feel dizzy, like I needed to sit down or I'd puke.

As we wound our way out of the labyrinth, Mom asked me if I was doing okay.

I told her I was okay. Just a little tired.

"I might be a little depressed. I think you're right about me getting out more."

"You'll let me know if it gets serious?"

"Yes," I said, not sure if it wasn't already serious.

Promise?"

"Yes," I said.

It would get serious sooner than I thought.

Because even in the calm at the center of the labyrinth, a ferocious thing had seeped into me. Even in the most peaceful moments of my life, it was working its way through my blood, into the comb of my bones, into the web of my veins, and eventually it wound its way through the labyrinth of my brain, passing through the blood-brain barrier, flowing into my spinal cord, seeping into my nerves.

I got home so exhausted I needed to take another nap. When I woke up, my pillow was covered in blood.

I wanted to scream, but the blood had trickled down my throat, and all I could do was cough, a harsh and scary metallic cough.

This is really bad.

A hot spike of adrenaline shot through my body, and I lurched out of bed, running into the hallway and then into the bathroom.

With the lights on, when I looked in the mirror, everything looked less frightening than it had in my half-awakened state. Blood on my nostrils and over my top lip, but I wasn't bleeding as badly as I thought I was. I grabbed some toilet paper, moistened it in the sink, cleaned my nose, and then sat on the toilet, pinching my nose shut with my head tilted downward.

My brain is leaking out of my nose.

Terrified, I checked the toilet paper for evidence of my demise but was relieved when I saw only a small spot of blood.

Just a nosebleed. I wasn't really a nosebleed kind of girl, but they happened from time to time, usually in the depths of winter when I'd spent too much time inside next to a heater.

Here, it was so humid it seemed kind of ridiculous that I'd get a nosebleed, but it could also probably be the stress of moving. And maybe the result of the pounding headache I developed on the walk back from the labyrinth.

But when I looked at myself in the mirror after the bleeding had decidedly stopped, I gasped.

I didn't recognize myself. Despite having moved to Hawaii, I was so pale I looked almost blue under the bright bathroom halogen light. Sure, I hadn't really spent much time outside, but not even in the depths of winter in Oregon would I have ever gotten this pale. My lips looked almost purple, and even though I seemed to be sleeping 16 hours of any given day, dark circles had formed beneath my eyes.

For some strange reason, I thought about the thing I'd seen lurking at the edge of the jungle. I couldn't shake the horrifying feeling that I was also becoming shadow-like. If I stopped paying attention, maybe I'd disappear.

"Have you guys seen any people lurking around the property at night?" I asked my parents, as casually as I could, over dinner.

"Like, trespassers?" Mom said, an edge in her voice.

"I don't know. Is there a reason why someone would be walking through the jungle near our house?"

"No," Dad said, "Unless you're talking about the night walkers..."

"The night walkers?"

"Yes. The ghosts of ancient warriors that sometimes walk through the jungle late at night, capturing the spirits of people who don't belong there."

Mom laughed.

I lost my appetite.

I didn't tell Mom about the nosebleed.

Mom was right. I needed to get outside more. Maybe I was going a little crazy—seeing things that weren't there.

I made it my resolve that I'd take a daily walk to the beach no matter how shitty I felt.

Just like the walk in the labyrinth, at first, I'd feel like I was trying to move through thick molasses, but eventually the resistance would give way to a rhythm and an unexpected feeling of strength.

The water at the beach by our house was lagoon-like. Sometimes I'd see a sea turtle swimming there, and other times, the ocean was empty but exhibited a strange, hazy smoke-like quality on account of the clear spring water mixing with the salty seawater. Sometimes I waded in the ocean, the warm water soothing my aching legs. Other days, I'd just sit with my toes in the sand and a book on my lap. The beach was often empty, an occasional family or couple or person going for a walk like me, but because the beach was only accessible by taking the Puna Historic Trail and not right off a big road or parking lot, I mostly had the place to myself.

Sometimes I'd feel into my body and sense that something was eroding me from the inside out, like a rust on my bones and blood, but maybe it was just the loss of home, of Oregon, of my comfortable friendship with Tay, or maybe it was just the way it feels to grow up. Next year would be my last year in high school, and I wasn't yet sure what I wanted to do. Yes, probably college, eventually. But maybe I wanted to take a year off to travel to Europe, see the real Labyrinth in Chartres Cathedral? Maybe I wanted to volunteer with Doctors Beyond Continents in Africa. Every time I had a chance to think about my future—unlived but expansive with possibility, I felt a little dizzy and nauseous. Possibility could be exciting, but it could also be paralyzing and overwhelming. When you can be anything, sometimes it's easier being nothing.

I sensed that I was getting weaker by the day, that the naps were lasting longer, and while I didn't wake up again in a pool of blood, I woke up clammy and cold from night sweats that drenched my sheets and left a round shadow in the pit of my pillow. Mom would try to feed me, but I found that my appetite had disappeared. I was never one to count calories, but I'd typically find it hard to resist anything involving cake or chocolate. But when Mom tempted me with mochi, these sweet little custard-filled rice cakes made at a Japanese bakery in Hilo, I'd often eat a bite or two and then feel too tired or sick to go on.

Mom didn't really comment on any of this. She knew intuitively that eating was a sensitive subject, especially for a teenage girl, and didn't want me to get hangups about food. For all she knew, I was just trying to get into bikini shape.

One day at the beach, something strange happened.

I wasn't used to seeing a lot of people, but while reading, I got the sense of someone watching me, no, not just watching me, but studying me. But when I looked around to scan the landscape for others, there was no one there. Eventually, the feeling creeped me out to the point that I got up and left.

As I walked the sandy trail back home, I couldn't help but sense a presence. Something there that shouldn't have been there. But when I looked back, there was nothing.

I looked down at the trail of footsteps I left behind me.

Just my two footsteps in the sand.

Then I got sick—with a cold. Well, it wasn't quite a cold, really, but more like a cough that racked my whole body and forced me to double over if I was standing up. The cough interrupted my sleep. In the middle of night, I felt something shift in my back, like my spine was unlocking, opening up to let something in, and then a terrible stab of sharp pain that made me cry out.

I'm dying.

It was the first time I let myself think it.

Of course, it was absurd. I was just depressed. Stress makes your immune system weak. I must have caught a cold on one of my walks.

But the cough got worse by the day, and eventually Mom had had enough of seeing me sick.

I'd been scared about what was going on inside me for weeks, but when Mom opened my bedroom door and said, "Get dressed, I'm taking you to the doctor," I'd never felt more terrified in my life.

Chapter 3

The doctor was a kind-faced blond woman who looked younger than my mother.

"What brings you here today?"

Mom looked at me to explain.

"Well, I've been feeling really tired lately. I sleep a lot during the day. At first, I thought it was stress from the move and the time difference from home, but it's been weeks now and I feel like I haven't adjusted. I've been a little more achy than usual, too. Headaches. Heavy legs. And now I have this cold, and this cough that won't go away that keeps me up all night."

"Oh, you moved recently! Where did you move here from?"

"Oregon. Portland. Well, Gresham specifically."

"How are you liking it in Hawaii?"

"Okay. I mean, I think I'd like it a lot more if I had more energy."

"Any other symptoms?"

I thought for a moment. I didn't know if the nosebleed was important to mention, but I figured I might as well be thorough.

"I had a nosebleed last week?"

The doctor nodded.

"Do you have heavy periods?"

I felt my face turn red. Mom and I weren't really into talking about our periods in detail, and the question seemed unrelated to nosebleeds.

"I don't know. I mean, I bleed, but I don't know what heavy would mean," but then I remembered how Tay sometimes would ask me to check her pants for leaks, and I figured this might be what the doctor meant.

"I don't get leaks," if that's what you mean.

The doctor nodded.

"Anemia is pretty common in young women your age. Let's order some blood work. I'm going to order an iron supplement just in case. I'll give you a call if you need to take it. It's most likely just that."

I felt a flood of relief. All this time, I'd been worried about having a mental disorder, or depression, or malaria, and it was probably just anemia.

I hadn't been eating too well since the move, so it all made sense.

The doctor sent me down to the lab, where I dutifully offered my arm. I'm strange in that I like to watch the needle go in. I find that it hurts more when I can't see what's happening.

I was still euphoric from the relief of having a reason for my unrelenting exhaustion, when I saw something that stopped me in my tracks.

He was sitting hunched on the same couch I'd been sitting in with Mom while we had waited for the doctor to call us. He was tall and thin, but somehow still muscular. He sat doubled over as if he was carrying an immense weight on his back. There was clearly something wrong with his back, though I couldn't quite make out what it was. Despite it being practically 90 degrees outside, he wore a black coat that covered whatever was going on there. He looked my age, maybe a year or two older, but he wasn't there with his parents or family. He was alone.

Despite the dark clothes he was wearing, his face looked illuminated. By which I mean, it looked almost as if it was lit from within. It's hard to explain. I'd never seen a face so beautiful in my entire life. I could tell even from across the room that his eyes were very light-colored, because they contrasted so strikingly with his brown skin. He looked like the male version of the Afghan Girl that had been on the cover of National Geographic years earlier. I took art history my junior year and had always found myself drawn to the photograph for reasons I can't easily explain.

The photo was the kind you couldn't look away from the moment you saw it, and this guy's face had the same otherworldly beauty to it.

All shame went out the window. I literally stopped in my tracks in the middle of that waiting room to stare. I mean, I stopped only for a moment, not long enough for Mom to notice or anything, but just for a flicker of an instant that somehow seemed to also last forever, long enough to take him in.

He looked down at the floor, as if he was deep in contemplation of something. He looked kind of sad, really, but for a moment, he looked up, and his eyes glanced my way. Just for a moment, as if he could sense my presence or sense that I was staring.

He looked surprised to see me. His face contorted in confusion.

And then, time moved on. I kept walking and broke my glance, and Mom and I stepped out of the doctor's office into the bright afternoon sun.

That afternoon, the doctor called.

I had anemia. She told me to start taking the iron pills right away and to call her if I didn't feel more like myself in a couple of weeks.

I waited expectantly for the iron pills to work, but in the days that passed, I only felt more exhausted. When I'd climb the stairs up to bed in the evening, I had to rest halfway up to catch my breath. I wanted so badly to believe that the answer a bad case of anemia, but as several days became a week, and then a week and a half, and I still didn't feel better, the old flicker of panic returned, eventually becoming an energy that left me nauseous and unable to sleep at night.

I told myself I'd give myself a couple of more days. How long were the iron pills supposed to take to become effective? The doctor had said two weeks, but maybe that meant that they just started working at two weeks, and that it could take days after that before my body recovered. I told myself I'd wait it out a few more days before telling Mom.

But I could tell Mom was already worried. She had noticed me pausing on the stairs to catch my breath. My early afternoon awakenings blended into afternoon naps, where Mom had to knock on my door to tell me it was time to eat dinner. Most nights I didn't want to eat, but Mom would remind me that not eating wasn't going to make my anemia any better, and the longer I wallowed in bed, the longer it would take for me to start feeling better.

"Use it or lose it," she said.

Mom's theory was that I was depressed and that my depression had led me to stop eating, which had led to the anemia.

I knew I wasn't going to win the fight to stay in bed, so I dragged my body out of bed, wondering if gravity had always been so strong. Even lifting my legs over the edge seemed to take all my effort and will. My body felt like it was slowly turning to stone. And even though deep down I knew that there was something terribly wrong with me, I couldn't help but wonder if maybe Mom was right. Maybe it was all in my head, nothing but a touch of teenage depression. If I could just get myself moving and make a few friends, the cloud and heaviness would clear, and I'd start to feel better.

Just a few more days, I told myself over pizza that night. In Oregon, I'd easily eat two or three slices, but now I could barely finish half of the slice that sat on my plate.

Just a few more days, and the iron pills will work, I said as I steeled myself and my thousand-pound legs for the climb up the stairs, knowing it would knock the wind out of me, knowing I'd be nauseous mid-way up and end up having to stop and rest.

I didn't make it a few more days.

I didn't make it to the top of the stairs.

Chapter 4

Mom heard the thud when my head hit the ground. Thankfully, I fell forward, hitting my head hard on the edge of the stairs. I didn't pass out or anything, but the sound of me hitting the stairs alerted Mom and Dad, who stood over me with a new look of fear in their eyes that I'd never seen before.

"Oh my God, what happened?" Mom said, her voice shaking from worry.

"I fell?" I said, knowing that wasn't the whole story.

"Maya?"

"I'm still exhausted all the time, Mom. I didn't want to come down to dinner. I just wanted to rest. My legs turned to Jell-O on the way up the stairs."

That's when I noticed the change in my parents' faces. Mom's face inexplicably shifted from deep concern to terror, and Dad looked like he had just seen a ghost or a vampire. Except the problem was that they were looking straight at me, as if *I* had become the ghost or vampire.

"What?" I ask, looking behind me, wondering if maybe the house was, in fact, haunted?

Before I got tested for anemia, back when Mom thought I was just depressed, I'd joke that I was so sick because the house was haunted. Needless to say, it didn't go over well when I suggested that Mom might need to call in an exorcist.

That's when I feel the trickle in my nose, like a runny nose, but I know it's much worse than a trickle–more like a gush of blood.

Oh no.

It's been years since Mom and Dad have seen me get a nosebleed, but that's the final straw for Mom.

"Okay. Enough is enough. We're going to the hospital right now to get some answers."

Seeing that I'd fallen down the stairs had frightened my parents, but the nosebleed has Dad worried I might have given myself a concussion when I fell down the stairs.

And so, even though it's already well past eight o'clock at night, we all load into the car to make our way to the closest hospital, way out in Hilo. The car ride out to the hospital was unbearably silent, the car suddenly saturated by an uncomfortable quiet that had never been there before, that I sensed (rightly even then) would now live beside us forever. The quiet made everything more uncomfortable.

I expected a crowded hospital and having to wait all night to see a doctor, but the waiting room was empty, and after taking my blood pressure, the nurse led me to a curtained hospital bed right away.

The doctors ran an IV into my arm with whatever it is they put in those IV bags. It was probably pain medicine because whatever it was, it made me feel a lot better right away.

I could tell that seeing my body relax in relief from the pain relieved Mom, which made me feel way better.

They rolled me into a CAT scan, which was kind of cool. They warned me that I'd probably feel claustrophobic in there, but I found it peaceful, like being in a white cave with a lot of echoes all around me. The doctors were searching for answers. Maybe if the doctors told Mom explicitly that there was nothing wrong with my brain, she'd finally stop with all the talk of me being depressed.

The CAT scan showed no evidence of bleeding in the brain, so I was all clear on that count, but the doctors told me that they were going to keep me overnight anyway to run some tests and try to figure out why I was so tired all the time.

A nurse came with a tray that contained what appeared to be like twenty vials of blood. They pulled so much blood out of me that I was shocked I didn't pass out right there on the hospital bed. Then, they rolled me upstairs to a room divided by a white curtain. I couldn't see if there was anyone in the bed next to us.

I woke in the morning to a hospital breakfast, which surprised me by not being completely awful. There was orange juice, eggs with cheese, and even ube pancakes.

Mom had stayed with me during the night, and the nurse had even brought Mom a warm coffee. Mom held the cup between both hands as if to keep them warm, like she used to do in Oregon.

"Do I get to go home today?" I asked. "I am feeling better than ever."

But even as I said those words aloud, a dark doubt crossed my mind. What if I was feeling better because of the pain medicine in the IV bag--and what if I'd start to feel bad again the second they disconnected me from it?

I shook the thought away.

"They're running every possible test they can run. Million-dollar workup, they call it. They are testing you for thyroid deficiency, lupus, diabetes, kidney disease," she paused, uncomfortable, and then added, "They also tested you for pregnancy and HIV, and for drugs. I mean, I told them that those tests were unnecessary, but they said they needed to cover all their bases as a precaution."

That made me laugh. This whole situation was absurd enough, but if my mother expected that I'd tell her out loud that *yes, I was still a virgin and not into intravenous drugs*, she would be waiting a long damn time. Still, I could tell that there had been an unspoken question in her pause.

"Oh. My. God. Mom! I've been lying in bed since we landed in Hawai'i. What do you think I'm doing late at night, sneaking out to have sex in the jungle with all the nonexistent boys in our neighborhood?"

I had expected our neighborhood in Hawaii to be populated by a plethora of brown-skinned, washboard-ab surfer guys, but instead our neighborhood seemed to be populated entirely by senior citizens well into their retirement and a few other middle-aged couples in their mid-to-late forties who had successfully managed to retire young. The plethora of hot surfer boys I'd imagined were nowhere to be seen—or maybe they were all on O'ahu. It didn't matter. O'ahu was an impossible hour-long flight away, anyway.

Mom could see by my scowl that I was done talking.

"I'm going down to the cafeteria to get some breakfast. I'm sorry all this is happening," she said, putting her hand lightly on my leg.

I felt my anger soften, but kept my angry stare fixated on a dusty corner of the hospital room, and I didn't look up until she left.

HIV.

Pregnancy.

I laughed. In my dreams I'd have the kind of exciting life that would put me anywhere at risk of either of those two things, especially given the fact that my parents basically moved us to a retirement community.

Of course, I didn't know then how shielded I was. I didn't know that Hilo had a terrible drug problem and that the doctors and nurses were accustomed to seeing girls my age come in pregnant, with all kinds of diseases, diseases that left them way worse than exhausted. It made sense for them to give me those tests.

My thoughts were broken by the sound of rustling in the bed next to me.

I'd forgotten that I was sharing a room.

I felt a flush of heat cross my face. We weren't alone, and whomever was in bed beside me had heard everything. I was so mortified that even though there was a curtain between us, I covered my head with the hospital blanket and breathed in the faint smell of bleach and lavender.

I heard another rustling in the bed. They were waking. Or, maybe worse, my conversation with Mom had woken them up.

Great. Just great.

I wanted desperately to know who I was sharing a room with, but that line of inquiry was interrupted by Mom's return, and then a visit from the doctor, who said that all the tests came back negative. I didn't have a thyroid condition, lupus, or a kidney disease. I didn't have HIV.

"You're not pregnant," the doctor said, matter-of-factly.

With that, I heard a stifled laugh come from the bed behind the curtain. They were clearly a *he*, and *he* sounded young.

Fucker.

The doctors explained that they could perform further tests, but that given my youth and my history, I was probably just exhausted and maybe depressed from the move, and my anemia was still bad, so they were going to give me an infusion.

"We'll also leave you with the phone number for behavioral health. In situations like this, a short period of taking antidepressants can be helpful," the doctor, a balding man in his late forties, said, handing Mom a sheet of paper with the phone numbers.

Mom looked at me triumphantly.

I scowled.

Another laugh from the bed behind the curtain.

The doctors returned an hour later with my discharge papers. Mom helped me pack my things. Dad came over with some fresh clothes from home so I wouldn't have to leave the hospital in my pajamas. They offered me a wheelchair, but I told them I could walk.

I was slow to leave the room. I wanted to see who I'd been sharing the room with all night, and I found it strange that even though I'd been visited by doctors and nurses and support staff all morning, not a single person had come to check on the guy sharing the room with me. Maybe he was just an old-timer, in for a long stay?

I got out of bed and traced a path through the room that would put me in a position to get a glimpse of his bed.

I glanced up, and felt a chill, then anger, then, for the first time since all this began, real fear.

Chapter 5

"Do you want me to roll the windows down?" We were making our way back to Hawaii Paradise Park from Hilo. It was a beautiful day.

Mauna Loa created its own weather, and even though it was the dead middle of summer and should have been nearly 100 degrees, cool breezes came down from the mountain, the way a cold current can sometimes cut unexpectedly through warm water in the ocean, chilling you unexpectedly.

I shrugged. I was still trying to make sense of what I'd seen, but my fear and confusion hijacked every reasonable thought my brain tried to propose.

When we got home, Mom offered to call Behavioral Health for me. She knew I wasn't going to do it myself.

"Whatever, Mom, I'll go to whatever appointment you make," I said, and made my way up to my room.

Whatever they had given me at the hospital had left me feeling great, and I planned to use my energy while I had it. Despite what Mom seemed to think, I wasn't just being lazy. But then again, good health has the quality of erasing the memory of what it feels like to be sick. The memory of the exhaustion hovered above me, a vague memory and frightening possibility, but in the glow of feeling better, it felt more like ancient history. All that was over now. The doctors at the hospital had made me feel better. That's all that mattered. And maybe they were right, maybe some depression medicine would help me feel this way all the time.

I put on a bathing suit—a one-piece I'd bought months ago back when I thought our little trip to Hawaii was just going to be a vacation. I packed a small bag with my water bottle, a book, and my journal.

Then, I bounced into the bright sunlight of a perfect day, making my way to the little path through the jungle that would take me to the quiet beach, where I'd have some time to think.

It sounds crazy writing this down, but if I don't write it down, I'll tell myself tomorrow I imagined it. The guy who had been in bed beside me all night at the hospital was the same guy I saw at the doctor's clinic in Kona all those weeks ago--the skinny one with the weird back problem, and the otherworldly eyes. I think they might be green, just like the girl in the National Geographic picture.

When I glanced into his part of the room, I figured whoever was in there would be asleep or looking away, but instead, he was looking right at me, and I swear, his stare, it did something to me, changed me in a way I can't explain. Does it sound cliché to say it pierced me to the bone? Either way, the thing that scared me about it was how worried he looked, and not just worried in a general sense. He looked worried about me. Specifically. Like it was a look of pity, and fear, or the kind of look you'd expect someone to give you when you've gotten a terminal diagnosis.

I know all of this is probably just in my head. The move to Hawaii has stressed me out more than I'm willing to admit, and the isolation is probably starting to get to me. People aren't meant to live like this--going weeks not talking to someone their age. I probably should try giving Tay a call again, but I know she's probably having the time of her life out there in New York, and I don't want to ruin it with her having to hear me whine about how much I don't really like it here in Hawaii.

The memory of the guy in the bed beside me faded away in the days that followed as the exhaustion returned. Within a couple of days, I was back to napping through the afternoon. Mom scheduled the appointment with the psychiatrist, and she was hopeful that antidepressants would help. I couldn't help but feel that Mom was in denial.

I wasn't getting better. This didn't feel like depression. But I wasn't a doctor, so who was I to say anything?

In the weeks that followed, I tried so hard to keep up with life. I'd drag my stiff body down to dinner every evening. When Mom suggested a trip to Kona to go shopping, I didn't say *no*. I didn't want her to think I wasn't trying.

"What we both need is a little retail therapy!" she quipped.

Getting an appointment with a psychiatrist was harder than she expected. The earliest possible appointment they could give her was three months out. Mom spent two whole days on the phone, harassing receptionists and doctors, and they finally relented and found her a sooner appointment, but it was still two weeks away. I could sense Mom growing more restless and desperate to *do* something, especially as she saw me grow weaker by the day.

On the car ride to Kona, I shivered in the front seat. Mom turned off the air conditioner and opened the window, flooding the car with cool air. The road to Kona climbed in altitude and the air was crisp and biting up here, even though the sun looked warm and inviting.

"That's just colder," I said, shifting uncomfortably in my seat. I couldn't seem to find a position anywhere these days where my body felt comfortable. Everything ached. My bones ached. My muscles ached. My blood seemed to ache.

When we finally got to the shopping center, I was covered in sweat. Somehow, I'd gone from being freezing cold to unbearably hot. In the weeks that had followed the hospital stay, Mom had a perpetual look of worry on her face, but as she saw me struggle to exit the car, I saw the worry flicker between panic and devastation.

The moment I got out of the car, nausea overtook me. I doubled over in the parking lot, puking up my breakfast, and collapsed to my knees, my body heaving, working to get every bit of breakfast out of my stomach. I knelt on the concrete long after the stomach spasms died down, tears coming out of my eyes now, desperate, hot tears.

"I can't do this anymore," I said, in between sobs. "I can't."

Sometimes the body's answer to pain is mercy. A warm white static crept across my field of vision. At first, it frightened me. I could feel it closing, like a window over my eyes. In a moment, all I would be able to see was white.

I fell backward, my eyes grazing a direct stare at the sun.

And I swear, the last thing I saw was his face. His green penetrating eyes. His worried expression.

I woke in a hospital room, Mom sitting in a big plastic recliner beside my bed. My head throbbed something awful.

"What happened?" I managed to sputter out.

My mouth felt impossibly dry, and I found it difficult to form the words. My tongue felt like a foreign object in my mouth.

Mom winced. She looked pale; the perpetual look of worry she now had on her face all the time was still there.

"You passed out in the mall parking lot. The doctors gave you a lot of medicine when you got to the hospital. They told me it might take a little while for you to wake up. They did some more blood work..."

She stopped.

I could tell she didn't want to go on speaking. The whole thing sounded bad enough, but what she had to say next had the forebodings of something far worse.

"The doctor says your red blood count is really low, way lower than when we did the blood work a couple of weeks ago. And way lower than when they checked for anemia at the hospital."

"And?"

"They say they are going to be running more tests. They don't know what's wrong, but they want to cover all their bases."

Mom paused for a long time again. I could sense she had more to say, but didn't want to say it.

"There's more? How can there be more than just tests?"

"They want to do a bone marrow biopsy," Mom said, her body sighing as she said it.

When Mom said the words *bone marrow biopsy,* the bed beneath me disappeared, and I felt myself falling, falling through space and time, falling through the center of the earth and the intense gravity there, falling through a wormhole that I knew would change my entire life.

"So, it's not anemia?" I managed to splutter out.

"It could still be anemia, but you've been on iron pills for almost four weeks now, and your red blood count is still low and dropping they don't know why. They've given you all these other tests to rule out other conditions. So, they feel that they need to do the bone marrow test to rule out any other serious conditions."

The bone marrow biopsy was as painful and awful as I thought it would be.

They released me from the hospital, this time with steroids and pain medicine, they said would keep me comfortable until they figured things out. The medicine did keep me comfortable, but not in the way it had kept me comfortable before. I didn't need to sleep all day. I could manage to sit on the patio with a book or a journal. Or I could join Dad in the living room to watch a baseball game. But the medicine made me angry and moody, and I was way snappier with Mom.

Mom got the call on a Monday morning. The doctor said he wanted us to come to the hospital in Kona. *This afternoon, if you can.*

I don't really remember the long drive over to the hospital. I remember the feeling of panic in my bones. The road climbed up toward the clouds, I felt the old chill return. And then the road descended back down toward the ocean, and I felt a flash of heat pass through my whole body that left me sweating and trembling at the same time.

We didn't meet in a doctor's office. We met in a small white conference room. This was new.

The doctor had dark hair and dark eyes and looked like he was about Dad's age.

I don't remember exactly what he said, but a few phrases stood out... *Leukemia... cancer in the blood and bone marrow... rare metastasis to the brain... high potential for organ failure... your daughter is in grave condition...*

Grave condition.

Grave.

Chapter 6

We drove back to Hawaii Paradise Park in silence.

The conference with the doctors hadn't lasted too long, but in the quiet of the car I managed to piece together more of what had been said. The doctor had explained that the first step was to start chemotherapy immediately. They would schedule me to start at the Kona Cancer Center early next week. But my cancer was advanced. If I needed something like a bone marrow transplant, I might have to travel to Honolulu, where the bigger hospitals were located.

By the time we left the hospital, it was already golden hour, that hour right before sunset, where the light turns everything gold and red. Mom held my arm as we walked to the car, our bodies forming long eerie shadows behind us.

The road home skirted the shoulder of the mountain, and I could see far out into the sea from the window of the car. The road was so vertiginous, it almost felt like we could be flying in an airplane or helicopter rather than driving.

The sun had set by the time we neared the town of Volcano. I noticed a red glow on the horizon but didn't think to consider that the sun had set behind us, and it didn't initially strike me as weird that we hit unexpected traffic. Mom and I had driven this road at least a half dozen times before, and we'd never hit traffic around Volcano.

But when we got nearer to the entrance of the park, I saw the billboard. Usually, it blinked an illuminated sign that said, "No lava visible in park." But tonight was different. The sign said, "Use Crater Rim Drive to access overlooks to view eruption activity." The sign blinked, and new words appeared, this time a warning, "Eruptions are highly unpredictable. Smoke, tephra, volcanic rocks, and glassy fragments can be emitted from the crater without warning."

"The volcano is erupting!" I said, managing to lift my body into a vaguely upright position, where I had previously been slouching to try to manage the pain in my bones, my back, my hip, my head.

"Can we see it?" I asked, less a question and more of a demand. If my condition was indeed *grave*, like the doctor had said it was, it's not like Mom and Dad would dare deny me my dying wish to see the volcano, no matter how exhausted they were from the day we'd just had.

"We might as well," Mom said, her voice small and distant, as if she were somewhere in the bottom of a deep well.

Dad nodded, and when we got to the park entrance, he turned the car to go into the park.

We were just one car in a procession of cars making its way to the volcano. On the side of the road, a parade of people walked along the road, presumably also making their way to the caldera. Traffic moved so slowly that the people walking passed our car.

The sky glowed red ahead of us. I'd never seen anything like it. The caldera glowed so bright red that the dark clouds above it reflected its glow. In places where the thick clouds above us broke, there were more stars there than sky. When we had visited Kona for our week-long holiday, Mom, Dad, and I had gone stargazing, and I'd remembered feeling breathless and a little dizzy under the night sky. Back then, I'd attributed my dizziness to awe, but not I wasn't so sure. In Hawaii, it feels like you're closer to space than anywhere else on earth, closer to heaven, some would say.

We got closer to the caldera, but I didn't feel closer to heaven.

In fact, the red glow of the caldera looked increasingly hellish the closer we got. In addition to the ache that seemed to seep down into my bones, I felt the waves of nausea coming, my body tensing up and drawing itself in, the way the ocean retreats backward toward the horizon before the tsunami comes. I didn't want to tell Dad to turn around or stop the car, but I knew that if we didn't get to our destination soon, I'd end up puking all over the car seat.

This nausea felt different than any nausea I'd ever felt before. I'd vomited before, when I'd had the flu, or after riding a tilt-a-whirl at the fair. But this nausea was something else. It originated from a deeper place in my body. It started mildly enough, a gagging feeling in the back of my throat, which I could resist at first, but found harder to resist the more I fought it. I felt my body heave from within; my whole being expelling everything inside of me that didn't want to be inside.

I asked Dad to stop the car, threw open the car door, and vomited into the highway.

"Maya," Mom said. I heard Mom struggling with the door latch as I spilled my guts onto the highway. She managed to get the door open and stood beside me, pulling my hair out of my face.

My stomach spasmed for minutes after. Dad suggested we turn around, go home, but I told him "What's the point?" I'll feel just as shitty at home as I'll feel here. We might as well see the caldera. The volcano's eruptions are hard to predict. This might be my last chance to see it. I tell Dad to keep driving.

"I want to see it," I said.

After what feels like forever, we reached a big parking lot at the end of the road. Dad pulled in, but the lot was crowded with cars and people. After driving circles in the lot for what felt like an hour, Dad finally found a parking spot.

Mom asked me if I needed help getting out of the car, but I told her, "No."

I can get out of the car on my own two feet. I'm not dead yet, I thought. I want to see the caldera on my own.

I walked ahead of Mom and Dad and made my way to the red glow. I just wanted a moment alone with the caldera. After emptying the contents of my stomach, I felt a little better, a little lighter, and I found myself shocked to be able to walk at a swift pace down the dark trail.

I turned on my phone to illuminate the path beneath my feet. I'd lost Mom and Dad, and knew they'll be angry I left them behind, but I didn't care. I needed this one thing just for me.

The path wound through devastated ground.

I hadn't brought sturdy shoes, only the standard local footwear—flip flops. I walked with care over the volcanic rocks, making a point to avoid stepping on the occasional scrub plant that had managed to survive in this impossible landscape.

The path turned, and I saw it—the edge of the world—a cliff up ahead, from which emanated a bright orange glow—like a witch's cauldron. Even though my legs ached and I felt echoes of the nausea returning, the adrenaline buoyed me, and my pace quickened. I found a spot along the guardrail where there was less of a crowd, leaned over, and look down.

My eyes didn't understand what they were looking at. Down there, down in the caldera, the ground glowed red, and a geyser of bright yellow fire spurted hundreds of feet into the sky. The lava boiled and flowed away from the fountain, crackling and spluttering bright yellow near the fiery geyser, and then redder, and finally black the further away the river flowed. Puffs of smoke floated up from the conflagration, glowing red, forming all kinds of shapes and figures in the sky, obliterating the stars.

"Hello, Pele," a voice beside me whispered.

I startled to realize that someone was standing close to me.

He must have arrived so quietly I didn't notice his arrival.

"Pele?" I asked, unable to take my eyes off the glowing fountain.

"Pele, destroyer and creator. She lives in this crater. *Halema'uma'u.*"

"Oh, yes. Pele, the Hawaiian goddess of the volcano," I said.

"If you look closely, you can see her," he said.

I look closely, wanting to see what he saw. Even though the eruption was spectacular, I didn't see a goddess down there. Only smoke and fire.

When I glanced up to see who I had been speaking to, I felt a chill pass over my body, then inexplicably, a disquieting sense of déjà vu.

I backed away from the crater edge.

Chapter 7

"I don't know why you had to go run off like that," Mom snapped angrily in the front seat of the car. "Given your... condition... you could have fallen, hurt yourself, gotten lost on the path. It's not like the reception out there is good."

I heard everything Mom was saying, and my brain has registered that she was mad, but I was somewhere else, back at the crater, trying to make sense of what happened there.

The moment I'd looked up from the crater, I recognized him, the face was unmistakable. It was the same guy I'd seen in the doctor's office in Kona, the same guy who had shared the hospital room with me in Hilo, after I'd had the fall and the nosebleed.

Around the caldera, the faces of the people around me glowed red. The caldera was so bright it reflected off people's skin. But even in the red hellish glow of the caldera, his face seemed to glow as if from within, a brightness more like a full moon on a clear night than a face shadowed by the glow of the eruption. Now that we were close, I could see his eyes were green—a striking, penetrating green.

But it was the way he looked at me that disturbed me the most. It was an intense expression, but also one of shock and not a little fear, like he had just seen a ghost.

Like I was the ghost.

From a distance, he'd looked thin and gangly, but closer, I could see that his arms were muscular and strong, like he could carry me back to the car if he needed to. In the light of the caldera, he didn't look sickly at all.

"You!" I said, my voice trembling a little.

I might as well have been throwing volcanic rocks at him rather than saying a word. He flinched and stepped back, like he'd been struck.

Then, I saw his face twist into pain, terror, and revulsion. Without saying another word, he turned around and ran away into the darkness, but not so quickly that I didn't get a better glimpse of his back.

It was his back that weirded me out the most. Lumpy and hunched and complex, like the works of a clock with intricate, beautiful machinery wound into it.

Lying in bed that night, you'd think that I'd be worried about my diagnosis, but all I could think about was him. Why did I keep seeing him everywhere?

I mean, the Big Island is a small community. We'd only been living here a few weeks, and we'd already run into a lot of the same people. Coming from Portland, where everyone is basically anonymous to one another, it was strange at first, but then became another normal thing we were starting to get used to. People expected you to remember their names here—everyone from the grocery store clerk to the guy at the gas station. The women at the bookstore always took the time to make small talk with me, to ask me how the last books she had sold me had gone, and

I found myself shocked that she even remembered which books I'd bought.

I suppose it wasn't too strange to be seeing the same guy everywhere. If he had a chronic condition like me, he probably had a lot of doctor's appointments, too. And whenever there's a big eruption, news travels fast, and people drive from all around the island to see it.

Maybe seeing him around wasn't so strange at all?

I would eventually learn I was gravely mistaken.

His presence wasn't random.

Nothing had been an accident.

But I wasn't ready yet.

The cancer ward smelled of disinfectant, and everything was a dull, depressing beige. My parents and I sat in big plastic chairs waiting to be called.

The doctor called us into the examination room. She was a slight woman who looked younger than my mother, but she got right to business.

"When we ran your most recent blood tests, we found a preponderance of abnormal white blood cells."

My brain went blank. I struggled to make sense of the words that were coming out of her mouth.

"Leukemia. You have leukemia. It's a cancer of the white blood cells."

Cancer. She said cancer.

"More specifically, leukemia is a cancer of the bone marrow. Bone marrow is this spongy tissue that grows inside basically every bone in your body. Normally, bone marrow produces all your body's blood cells, including the red blood cells that deliver oxygen to every cell in your body, and the white blood cells that help you fight infections, like colds. With Leukemia, the body produces unhealthy blood cells, which supplant—I mean, they replace, the normally functioning cells, leading to the symptoms you've been experiencing. The fatigue, the bone pain, for example. Have you noticed more frequent infections like colds or wounds that won't heal?"

I remembered my cold, how the cough had lasted for weeks, and had kept me up at night.

I felt my blood boil and transform in my veins, but not in a cancerous way. This was anger. This was rage.

"Just cut it out of me. Can you just cut it out of me?"

Her face grew serious.

"It doesn't work like that," she said. "It's not just in one body part that we can cut out. It's everywhere. It's in your blood, your bone marrow..."

No. This didn't make sense. I felt furious. Why couldn't they just cut the damn thing out, but then I realized that it was my blood itself that had spoiled. The cancer couldn't be cut out because the cancer was me. I was the cancer.

"Your cancer has spread to other parts of your body. To your brain..."

At this point, I lost track of what she was saying.

The words got more complicated and much more terrifying. My mind and spirit retreated to a small, quiet place deep inside my body where the worst of it couldn't reach me.

"This kind of Leukemia has a very poor prognosis...."

I retreated further inside myself. Did this mean I was going to die?

She said other things. My body was weak. A bone marrow transplant would likely cause more harm than good. High mortality rate...

The room began to spin, and I noticed the white clouds around my eyes closing in again. This time, the doctor was there to catch me to stop me from falling off the doctor's bed and hitting the floor.

I woke in the same room, the concerned faces of the doctor and my parents hovering over me.

"Syncope," the doctor said, her voice signaling less concern than I would expect given the fact that I'd just gone unconscious in the middle of a doctor's office.

"What?" Mom spluttered out.

"Fainting spell," the doctor said. I'm going to get you a glass of orange juice." She returned with a bottle that contained a photo of an orange on it.

"The sugar will help. This is a lot to take in, I know. I'm so sorry. But right now, we need to focus on the first step, which is a course of chemotherapy to get your cancer cell numbers low so that maybe you'll be able to qualify for a bone marrow transplant later. The chemotherapy regimen will last a couple of weeks, and the medicines you'll receive will be very intense. You'll need to stay in the hospital to protect yourself from infection. The next few weeks are going to be difficult," she said, but she grabbed both my hands, knelt in front of me, and looked me in the eyes, "but we are going to get through this, okay?"

I nodded, not sure if I believed her.

"You'll need the support of your family and friends," she went on. "You'll stay in the hospital while we administer chemotherapy treatment, but once we're done, and once we're in the clear, you should be able to go home again."

I nodded, trying to take everything in, but it all felt overwhelming. Things were happening so fast. When the doctor said *home,* I almost wanted to laugh; our house in Hawaii Paradise Park hardly felt like home to me. And when she mentioned that I'd need the support of my friends, I flinched. Tay had no clue what was going on. It's not like I had a chance to tell her; we hadn't really talked since the move, except to send a few texts back and forth about where we were in the world. Things like "Getting on the plane to fly to New York, so excited!" And "We just moved into our new house!" followed by a picture of my new room and the yard. Every few days, we'd send each other a photo, but nothing more. I hadn't bothered to tell her about how sick I'd been feeling. Part of me had still believed it was all in my head.

"We have you scheduled to be admitted tomorrow. Rest up tonight. Eat a nice big dinner. This will be a longer hospital stay, so you might want to think about what things you can pack that will make you feel more comfortable. Things like books, journals, warm cozy sweaters..."

I nodded. Mom nodded. For the first time, she didn't look worried. She had the look of someone preparing for a long run.

Dad had a dazed, faraway look, like he was only halfway here. I could sense him retreating within himself. He was there, but might as well have been in Alaska.

You'd think that being told you have cancer would leave you in a state of complete and utter panic, but as we walked out of the doctor's office, I felt relief. For the first time in weeks, I didn't feel scared, or anxious, or worried. I finally had answers and that was something.

I felt present. Present with my exhaustion, present with the smell of disinfectant in the halls, present with the warm sunshine on my skin when we left the hospital and walked across the parking lot. For the first time in a long time, I felt like I was really living.

On the way home, I asked my parents if they could take me to the bookstore. I figured if I was going to spend weeks in the hospital, I might as well have good books to read. I did a quick Google search of cancer books, and books about Leukemia, and made myself a little list of required reading.

Mom saw my little stack of books, and her mouth went slack and her face went pale, but this wasn't about her.

While browsing, I also found a few thrillers that came highly recommended by the staff and figured I'd bring a couple of those along for the ride as well. Before I left, I picked up a small black journal, where I figured I'd write down my thoughts.

Back in the car, Mom asked me what I wanted for dinner.

It all felt so final. What did I want to eat for what might be one of my final meals? I didn't have much of an appetite.

Pizza seemed like it would be the most palatable option.

At the dinner table, I picked at my slice, unable to finish it.

In bed, that night, I Googled my specific diagnosis, a word I couldn't pronounce, much less barely spell. The information seemed highly conflicting. Apparently, my cancer was typically diagnosed in older patients. Younger patients had a better prognosis, but the prognosis was grim if the cancer developed into full-blown leukemia, as mine had.

In other words, I could have a year to live, or years to live, but the internet seemed unable to give me a clear answer. =.

I realized that the more research I did, the worse I was going to feel.

I texted Tay.

Hey, was wondering if you have time to Zoom, like tonight. I know. It's late notice, but it's kind of an emergency.

The message read "delivered" all night. I couldn't sleep. Between doing Google searches on my cancer and checking to see if Tay had read my message, I spun myself into a full-blown anxiety attack. Not being able to distinguish between whether the shortness of breath was my anxiety or the cancer that had spread to my lungs, I decided that it was likely just the cancer. I was tired of people telling me that this pain was just in my head, and it was something of a relief to know that had not been all in my head after all. It wasn't depression or anemia. It was cancer. Fucking cancer.

The next morning, Mom helped me pack a bag for the hospital. I'd donated all my cozy sweaters in Portland, but at least I still had kept one of my softest blue beanies.

Mom promised she'd buy me more sweaters. I told her it didn't matter. Mom insisted that it did.

As Mom and Dad drove me to the hospital to be admitted, I tilted my face up to the warm sun, trying to soak in it. Was this the last time I'd see the blue sky so wide above me? The last time I'd seem the ocean?

I couldn't help but keep checking my phone.

The message to Tay sat stale in the void.

Delivered.

Unread.

Chapter 8

Inside the hospital, a nurse brought me to a cold gray room with two double beds and heavy blue curtains blacking out the only window. My bed was the one closest to the door, but because the other bed was empty, the white divider curtain had been pushed to the side of the room. I opened the window curtains to let in some light. The view outside the window wasn't half bad. We were, after all, in Hawaii, and from my window I could see buildings, and beyond them, the sea. It was a calm day, the kind of day that made the line between the sky and horizon blur, my eye straining to differentiate between earth and heaven.

I was scheduled for surgery in the afternoon, where doctors would implant a central line in my chest so that they could more easily deliver chemotherapy and other drugs during my hospital stay.

When they wheeled me back to my hospital room, I noticed that the white curtain dividing the two beds had been pulled shut, and the blue curtain covering the window must have been drawn because the room felt darker than it had been when I left it. Mom napped on a plastic recliner that had been tucked into the corner of the room beside my bed, and Dad sat stiff on a plastic chair beside her.

When the nurses were done fretting over me, I grabbed my bag of books and, without looking, lifted the first one out. It was a book called *Mortality.*

This didn't feel auspicious at all.

I hardly had time to settle into reading before a nurse came in carrying two IV bags containing the first of the chemotherapy treatment.

She explained to me that eventually, the chemotherapy treatment would leave me without an immune system. It would kill off the cancerous white blood cells that had poisoned my blood, but it would also kill off the remaining healthy white blood cells I had. White blood cells are what fights infections in the body. Without white blood cells, I would be vulnerable to all kinds of illnesses. Going forward, I'd have to be careful about contracting any infections. Mom and Dad would have to wear surgical masks when they visited, and whenever I was around anyone, doctors and nurses included, I'd have to wear a surgical mask as well. Even the tiniest infection can be disastrous. Even a small sniffle would be considered an emergency.

Other than the warnings of my impending vulnerability and potential doom, the day passed uneventfully. Mom and Dad took turns to get food from the cafeteria; Mom and Dad took turns to sit vigil over my bed and watch me read. Nurses shuffled in and out of the hospital room, checking my temperature, my blood pressure, and asking me if I needed anything.

I had never been watched so closely in my entire life, and by the time the sun set outside my lone little window, I was ready to be left alone.

I could tell Mom and Dad were exhausted.

"Go home, guys. Get some rest. Come back in the morning, okay?"

Mom said, “Absolutely not. I’m not leaving your side.”

“Remember what the doctor said about this being a marathon, not a sprint? Things are going to get harder in the coming days. Go home tonight. Get some rest.”

I didn’t know from where within me I found that wisdom. It felt like some other person was speaking through me, rather than me saying the words coming out of my mouth.

Mom and Dad resisted, but they eventually relented.

“We will be back first thing in the morning. And if anything changes, all you need to do is call, and we will turn right around and be back.”

I nodded.

“Are you sure?” Mom said, slowly packing her bag.

“Yes,” I said.

But when they shut the door behind them to leave, I found myself shocked to feel the hot tears on my cheeks.

Leilani, my night nurse, a small, but spunky Asian woman who wore a plumeria behind her left ear, came to visit me not long after my parents had left. I’d managed to wipe the tears off my face by then, and I hoped that she couldn’t tell I’d been crying.

“Ready to go to bed?” she said.

I wasn't sure, but decided I'd go along with the protocol.

She gave me sleeping medicine in a clear white cup, watching me swallow it before she left.

"Get some good rest, dear," she said, closing the door softly behind her.

The sleeping medicine was potent. I didn't so much as fall asleep as drop like a stone into the dark well of it. My sleep was dreamless. In the darkness of it, I felt the currents of anxiety and fear flow through my body. At night, fear and anxiety were free to run rampant, my conscious mind unable to numb or push them away with distracting thoughts or jokes.

It must have been dead in the middle of the night when I heard the wail come from the bed beside me, and a thud, as if someone had just fallen thirty thousand feet into my neighbor's hospital bed. The curtain was drawn closed, but I could hear distinct rustling and movement coming from behind the curtain. I hadn't remembered someone being there when Leilani had come in to give me my medicine, so this new patient had to be a recent arrival.

"Hello?" I said, half expecting not to get an answer.

A long pause followed by silence. They had stopped moving.

That's when I felt the world tear open with a scream of pain. When I opened my eyes, I saw that I had somehow fallen onto the floor.

In a moment of horror, I realized I had been the person screaming.

Finally, I heard his voice croak out the tiniest "hi" from behind the curtain. The voice seemed to come from the bottom of a deep well, a long distance away.

"Do you need me to call a nurse?"

"Oh no. Please don't," I said.

"Are you sure?" he said.

I can't explain it, but the voice had a calming effect on me. I hadn't realized my heart had been pounding in my chest the whole time until it wasn't. It had never struck me before that peace and calm could be something perceptible. I'd always imagined feelings like peace as the absence of things. The absence of fear, the absence of anger, the absence of anxiety.

"More importantly," he said, his voice working through my mind and body like a massage, "how are *you* doing? I was starting to get a little worried there."

"What do you mean?"

"I mean, you were moaning and tossing and turning, and you looked like you really needed a nurse for a moment there."

That sounded like the most absurd thing I'd ever heard.

"If there's anyone in this room that needs the nurse, it's you," I shot back, indignant at the accusation that it had been *me* that had awakened him, rather than the other way around.

I struggled to my feet, but the more I tried to stand, the more I just kept falling back down.

His soothing voice broke the silence, “Do you think it would be okay if I came over and helped you back into bed?”

I felt my face grow red.

“If you’re not comfortable, it’s okay,” he added quickly. “I just don’t think it would be all that comfortable for you to spend a night on the floor like that.”

He had a point.

“Yes, I guess,” I said.

I heard stirring, the movement of someone in the other bed getting out of it, and the sound of his feet hitting the floor. The curtain rustled. I peered into the darkness where the white curtain ended between our beds. I saw his long, fingers first. Strange. Alien. Otherworldly. I felt a chill spread over my whole body.

But when he pulled aside the curtain and finally managed to show his face, all my fear and hesitation slipped away, replaced instead by stone-cold terror.

Chapter 9

"You," I said, sitting up in bed, pulling my legs up to my chest in a defensive posture. "You..." But as much as I tried to articulate my terror and confusion, my stupid mouth only managed to mutter *you* repeatedly.

The curtain covered the rest of his body, but his face was unmistakable. It was the same guy I'd seen weeks earlier at the doctor's office in Kona. The same guy who had stood beside me and then run away at the caldera. It occurred to me with a chill that he was probably the same guy who had been stalking around in my backyard. And now, he was here, in my hospital room.

His mouth softened into a smile, but his stare was just as intense as it had been at the clinic in Kona, wide-eyed, like the Afghan girl in that National Geographic picture. Even though I knew I should be terrified by this stalker's presence in my hospital room, I found myself unable to take my eyes off his beautiful face.

Because it was beautiful.

Otherworldly. And even though the room was as dark as death, his face had the quality of being illuminated from within.

Just when I thought we'd be stuck in an eternal stare down for the remainder of the night, I noticed a change pass over him. Was it sadness? Pity? Fear?

He was the one to flinch first, his eyes flickered away, and then in a quick motion, he offered me his hand and helped me up. As soon as I was standing and steady on my feet, he backed away, disappearing behind the white hospital curtain, and the room got inexplicably darker without him there.

I heard the bed creaking as he got back into it.

We sat in silence for what felt like an eternity. My mind spun with things to say, but I couldn't seem to form a complete sentence worth uttering. I wanted to ask him if he was the same person I'd seen in the clinic and at the caldera, but before I could bring myself to ask a single question, I felt the effect of the drugs Leilani had given me earlier, and I fell into a fast and deep sleep.

Mom and Dad were sitting in their usual spots when I woke, and the curtain that had been closed in the night was pulled open, revealing an empty bed.

"Where did he go?" was the first thing that came out of my mouth.

"Where did who go?" Mom asked, a shadow of fear and worry crossing her face as she spoke.

"There was a guy there," I said.

Mom's brows furrowed.

"Well, when *we* got here, the bed was empty, and the curtain was open. Maybe they moved him to his own room so as not to disturb you? Given the fact that you're supposed to be in quarantine, I'd be shocked that they'd put another patient in this room with you. The nurses said you had a rough night last night."

While my sleep was hardly restful, I wouldn't necessarily call last night a rough night.

"It was okay," I said.

When I said that, Mom got up from her recliner to grab my hand.

"You don't need to be strong for me, okay? If you had a rough night, you can tell me you had a rough night."

"Okay," I said, confused. "But I didn't have that bad of a night."

"Okay," Mom said, but I could tell she didn't completely believe me.

I felt pretty good that day and asked my day nurse if it was okay I walked around. She said it was okay, as long as I was accompanied by someone, and as long as I didn't leave the hospital grounds—and only if I promised to return to the ward if I started feeling sick.

I told Mom I wanted to read in the hospital garden. It wasn't really a garden, but more like a little outdoor space with three picnic tables around which the hospital had planted a bunch of thoughtfully selected tropical plants to give the space the feeling of a garden. I dragged the IV pole on wheels with me and settled into one of the empty picnic tables. Three doctors in bright blue scrubs silently ate their sandwiches, ignoring one another at one of the picnic tables.

Mom sat beside me, but after a few minutes of me asking her if she maybe wanted to go to the cafeteria to get a coffee, I realized she wasn't going to take light hints.

"I feel like I've been under observation for the last 24 hours. Can I have just thirty minutes to myself where I can breathe?"

Mom's face contorted into hurt and sadness. I knew this wasn't easy for her, and my request wasn't making it any easier.

"But the nurse said you shouldn't be alone."

"Does it look like I'll be alone? There is, like a whole ER's worth of doctors, right there," I said, gesturing at the picnic table where the bescrubbed doctors with dark circles under their eyes ate their lunches in silence.

Mom looked over to the doctors and then looked over at me. I could see her perform some kind of inner calculation in her head, resolving at last on some conclusion. She just nodded her head.

"A half hour. I'm setting a timer on my phone. Promise me you'll go nowhere else while I'm gone."

"Promise," I said.

Mom walked away, her shoulders hunched. I could see this whole thing wearing down on her, erasing the strong, confident woman I'd known my whole life, replacing her with a woman who made herself small.

The diagnosis of cancer had been terrifying, as if an astronomer had somehow identified a black hole right outside the atmosphere that had been there all along. I could feel its dark and terrifying pull. I didn't know what existed beyond the event horizon, but I didn't want to know. The future lay before us, perfectly silent and unknowable and unspeakable, waiting for our arrival. But maybe the black hole wasn't cancer at all, maybe it was me, maybe I was the black hole. The doctors had given me the diagnosis, and just like that, everything I'd been and everything I'd thought I'd be disappeared. They took away my clothes and replaced them with a nondescript hospital gown that didn't even have a back. But that was the least of it. My own parents treated me differently now. They spoke delicately and euphemistically. As much as I wanted to talk about how scared I was I might die, it was a conversation none of us dared to broach.

Mom felt a million miles away, and Dad felt like he'd gone to a whole other galaxy.

It made me sad to see Mom that way, but her worry and silence felt like a hot, weighted blanket draped over my head on a hot summer day. It was just too much. I needed room to think, space uninterrupted by Mom and Dad's worry, and the nurses' check-ins, and the doctor's impromptu visits.

Finally, alone with myself—well, mostly alone, if you didn't count the zombie doctors, who still hadn't said a single word to one another the entire time they'd been sitting there—I realized I didn't know what to do. I could read my book, but I could do that just as easily in my hospital room.

I tilted my head back to look at the blue sky through the wide plumeria leaves above me. The tree was shedding its flowers, and they browned on the atrium ground. The space smelled sweet with the scent of their death.

I know.

I should call Tay. I did the quick math and realized it was late afternoon in New York. Maybe I could get in touch with her if I called now.

The phone rang quietly in my lap. I stared at the black screen, half expecting her not to answer, but then the screen flickered on. Tay pointed the camera up at her face, a canyon of buildings behind her.

"Tay!"

"Maya!"

"I haven't been so happy to see you in my entire life."

"Me too!"

"How are things going in New York?"

Tay's ears turned red, and she leaned into her phone receiver and whispered, "Maya, I met a *guy.*"

"Tell me everything."

She had met him in one of her public affairs classes. He was from Florida.

I asked her to describe him.

"He's built like a rock climber, with strong arms and broad shoulders, but intelligent, and shy, and has no idea how attractive he is."

His name was Luke, and from that first day, they had been inseparable.

"Has he *kissed* you?" I whispered, not wanting the doctors around me to hear, knowing that they probably didn't care about whether a teenager in New York had been kissed or not. But I cared.

"He kissed me in front of the Saint John the Divine after taking me out for coffee and dessert at the Hungarian Pastry Shop right by Columbia. It was so romantic."

I wanted to be happy for her, but instead I just felt angry. Little waves of rage coursed through my heart. I felt a deep rift forming between us, as the waves of jealousy rolled over my chest. I'd never been kissed and probably now never would be. Who would want to kiss me?

A fault line that perhaps had been there all along cracked open between us. Maybe it started with Tay's good grades and my mediocre ones. Maybe it had grown larger when she decided to spend this summer in New York rather than hanging with me at the mall bookstore like we usually spent our summers. Maybe the rift had been fully formed when Mom and Dad moved me to Hawaii. But now that she had kissed a boy, the rift became a fissure, a deep canyon. We were on two different tectonic plates.

"Is he your boyfriend? How do you plan to do the long-distance thing?"

Tay's face grew sad when I mentioned the words "long distance."

I mean, surely she had to have thought of it. He lived in Florida. She lived in Oregon. They lived as far apart as two people could live from one another and be on the same continent.

"We haven't really talked about any of that yet. I mean, it's all been happening so fast. We live so far apart. Me in Oregon, and him in Florida. But we've both talked about applying to Columbia for university and how awesome it would be if we ended up in the same place next year. I mean, he keeps asking me if I'll call him every day when the program ends, or if I'm going to just forget about him and move on to another boyfriend..."

"So, he is your boyfriend!" I say, trying to mask my envy with a smile.

"I mean, it's not like anyone's asked yet, but I guess. I mean. Yes, I guess you could say we are dating."

Tay laughed a little when she said the word dating. It was comforting to hear her laugh. It's a familiar sound. It feels like home.

"But enough about me, how are *you*? How's *Hawaii*? Ohmygawd, I'm so jealous. I can see palm trees behind you. Kissed any surfer boys yet?"

I pause, not sure what to say. She's so happy. First love, or whatever. I've never seen Tay go this gaga over a guy, other than Robert Pattinson, when she and I went to the movies to see the whole *Twilight* saga for a matinee screening.

Tay was always too smart for the guys in our high school, even the nerdy ones who took all the AP classes. But this Luke guy was different. It was obvious she really, really liked him, and I had a feeling that if she did get into Columbia and he got into Columbia, his choice to go there might make a difference in her choice of university—might even rule out her choice to go to Harvard or Berkley closer to home.

I didn't want to darken her glow.

"I'm doing great, Tay. Just great. Haven't kissed any surfer guys yet, but my parents took me to see the volcano. It was erupting."

"Oh, I'm so jealous," she said, but I saw her gaze trail off and her whole face light up.

The phone went dark. She put the screen to her chest. Through the muffled speaker, I could hear her laughing.

She lifted the phone up to her face, her face red, glowing, happy.

"Hey Maya, is it okay if we talk later? Luke wants to take me on a subway ride downtown to the South Ferry."

"Have fun," I said, pushing back the tears.

When the call went dead, the tears came. I wiped them away just in time for Mom. I didn't want her to see that I'd been crying.

That night, after Mom and Dad left, I listened for the sound of someone moving in the bed beside me. But as I fell into a heavy medicated sleep, the curtain remained open, and the bed was empty.

When I woke, he was standing over my bed, with a concerned look on his face. What surprised me the most was that I wasn't surprised to see him.

I could have sworn that I was dying, and he was there to take me wherever it is we go when we die, because I felt like I couldn't breathe, and my whole body hurt something awful, but then his hand grazed my cheek. It was so warm and calming, and I felt a little thrill pass through my body, like my insides were turning to caramel. I didn't want him to stop, but the more I stared into those penetrating green eyes, the more I found my body waking up from whatever twilight sleep it had been in.

I sat up in bed, and he backed away from me, as if shocked that I had the energy to move so quickly.

"You!"

"Me?" he said, still backing away from me as if I had the plague or something.

"You are the same guy I saw at the clinic in Kona. And you were there by the volcano. You ran away."

His lips parted into a shocked smile.

"I don't know what you're talking about. We just happen to share the same hospital room, and you sounded like you were in pain, so I decided to check on you. Clearly, you're not in pain now. I'm sorry I bothered you," he said, retreating behind the curtain, back to his side of the room.

"Gaslighting isn't a good look. Where were you all day? You weren't there in the morning."

I heard him getting back into bed.

"I was getting treatments in another part of the hospital," he said, his voice exasperated.

We sat in silence for a long time.

"I'm sorry," he said. "You're right. It was me."

"What?"

"It was me, okay? It was me at the clinic and me at the volcano, and me last night and me now."

"Are you *stalking me*?"

He laughed, a smooth-sounding laughter that crackled through the room, like a single violin note that rings before the symphony starts.

"No, I'm not stalking you. Kona is a small town. The island of Hawaii is not as big as people like to think it is. People run into one another. We're both on the same cancer treatment circuit, it seems."

It wasn't entirely untrue. Even though everyone called the Island of Hawaii the Big Island, it was hardly big by any standards. It was more like the size of Connecticut. Bigger than Rhode Island but not by much. The explanation made sense, but something still didn't seem to add up for me.

He went on, his voice breaking the darkness, softening, growing tender, "I'm sorry if I scared you. I was worried about you. You sounded like you were in pain. I waited and waited for the nurses to come, but when they didn't come after a while, I decided I'd check on you myself."

"Well, I'm not in pain now," I said. Was that true? Was I *not* in pain? I did feel a little breathless, but for the most part, felt about the same I'd been feeling for weeks, which wasn't great, but I wouldn't say it was on death's door or anything.

"I'm glad you're not in pain."

We sat in silence, my heart pounding. I didn't know why it was pounding so hard. Maybe it was all the medicine coursing through my body, but maybe it was something else.

Maybe it was him.

"So, what's your story?" I said, breaking the silence that felt interminable.

"What do you mean?" he asked.

"You know. Who are you? I don't even know your name."

"Gabriel."

When he said his name, some spark of recognition opened within me, like I'd heard his name before somewhere (of course I had, it wasn't an uncommon name). But it was more than that; I felt like I'd already heard his story elsewhere, that I already knew who he was, that he didn't need to tell me.

"I, well, I guess you could say I landed in Hawaii a few weeks ago..."

"Interesting. I did, too."

"Well then, it makes more sense why we'd be running into one another. We're clearly both doing the 'just landed in Hawaii circuit."

I nodded in the dark.

That's when the screens above my head that had been monitoring my heart and breathing all started to beep all at once, and I felt my breath catch in my throat, not like a cough, or a sneeze, but like someone was sitting directly on top of my chest, making it impossible for me to breathe in or out. I gasped for breath, tried to call out for help, but already I could see the white stars in the periphery of my vision closing in, piling up like snow.

The last thing I saw was his eyes. Rather than worried or frantic, like Mom's eyes would have been, his face was calm, inviting.

"You are safe. Everything is going to be okay," he said.

I looked up into his beautiful face and soft, thick lips. Even though I was probably dying and couldn't breathe, all I could think about was how much I wanted to kiss him. Yet, the more I wanted to lift my body to grow closer to him, the stronger the force of gravity seemed to become.

He looked down at me in that moment, a look of shock on his face, but also something else, tenderness? Lust? I couldn't make sense of it.

Everything went black.

Chapter 10

I woke with Mom's hand on my forehead.

"She's waking up, thank God," Mom said. Her voice sounded distant, weak with worry.

For some reason, I couldn't see her face.

I could hear Dad's feet shuffle to my bedside, but my head felt like it weighed ten thousand pounds, and for some reason, I couldn't turn my neck to look at him.

I felt a hand on my arm.

"You had us really worried there for a minute, hon," he said. His voice also sounded distant, muffled, as if it was coming from behind a thick curtain.

As much as I was glad to have Mom and Dad by my bedside, my first thought was *him. Gabriel.* Where had he gone?

"Where is he?" I tried to say, but no sound came out of my mouth, and when I tried to speak, I felt like I was choking.

I gasped against something that seemed to be holding my voice prisoner.

"Where is he? Where am I?" I gasped. Mom's face finally came into view, and I saw why it had been so muffled. She was wearing a white face mask. Dad was too.

Mom shook her head, and then, very slowly, like the way she used to talk to my grandfather, who was diagnosed with Alzheimer's last year, she explained, "You have a tube in your throat that's helping you breathe. You're in intensive care. In isolation. You have no white blood cells in your body to protect you against infection. You went into a crisis a few days ago and have been asleep since then."

"Gabriel," I asked, and the sound somehow made it through the tube, sounding more like "Gab."

Mom shook her head. It was clear she had no idea what I was trying to say. The machines above me started to beep again, and I saw Dad's face twist into terror and then panic.

I need to get out of this bed and figure out what's going on. Why am I here? Why am I trapped? Where's Gabriel? I grab at the tube coming out of my mouth and pull, trying to get it out of my throat, but before I can pull it out, the room becomes crowded with nurses and doctors, all frantically pushing buttons, touching my tubes, and then I see the white stars again crowning away my vision, and I'm gone.

Chapter 11

Gabriel sits crossed-legged in the center of a white open expanse. The open expanse has neither horizon nor walls, nor sky, nor ground, though he's sitting right in the middle of it. I know it's the middle, because where else would we be, but in the middle of it all?

He looks so small compared to the blank expanse around him. I can make him look very small if I take the wider view of the space, or I can make him very large if I get close to him. His eyes are closed. He appears to be meditating. I don't want to disturb him.

It's hard to explain. I feel so much love for him, even though I don't know him from Adam.

Does he know I'm here?

What is this place? Where am I?

I am everywhere.

When I wake, the tube has been removed from my throat, but my throat feels raw, like it's been sliced open from the inside.

The room is big, white, and windowless. There is no curtain, and no other bed. No Gabriel. My body hurts. I feel like I might have imagined him, imagined all of this.

How am I even still alive?

Mom and Dad sleep together on the big green recliner tucked into the middle of the room. They're both wearing white gowns and masks. They hear me moving and wake up.

"How are you feeling today, dear?" Mom asks, as if nothing horrible has happened and I've just woken up in my own bed. Acceptance takes a long time to come, but when it does, its effect is total.

"Let me call the nurse and get you something to drink."

My throat feels so raw the idea of drinking anything sounds about as appealing as drinking a cup of sand.

"Please, no," I croak out.

"Oh, don't talk, honey. The medicine is doing its work. We have to be very careful that you don't get sick."

Everything comes back to me all at once. The chemo. The night I woke with the tube in my throat. Gabriel.

"How many days has it been?" I ask, every word hurting as I speak it.

"It's been a week, hon," Mom says. She looks away. It might as well have been a year. There's a huge gulf between us, now. The sick and the well. The healthy and the not. The one who sees everything and the person going through it.

I pull myself into a somewhat sitting position in the bed.

I reach to brush my hair out of my face, and a clump gets tangled around my fingers, and then detaches from my scalp.

I want to look at myself in the mirror.

Mom helps me up and holds my arm as we make our way to the bathroom. I feel like I'm a hundred years old.

I stand in front of the mirror, and for the first time in a week, get a glimpse of myself. I don't recognize her, the girl in the mirror. My face is bloated and pale. My lips are chapped and bloody. My skin tone is splotchy and red, like there's been a horrible rash all over it. And my hair is coming out in clumps—I'm half bald.

Who is that girl?

I reach to brush the hair out of my face, and a clump falls into the sink.

Morbidly curious, I pull my hair and more comes out in my hands. I look like an abused doll who has gotten half its hair pulled out.

When I walk out of the bathroom, Mom gasps. Dad looks away. I think I can see tears in his eyes.

I had taken one last look at myself in the mirror before I left the bathroom. Bald patches cover my head in weird places.

That evening, Mom helped me brush the last of the hair out. Dad found the pink beanie in my bag, and I pulled it over my bald head.

I asked them to go home again. I wanted to be alone. I wanted to be able to cry freely without worrying them.

Chapter 12

A maddening week followed. Doctors and nurses walked in and out of my room to give me a new infusion of blood or pain medicine, or sleeping medicine.

I wanted to leave the hospital. I fantasized about it, dreamt about it. One afternoon, I dreamt that I was standing at the edge of the caldera, watching the eruption. I saw a woman crawl out of the red fissure in the earth. She was me. She was Pele. She was screaming.

The pain in my body grew so unbearable that I jumped into the fissure to join her.

I couldn't eat. I barely could sleep. The pain medicine helped, but barely. They gave me a morphine pump, but I couldn't get enough of it, pumping myself into a stupor and eventually into sleep.

Some days hurt less than others. On those good days, the nurses, seeing that I was getting antsy, would let me get out of bed to take walks around the cancer ward.

One morning, I woke up alone and slipped out of bed. It was early morning, the time when the nurses changed their shifts, and when everything in the hospital is still quiet.

I walked down the hall, dragging my I.V. pole behind me, passing open rooms, where people lay in various states of suffering.

I walked until I reached an open door with a big red EXIT sign on it, and I slipped inside. It was an emergency stairwell, and I think it was just the grace of God that I didn't set off an alarm or anything. The light in the stairway was softer than the bright halogen of the hospital. I immediately felt calmer and safer in there.

I sat down on the top stair and took a deep breath. Finally, alone. No one would barge in on me in here to check my vitals or check that I had enough meds in my I.V. bag. No one to ask me if I needed anything or if I had any new pain.

Just me, and the pain, for once.

It was a relief.

That's when I felt the warm hand on my shoulder.

I looked up. It was him.

Gabriel.

I felt so many different things rush through me at once as I looked at his hunched figure, leaning over me in that shadowy stairwell. It had been at least a week since I'd seen him last, since he'd last touched me, and I didn't want to admit that when the pain subsided enough for me to think about things other than my impending death or fleeting mortality, my thoughts sometimes drifted over to *him*.

Who was he, really? I realized that he'd hardly told me anything about himself. He had said he wasn't from around here, but where was he from? How old was he? He looked a little older than me, but not by much. Why was he always so worried about me? Why did he even care?

My thoughts were broken by his soft voice in my ear, “Where have you been, stranger?”

“Busy dying. What about you?”

He laughed. I could tell he didn’t want to laugh, but he did.

I didn’t want to look at him. I didn’t know what I would feel if I looked at him, and it scared me a little. When I finally turned to face him, I held my breath. I didn’t know what I was expecting. He was so beautiful, a crooked smile on his face. He glanced away, just as quickly as I looked up.

I didn’t break my stare. I wanted him to look at me. I wanted him to touch my face again, like he’d done last week.

But he didn’t look at me, not directly. He looked past me, clearly trying not to smile. I could tell he liked the way I was looking at him.

“I’m so sorry,” he said. “It was not supposed to go this way. I messed everything up. I, just, I don’t know.”

“What do you mean by that?”

He shook his head.

“I shouldn’t be here,” he whispered. That was obvious. He wore a big black jacket. He wasn’t in a hospital gown, the garb of a citizen of the country of the sick.

“Yeah. I shouldn’t be here, either, but here we are.”

“No. No. I really shouldn’t be here. I should go.”

"Oh," I said. "What are we supposed to be, then?" I said, finding myself flirting with him despite myself.

This made him smile, but then he grew serious.

"No. We aren't supposed to be anything at all."

I felt my face grow red with shame. I stood up and pushed my way past him, the bright lights of the hospital hallway making my eyes ache and then tear up.

I told myself it was just the lights.

I'd heard enough boys tell me that they didn't "want to be anything" to know that he wasn't interested in me; that he was trying to let me down gently. Why would he be interested in me, anyway? I was practically dying. I mean, I hoped I wasn't dying, of course, but I was sick, and my body was falling apart, and who would want to date that, much less be around it?

I'd noticed as I pushed my way past him that he didn't have any I.V. with him. Maybe he was leaving and wanted to say goodbye to the pathetic girl who had had a medical emergency in the bed beside him. But there was something else about him, something that seemed to glow from within.

He was beautiful, and I was... bald.

I crawled into my hospital bed, covered my head with the bedsheets, and cried.

As I cried, a thought occurred to me that gave me chills. What if Gabriel wasn't human at all?

The days passed, and I slept through most of them. Mom and Dad stayed with me during the day and left at night. I half-expected Gabriel to come visit me when I'd wake up in pain in the middle of the night, but he never did visit me again. He was gone.

Mom sometimes asked me if I'd told Tay about what was going on, but I shrugged her off. Tay sent me pictures of her and her new boyfriend: here they are at the MET in front of a naked Greek statue. Here they are at Coney Island, taking a selfie on the Ferris wheel, the ocean big and infinite behind them. Here they are at some diner in the middle of the night, feeding each other apple pie à la mode.

I tried not to feel too angry and left out. But sometimes I'd find myself shocked at the force of my own rage. It seemed to come out of nowhere, like a terrible weather system that left me scowling and staring into the void.

I should be out there living my life, not lying here in a hospital bed trying not to die. Mom and Dad were never good at being around anger, and they'd tell me they needed to go get lunch or make a phone call whenever they noticed my face darken.

I had planned to read a bunch of books during my hospital stay, but *Mortality* sat unread on my bedside table, and I spent most days too sick or exhausted to do much of anything but watch television and stare into the void, my soul fuming.

I was surrounded by my parents, and doctors, and the hospital support staff, but I'd never felt so alone in my entire life.

I lost track of time. One morning, my doctor walked into the room before the nurses had had a chance to check my vitals. This was unusual. My doctor usually visited after the nurses had done their poking and prodding, and after the hospital staff had brought me breakfast.

His mouth was covered by a mask, but from the look of his eyes, I could tell he had bad news.

It was difficult to take in what he said. My blood counts were not improving. The treatment wasn't working.

I saw Mom physically collapse into the chair. Dad looked away. I think I saw tears in his eyes.

"So, what's next?" I asked, quick to get down to it.

The doctor mentioned that there might be some clinical trials that they could try, but that I wouldn't qualify for any of them while my body remained so weak from the chemotherapy.

"The best thing you can do right now is go home and get stronger, and we'll prescribe you medicine to keep you comfortable."

"Does this mean that I'm dying?" I asked.

The doctor bit his lip.

"With the fact that your cancer has spread, I'm worried that any treatment we try right now will just make you sicker or could kill you without adding much benefit."

"But does that mean that I'm dying?"

The doctor looked away. It occurred to me that even doctors had trouble admitting difficult truths.

"Right now, just focus on getting stronger, okay? We'll discuss the next steps in a few weeks when your body has had some time to recover."

And then, the doctor left the room quickly, like he was trying to run away from a conversation he didn't want to have.

Mom looked away. She was trying to hide the tears. Dad didn't say a word. He didn't look sad at all. He looked angry.

After spending just over a month in the hospital, the day finally arrived when I was stable enough to go home. They stopped the chemo, which meant that for the first time in weeks I started to feel much better.

A nurse said that palliative care would call for an appointment in a few days.

"Isn't palliative care for people who are dying?" I asked.

The nurse grew pale and seemed to fumble her words.

"No. No. It's not like that. Palliative care is for anyone with a chronic condition. It's all about managing pain right now so that you can have your best life now while your doctors figure out other options. It goes alongside your regular treatments."

The whole thing was incredibly overwhelming.

Why couldn't they tell me if I was going to die? Did they not know? Or did they just not want to say the unspeakable?

I knew I should have been worried about dying as my parents drove me home, but somehow, all I could think about was Gabriel telling me "he shouldn't be here" and that we "shouldn't be anything at all."

Chapter 13

It felt strange to be back home, mostly because home didn't really feel like home. After all, we'd only just been living in the house for a few weeks before I got really sick.

It felt wonderful to be out of the hospital. In the evening, I'd lie on the grass in the yard, feeling the cool air on my face, watching the stars blink on, feeling the heat come off the tiki torches as Dad lit them, one by one.

Mom hovered around me uncomfortably, knocking on my door at random times to make sure I was still breathing. I could tell that without the monitors at home to check my heart rate and other vitals, she was worried that I'd just drop dead in my room, but she was too terrified to tell me that this was her worry, so instead, she just checked up on me every hour, which left me basically without privacy.

We hadn't really talked about anything since we left the hospital. The doctors had a sense of urgency when they talked about the clinical trial, explaining that they wanted to give my body some time to recover before they started, but also warning me that if I waited too long, I might lose the option entirely if I got too sick. Even so, the thought of choosing to pump more poison in my body when I might die anyway sounded like an awful bargain.

I wondered if there might be another better option, but couldn't imagine it.

Tay called me. Her eyes were red and puffy, and I could tell she was in her room back in Portland. Her summer program had come to an end.

I pretended that my camera was broken so she wouldn't have to see me. My voice sounded healthy at least.

"It hurts so much to be away from him."

I didn't want to laugh, but I had to suppress my laughter. She had no idea.

"At least you can talk on Zoom and stuff."

"It's not the *saaaame*," she said, her voice taking the pitch of a small animal wail, when she said the word same.

"Did you guys *do it*?" I asked. I wasn't sure if it was rude to ask, but it was the one thing our conversation seemed to circle around whenever we texted or talked.

She smiled, and grew silent, and her face got very red.

"Oh my god. You guys did it. You *did it*. You're not a virgin anymore."

Tay buried her face beneath her pillow.

"And you're not going to tell me anything?" I said, feeling the old anger rise. There it was. Out of nowhere.

Tay extracted herself from the pillow.

"I don't know how to describe it. Like, you hear people talk about it in this clinical way, like it hurts or it feels good, but it wasn't like that at all. It was just two people in love, connecting in this special way. It's so hard to put into words. Like there was no boundary between him or me, or me and the world. Everything was just one thing, and the whole world, for just one moment, made radical sense."

"You said the word *love*," I said.

Tay buried her face in the pillow again, and I could see that the tears had returned.

"I just miss him *so* much."

The anger washed over me in waves. I still hadn't told Tay about my diagnosis. The fissure between us had grown deeper. I felt like we were standing on two different sides of a canyon, a roaring river between us. On her side—life, and sex, and relationships, and a future. On my side—doctors talking about palliative care and experimental trials.

I knew that Tay would do everything she could to help me if she knew. She might even convince her mother to fly her out here.

I got the sense that it wouldn't matter. There was no helping me through this one. Telling Tay the truth would make it real in a way I wasn't ready to make it real. It would change things between us and I didn't want things to change.

Mom knocked on my door.

"That's my mom calling me down to dinner," I said, grateful to have an excuse to drop the call without being rude. "I'll call you tomorrow," I said, not sure if I would call.

I decided to take a walk to the beach. Mom was nervous about me going there on my own, but I told her that I might as well die right now if I can't have some sense of normalcy in the meantime.

The mention of the three-letter word caused Mom to relent just a little, but she made me take my phone, and she said that if I wasn't back in an hour, she would send a search party. I knew she wasn't joking.

It hurt to walk. It hurt to breathe. I had to stop and sit down several times because I felt like I was going to throw up.

I made it to the beach and sat down in the sand with my journal.

After so many weeks of people attending to my every bodily function, it felt good to be alone at last, free of Mom and Dad's worried looks, free of having to perform "being strong" so they wouldn't have to worry about me dying. It felt good to not have to try to pretend that things were normal or okay.

I felt the hot tears on my cheeks, followed by the familiar rage.

It was like a storm—the rage. This energy that washed over me in waves, leaving me unable to think about anything else but the anger.

It made the tears go away.

That's when I felt the hand on my shoulder. My body went cold when I looked up and saw who it was.

Chapter 14

"Gabriel," I struggled to my feet. "What the hell are you doing here?"

He stood above me, his body hunched. Something was really wrong with his back, like he was carrying something heavy there, some deformity. From my angle, I couldn't tell exactly what it was. Even though it was practically 100 degrees outside, he was wearing a heavy blue coat, and black pants, and closed-toe shoes. He didn't fit the landscape at all.

"I was walking along the beach, and saw you, and even though I know the reasonable thing to do is to give you space, I couldn't help it. I just *had* to say hi."

His eyes are so intense. A little electric current passes through my body. I like that he's looking at me. It feels so good. I don't want it to end.

I stand up to face him, and I become aware of how close we are, our bodies almost touching.

"I thought you said we shouldn't be friends."

He broke his stare, and sighed. "It's not the best idea, but whatever. It's not like I'm going to get stricken down by God or anything for talking to you."

I could feel a subtext forming beneath his words. I'd lost a lot of weight in the hospital. I was skinny now, but not in an attractive way. I was skinny in a "I'm dying" kind of way. He wasn't going to be stricken down by God for talking to a dying girl, is what he meant.

"I'm glad you're out of the hospital," he said, struggling to find something to say that didn't involve the weather or my impending doom.

"Yeah, tell me about it."

Out of nowhere came a big gust of wind. It happened sometimes in Hawaii. Some motion of wind from high up in the mountains made its way down to the coast, bringing a sudden and unexpected gust that could sometimes be dangerous if it dislodged a loose palm branch onto the head of an unsuspecting tourist or motorist.

"Hey, look," he said. "I have to go now. But I was wondering if you wanted to come with me tonight to Mauna Kea to see the stars?"

I'd been wanting to go since we moved to the island, but I'd heard you needed a four-wheel drive to go there, and my parents didn't have one.

"I'll bring a Jeep," he said, as if reading my mind.

I struggled to breathe as he said the words, and not because I had lung cancer, but because being around him literally took my breath away.

"Okay," I said, cautiously. "What time?"

"As soon as the sun sets, I'll be waiting in the car outside your house," he said, and then, without saying another word, he backed away from me, until he was completely enveloped by the monstera and ginger of the jungle. Then, and only when I could barely get a good look at him, he turned around and disappeared into the shadows.

I sat in a daze, alone on the sand, my mind spinning.

How did he know where I live?

More importantly.

Did Gabriel just ask me on a date?

And how the hell was I going to explain this to Mom?

I walked home slowly, stopping a lot to catch my breath.

When I came through the front door, I could see Mom was relieved that I was back.

"How was it?" she asked, trying to sound as casual as she could.

"The water was nice and warm," I said, and then told her I was tired and was going to go back to bed.

I tucked myself into bed and wondered if I should text Tay and tell her that I have a date but decided not to say a word. I set my alarm, and slept into a deep, peaceful sleep, the most peaceful sleep I'd had in months.

Chapter 15

I wake to the blaring ring of my phone alarm. The sun sets around 7 p.m., but when I sit up and look at my clock, I see that it's already 6:15 p.m., and I'm running late before I've even started. I've somehow slept through the whole day. I drag my aching body out of bed and make my way to the bathroom to take a shower. I half expect everything to hurt, but somehow, I feel almost like I'm floating as I shower and brush my hair. It's the adrenaline. I can't wait to see *him*. My heart pounds harder at just the thought.

Afterward, with a towel wrapped around my body and my hair dripping, I rifle through the two bags of clothes I brought to Hawaii from Portland, trying to find something to wear.

I find the flower-patterned dress I bought at a thrift store when I started high school. It is from the 90s, from the era where girls wore babydoll dresses with floral patterns. The dress has spaghetti straps and falls just above my knee. I decide to not wear a bra. I'd never really felt the need for one.

I could tell it kind of horrified Mom, who sometimes would pull me aside and whisper, "Maya, I can see your nipples through that dress." But Mom would never dare make me change my clothes because it made her uncomfortable. Bodily autonomy was very important to her.

In the bathroom, I consider whether to wear makeup and decide against it. I don't want it to look like I am trying too hard. I put on my pink beanie to cover my head, throw on some lip gloss, and take a long, hard look at myself.

I still look very sick, and I have no idea why anyone would want to go on a date with me, but I know that if I stand there scrutinizing myself for a moment longer, I'll lose all courage and crawl back into bed. So, I shut off the bathroom light, plunge myself into darkness, open the door, and make my way downstairs, hoping I can slip out of the house without Mom making a big deal of it.

But Mom is sitting on the couch watching some home renovation show, and the moment she hears my feet creaking on the stairs, the show goes off and she's standing in front of me appraising me head to toe. Her mouth grows stiff, and then she opens it as if to say something, but she stops herself, shakes her head, and then nods.

"Where are you going all dressed up like that?" she asks, clearly suspicious.

I look out the front window to see if he is here yet, but there is no sign of a Jeep outside, not yet. I hope he will come soon. The last thing I want is Mom asking more questions. Thankfully Dad is nowhere to be seen.

"I was hoping to maybe take a walk to the labyrinth. There's a drum circle there tonight."

Mom eyes me up and down and doesn't say a word for what feels like forever.

Just when I think I might die from the silence between Mom and me in the living room, I hear a car pull up in front of the house, and hope Mom doesn't hear it too.

"Well, have fun," she says, turning back on her show. "And take your phone with you. And call me if you need anything."

I try not to dash out the door, but I move swiftly. Gabriel is waiting in the driver's seat, looking as stunning as ever.

The seats of the Jeep are set high up, and between feeling like my lungs don't work, and my aching limbs, getting into the car feels like an athletic event. He offers me his hand, and I take it. I grab his arm for extra purchase, and I can feel the hard muscles tensing beneath his skin. I can see every vein in his arm shift as he pulls me up onto the seat. His arm is so perfectly formed, it's like looking at a Renaissance statue. It's not just his arm that's perfectly formed. My eyes make their way to his chest. He's wearing a form-fitting black shirt covered by a jacket, but I can see his chest perfectly, the shirt hugging his muscles. His back is covered by an unseasonably heavy jacket, and he still looks a bit hunched over in the seat, as if accommodating an immense load he's somehow carrying on his back.

A little wave of electricity passes through my body. I don't want him to let go, and I don't want to think about his back. With one strong pull, I'm up.

I hardly have a moment to catch my breath. Gabriel hits the gas and we're off.

"So, what changed your mind about seeing me?" I ask, as soon as we're far enough away from my house that I know there's no chance Mom will hear, and less of a chance that Gabriel will change his mind about me and turn around.

"What do you mean?"

"You said that you shouldn't see me and that we shouldn't be anything at all."

He shakes his head, "No, it's not a good idea."

"Why?"

"Because of what happens next," he says, with a flutter of his hand.

It takes me a moment to understand, but then I get it.

He must know I'm very sick. It occurs to me that he probably thinks I'm dying. He doesn't want to get too attached. For all I know, he might be dying too and might not want to get too attached for his own reasons.

He hasn't taken his eyes off the road. In the distance, the sky has turned a bright red, just like an eruption.

"It's like you're taking me to the mouth of hell," I say, laughing, deciding it's best to change the subject. But he doesn't laugh.

I stare out the car window at the passing forest that looks like it belongs in Medieval Bible, the dark trees look like paper cutouts framed by gold leaf. It's so beautiful.

I don't want to think the next thoughts, but you can't unthink thoughts once they arrive.

I don't want to die. I want more. I want more sunsets. More days of gold leaf skies. More first dates. More first kisses.

Like an ocean swell from deeper water, the waves of rage rise and crest inside me. I've been angry before, but this is a new kind of energy, an anger born of deep loss. For months now, I've felt trapped in my own body, my spirit strapped to a dying animal. The animal is frantic, bucking at its reins, aching to remain, while the spirit strains to slip away from the prison of pain the body has become. The spirit wants out. The body wants to go on.

The rage boils through me. My limbs hurt, but they also want to hit things.

I can tell that Gabriel senses the rage. He doesn't take his eyes off the road, but he puts his warm hand on my hand, and the rage settles into an electric current that passes through my body and resets it. I can sense his body's closeness, how it feels less like a body made of cells and atoms, and more like an energy, like a magnet, drawing me closer. His hand on my hand feels so good, but I get the urge to touch the rest of him, and for a moment, his hand tenses up almost as if he can sense my thoughts. I slip my free hand under my legs, just in case, and find myself grateful that he doesn't take his hand away. I want him to hold my hand forever.

I sneak a look at him and see that his knuckles are white from his hard grip on the steering wheel. He looks tense, too.

I try to focus on the scenery rushing past, but I can't focus on anything, not like this. I try to take a deep breath to relax, but with each shaky exhale, I feel my body tingle with electricity, coupled with a craving to kiss his lips that I've never experienced before. A hunger.

"You want to know why I decided to see you, even though I know it's not a good idea?" he says, interrupting my silent torment.

"Yes. Why?"

"I think I've sent you down the wrong path, and I need to help you find your way back to the right one."

"What the hell does that mean?"

His brow furrows. He looks worried.

"You know about free will, right?" he asks.

I nod. I'd always been interested in philosophy, so when I got a chance last summer to take a summer college course with Tay at the community college, we both jumped on the opportunity.

One of the central debates in philosophy was whether humans had free will or whether their actions were determined by outside events. Some philosophers believe humans have free will, which means that humans can make choices that determine their destiny. Other philosophers are not so sure that free will exists at all; they're not so sure humans have choices. Determinists believe that everything is controlled by prior causes and the laws of nature. According to the deterministic philosophers, our brains are wired a certain way when we're born, and then things happen to us. We think we're making decisions, but really our decisions are based on the way our brains are wired and the things that have happened to us, which are themselves the consequences of other causes, and no one has any control over any of it.

"Yes, I know about free will," I say out loud, realizing that Gabriel probably didn't see me nod.

"Let's say that free will exists in a very limited sense," Gabriel says. "Of course there are some constraints to free will. There are natural laws. So, you can't just will yourself to have the ability to fly or something silly like that. And there are other natural constraints based upon how each person's brain is wired, and the random and not-so-random circumstances that can arise in any given life. But let's just say, for the sake of argument, that due to the great mystery, or quantum mechanics, or God, whatever you want to call it—there's this unique thing that happens when a person becomes conscious. You could say that free will is a property of consciousness or that it gets entangled with consciousness—or something like that."

"Okay," I say, struggling to follow him, "but what does this have to do with you deciding to see me tonight?"

"So, natural laws... there are things that will just happen to you in your life that you have no choice or control over."

"Like cancer?"

"Yes, like cancer. But there are things you can control. Things within your sphere of choice."

"Like what?"

"Like who—or what—you choose to love," he says, not taking his eyes off the road.

I feel my face grow hot. But I'm still not fully understanding him. He senses this.

"Sometimes events outside of the natural laws affect what happens within the natural laws, and then these events have an impact on a person's free will."

"What kind of events?"

Gabriel opens his mouth to speak but then stops. I can sense him struggling with what to say next.

"Maya, I don't really have a choice here. But you do," he says, not taking his eyes off the road. I like the way my name sounds when he says it. I want him to say my name over and over.

"A choice?"

"Yes. The same one I had, a long time ago. You can choose who to love. But you cannot choose me."

"What if I've already chosen?" I say, quickly, feeling suddenly, inexplicably angry.

"You don't understand. You *cannot* choose me. It's impossible," he says, growing frustrated with me, like the way a parent might get frustrated with a child that's just said something is unfair, or the way a teacher might get frustrated with a student who doesn't understand a simple concept after the fourth explanation.

Even so, I almost laugh. I like a good dare.

"You can't change someone's feelings," I say.

"True," he says. "But that's not what I mean."

"Then, what do you mean?"

I can see his jaw clench tight, the muscles in his jaw twitching with frustration, or anger.

"What do you mean?" I ask again, but he doesn't answer. I feel it again, the energy of the rage swirls through me. Part of me wants to will it away, but another part of me knows that the rage is protective. I don't want to talk about choosing someone else. I want to touch him.

The anger is protective. It obliterates the possibility of other emotions, like sadness or fear. If I'm really going to die, which I refuse to believe is happening, I need the rage.

But Gabriel doesn't take his hand off my hand, and the gesture softens me even though I don't want it to. Gabriel's hand on my hand melts the locked ice of my tears, and I can feel them now, falling down my cheeks, soaking my flower dress, soaking into the Jeep's brand-new cushions.

He can see me crying out of the corner of his eye as we pull onto Saddle Road, driving directly toward the horizon, which has blossomed into flame with the setting sun.

“I don’t want to spend my time on this earth avoiding things out of fear. I decided that whatever is happening is happening for me, for a reason, and it’s my job to live it. I feel like you were put in my way for a reason,” I say.

“It was a mistake,” he says. “I didn’t know why you could see me those first few times. You must have been sicker than I thought you were.”

My head spins. I don’t know what to make of what he’s saying.

“What the hell are you?” I finally manage to say. “Like, do you have an Instagram profile I can stalk?” I ask, casually. I don’t want it to be weird if I friend him later.

“No. I don’t have a phone. No technology. You don’t want to waste the precious time you have on the internet, do you? You know those billionaires just make money off your attention, right?”

“Wait. You mean to tell me you not only don’t have a phone, but you also have no social media? None at all? Like no Instagram or Facebook? How do you even *live*?”

“Nope. I just believe that our attention is the last thing we really have. Like, so many people are poor in this world, right? You know, the top 1% owning like 70% of the total wealth in the country while the bottom 90% are left with the scraps? People work, like three jobs, just to survive, and then they spend their remaining waking hours on a screen, getting all worked up about whatever an algorithm has decided to get them worked up about. Did you know that when girls delete a photo of themselves, the algorithm will feed the girl an advertisement for beauty products, because it 'knows' she's feeling self-conscious? I don't understand why anyone would use their precious free will to participate in that, why anyone would want to spend the precious free time they have on this planet putting their attention on something they cannot control, something that controls them."

"But it also has the power to connect us," I snap back, feeling defensive. "Like, I don't know. Maybe I could go on there and find other teens who have my diagnosis and feel the tiniest bit less alone? Like, I can learn about the lives of girls on the other side of the world who have my same struggles—and see what their challenges are, and what their hopes and dreams are, and it might help me feel less crazy for being in this specific body with these specific pains. And when I'm sad or angry, or having a bad day, I can connect with artists and poets and feel more human thanks to what they have written. Like, on a day where I otherwise might have felt nothing, they help me to feel *something*. And I can read the words of wise therapists with their free tools to help me work through my depression and anxiety. I mean, Mom can afford to send me to therapy, but what about the other kids who can't afford it? Those resources are a lifeline. And I can get great book recommendations. And makeup advice. And recipes. And after the Japanese tsunami, people on different sides of the city and the world were able to learn that their loved ones were safe and okay even when all other lines of communication had gone down..."

"But even though those groups exist—for other kids with your diagnosis—you haven't joined them, have you?"

"No."

"Why not?"

I don't have a response.

We turn onto the mountain.

I can feel Gabriel's attention pulling away from me, he has a knife-blade focus on the road, and I don't want to distract him.

I've never been to the top of Mauna Kea, but I've heard it's a sacred place. The sky turns deep purple as we drive up into it.

"Do you go to school?" I ask, trying to get a gauge of how old he is. I really want to ask him if he's dying, or if he has cancer like me, but I hold my tongue.

"Naw. I don't go to school," he says, but doesn't offer anything more.

"Do you work?" I ask.

"Yes," he says, his eyes drifting over to me, and then flickering back to the road. He's a nervous driver. His knuckles are white. "But it's kind of hard to explain."

"Oh?"

"I help people with transitions," he says, quickly. I can tell right after he says it, he regrets it, almost like he's said too much.

The road has darkened before us. Gabriel flicks on the headlights.

"Transitions?"

"Yes, like a doula. But for death. I guess you could say I'm kind of a death doula."

"So, you work at the hospital?" I can feel the rage energy kindling in my body again, flickering up through my throat and into my head and heart. *I'm the only one who's dying.*

"No, no. Not quite."

I bite my lip. The landscape has become lunar. There are no trees, just the rough contours of volcanic rocks that form strange angles under the dim blue moonlight. It doesn't feel like we're going anywhere, but before I know it, I see clouds below us. Each time we turn a corner, I'm convinced we've finally reached the top of the mountain, but the road just keeps going, up and up and up, into the stars.

I can see Venus just over the horizon. The first star. I know others will follow.

"What's wrong with your back?" I ask. I can't believe the words coming out of my mouth, but I get the sense that he's hiding something from me. I've heard of birth doulas, but the idea of there being death doulas sounds absurd.

"Guess," he says, his auburn eyes flickering toward mine, and I melt.

"I don't know. Scoliosis? Poor posture? Cancer?"

He doesn't take his eyes off the road, but he shakes his head, "no."

"What if it's not a disease at all? What's if it's my superpower?" he says, his eyes flickering my way again.

I feel a thrill go through me.

In the short period of time that I've lived in the land of the unwell, I've heard some people talk about how disease can be a superpower. How facing one's mortality can bring wisdom and insight, and all that bullshit.

"That's bullshit," I blurt out loud, the rage breaking through the electric current, finding its way out through my mouth. "Mostly I'm just angry... and scared."

I stare at him, wondering why I suddenly believe him. Whatever is going on with him--it wasn't scoliosis or cancer or poor posture. It was something else.

"So, what is it, then?"

"I wish you'd just drop it," he snaps back. A gust of wind seems to rattle the car, shaking it on its tires. We're still going up, up, up.

I let it drop, but I steal a glance at his back and know that I'll figure it out eventually. He can't keep whatever is going on with him from me forever. But then again, it's not like he's asked me about my cancer or anything. I can't blame him for wanting to keep our first date lighthearted. Even so, we can only pretend for so long, before...

I don't want to think it. But the thought completes its loop in my mind like a reflex.

Before one of us dies.

Chapter 16

We turn a corner and arrive at a big building, but the mountain keeps going higher. A man stands beside a gate in the road and tries to convince us that it's safer for us to stay in the parking lot below, but Gabriel is having none of it.

"You can see just as many stars from down here as up there," the official with the ranger's hat says.

"We have the required four-wheel drive and intend to drive to the top," Gabriel says.

The man shakes his head and waves us through.

"I have something to confess," he says.

"What?"

"I've never been up here."

"That makes both of us."

The top of the mountain feels more like we're in Antarctica than Hawaii. The ground is as black as coal, with patches of snow in between that never melt. From where we stand, the earth below us is shrouded in a sea of clouds. We're surrounded by telescopes as big as buildings. Their white domes dot the landscape like strange igloos, houses for the sky people or whoever it was that lived here. A road slices through the lunar landscape, interrupting the wildness of the place with a single trace of civilization. Nothing human up here looked like it belonged here.

I shiver. It's cold up here. I'd only brought my spaghetti strap dress.

Gabriel glances my way and sees that I'm cold.

"Did you bring a jacket? It gets cold at the top of the mountain at night."

I shake my head *no*, unable to stop myself from shivering.

He leans into the back of the car and pulls out a thick blue blanket, wrapping me up in it, but I don't feel the blanket at all, just his arms, embracing me as he pulls the blanket tight around me.

Above us, a sky as dark as the nice wine my parents sometimes drink to celebrate their anniversary darkens more. If I strained my eyes, I could see the first faint stars break through the blue-black gloaming.

The place is so quiet. I can hear my heart pounding in my own ear.

A sea of clouds surrounds us. To the south, I can barely make out the summit of Mauna Loa, the other taller volcano on the island. I'd heard that it had erupted not too long ago and tried to imagine what the mountain would look like, covered in fire, oozing rivers of lava.

Gabriel walks down the road a little, toward a patch of white on the ground.

"Come here, let's touch the Hawaiian snow."

I follow him, wrapped in my blanket, and lean down with creaking body to touch the cold snow.

My breath catches in my throat, and I find myself gasping for air, but no matter how deeply I seem to breathe, I just can't get enough air. I don't want to tell him I'm having trouble breathing.

I'd always been one to feel a little lightheaded in higher elevations, but this time felt different. I find myself really having to focus on my breathing. No matter how deeply I inhale, my lungs seem to be unable to get enough air in them. The lack of oxygen makes my arms and legs ache more. I feel a sudden piercing headache slice through my eyes and brain, like a hot knife cutting into my skull. Just walking a few feet down, the road to the snow has left me winded and hurting.

Before I realized what was happening, I felt my feet leave the earth. He had swept me up into his arms to catch me and pressed my body against his hard muscled chest. I felt my body swoon, forgetting for a moment that I couldn't breathe, forgetting that I inhabited a body on planet earth, a body that was dying, a body that was hurting.

The sky above us had darkened completely, and it was dazzled with stars. The long, white band of the Milky Way stretched above us, like a road of light.

I couldn't tell if it was my body making me dizzy, or if it was Gabriel holding me so close, or the stars.

It didn't matter. For a moment, none of it mattered.

I could die right now, and it would all make sense, I thought to myself.

And then I did. Well, everything went away. Or *I* went away.

Chapter 17

I woke in the car, my head pounding and my lungs gasping for air, Gabriel driving way faster than it seemed safe. The landscape blurred past us like a dream.

"Am I dead?" I asked, knowing quite well that I was stubbornly still alive. Everything hurt to prove it.

"She wakes!" he said, clearly relieved that I had re-joined the world of the living, however tenuously that re-joining was.

We had made it far down the mountain. I could tell because I could breathe a little better, even though my body still ached something awful.

"Well, I ruined that," I said, glowering, feeling the old rage energy rise. The rage had the effect of easing my pain just a little. Like a morphine drip of anger. I'd heard somewhere that anger could be protective, but this was the first time in my life that I felt it in real time. The angrier I got at my illness, the better I seemed to feel physically.

Gabriel could see my clenched jaw and tight fists.

"Don't do that," he said.

"Don't do what?" I retorted, the words coming out of my mouth like barbs.

"That," he said, gesturing at my clenched fists.

Somehow, he could feel the rage radiating off me, like heat from a hot plate. And him telling me to not be angry had the effect of just making me angrier.

We drove in silence into Hilo. When he turned into town rather than down the road that would take me home, I sat up with a jolt.

"Where are we going?"

"To the hospital. You passed out."

When we pulled into the hospital parking lot, the last thing I remember was the acid-colored yellow lights of the parking lot. All the lights in Hilo are dimmed to prevent light pollution from reaching the telescopes. Even so, the light looked so bright as I slipped into my own darkness. Brighter than the sun, than the stars, than anything I'd ever seen before.

Chapter 18

I awoke to the sound of machines beeping in my ear, eyes blurry, body tired.

A curtain divided my bed from the other beds. I still felt fuzzy from the drugs and the pain. *This place is like a factory for the dying*, I thought to myself.

Gabriel was gone.

And then I remembered everything. The beautiful night sky. My passing out. Gabriel taking me to the hospital against my will.

And yet, I was alone. I wondered where everyone was.

The world seemed divided from me by a thick veil. Life ambled on around me, nurses checking vitals, janitors wheeling brooms and mops through the hallways, visitors holding lattes-- and between the world and me was my dying body. It wasn't exactly that I wanted *out* of it. It was more like I wanted to return to what my life had been before we'd moved to Hawaii, when I could move through the world without giving my body a second thought.

With bitterness followed by a deep pang of sadness, I realized those days were over.

In the hours that followed I swirled through the void, waking occasionally, to bright lights, or masked faces. I woke shivering. Two nurses with blank faces piled blankets on top of me, but the cold came from deep within me, not without.

One hundred layers of blankets wouldn't warm me. I slept a dark, formless sleep. I woke unsure where I was, until I heard the beep of the machines and remembered. I dreamt that Gabriel and I were walking together through the woods, trying to find a waterfall. He walked ahead of me, and in the dream, there was nothing wrong with his back. Instead, where the weird hunch had been, there were two dazzling wings, the color of rainbows.

"We're almost there," he said. "But take your time. We'll do this as quickly or as slowly as you need."

In the dream, I found it difficult to keep walking. I wanted a closer look at his wings. Of course, he had wings. That made perfect sense.

When I woke, I was back in the hospital room.

"I don't want to be here," I said, at one point, not sure if anyone heard me.

But Mom was standing beside my bed. Before I slipped back into sleep, I realized that she might think I meant that I didn't want to be alive, or on this planet, when I really meant that I didn't want to be in the hospital. It didn't matter. Before I could rouse myself enough to clarify my intentions, the warmth of sleep wrapped around me and swept me away.

In another dream, Gabriel stood in the middle of a moving river, holding a brain in his hands.

"Are all your thoughts in here alone?"

I laughed. It was so ridiculous. That all consciousness—all my thoughts and feelings, and love, and anger, and rage, and fear—could be held in that pulsing ball of jelly that Gabriel could hold so easily in his two hands. It seemed both entirely logical and entirely absurd. It's easy to forget that we're all just brains and meat.

"But what does it mean, Gabriel?"

His face grew very serious then, and he lowered the brain into the river. I watched the water carry it away, as it sank, and I felt myself slip into nothingness and back into the dark of unconsciousness.

I woke in a hospital room, half-shocked to still be alive, Mom and Dad sitting beside my bed. Mom's hair was uncombed, and Dad looked like he hadn't shaved in days.

We didn't say anything. Mom was crying and didn't try to hide it.

"You've been very sick for the last few days, so I think we need to catch you up on what has happened. Would you like me to do that?"

I nodded.

"Okay. We have a lot of things to discuss, but first, maybe you can tell me what you understand is happening?"

"Well, I was diagnosed with leukemia, and it's a bad case. I don't think the doctors have a cure for it."

He nodded, “Yes. You have a very serious case. The best treatment would be a bone marrow transplant. Do you know what that is?”

“Yes, it’s when you take the bone marrow of someone healthy and put it in my bone marrow.”

“Yes,” he said, nodding. “But in order to have a bone marrow transplant, doctors need to be able to get your cancer counts lower than they are currently, and your body needs to be stronger than it is right now.”

“And my counts are not low. And my body isn’t strong.”

“No.”

“Is there anything you can do to make the counts lower? Anything to make me stronger?”

“Well, you have a mutation that makes getting those counts down very difficult. And your cancer has spread, which complicates things further. There are experimental drugs you could try, but you’d probably have to travel far away with your family to another hospital on the mainland. But we think you’re too sick to travel safely right now. Besides, it’s not likely those treatments will work given your mutation and metastasis. If you were strong enough, you could travel to O’ahu to see about a bone marrow transplant, but we don’t believe you’re strong enough for that.”

“So, I’m just going to die?”

The nice doctor fell silent. I could tell he was trying to find a way to tell me the bad news I knew he was going to tell me, but he didn't have to say a word. His face said it all.

He nodded.

"If we cannot get the counts down, you will die, yes. And without a bone marrow transplant, you will die."

Mom looked like she'd been hit in the head with a baseball bat. For the first time in my entire life, I saw Dad choke back a sob.

"What matters now," the doctor said, turning to me. "Is what matters to you, Maya. The kind of treatment we'll provide for you now will be influenced by what is important to you, what kind of life you want to live with the time you have left. Do you understand? It's important that you think about what you value, and about the things that make your life meaningful to you. Our goal right now is to give you the best day possible, for as many days possible."

I tried to make sense of the words he was saying to me. *The time you have left.*

I didn't know what to say in response. What do you say to someone asking you to think about what makes your life meaningful? Just a few months ago, I'd been looking forward to my senior year in high school, my future sprawled out before me, an empty journal, pure possibility. I'd been looking forward to maybe someday getting a boyfriend, or at the very least, getting to kiss a boy before I turned 18. All of that felt very far away, now. Gabriel didn't have social media, much less a cell phone, so it's not like I could call him up and ask if we could get a re do. Our date had ended with me passing out, and him having to drop me off at the hospital. I know I'd been very angry at him. The chances of him wanting to see me again were basically zero.

I felt stupid even thinking these thoughts. Here was a doctor asking me to answer a fundamental philosophical question—and I was sitting here in a hospital room thinking about *a guy.*

"I mean, think about it. Do you have a bucket list? Are there activities you'd like to spend your time doing? Seriously, think about it. We'll talk later," he tapped my leg and the conference was over.

The tears streamed freely down Mom's face. Dad stared blankly ahead, like he had just been introduced to a ghost. The thought made me laugh.

The ghost was me.

I was a dead woman walking.

What made my life meaningful?

Mom and Dad napped in the big blue recliner. With their bodies intertwined like that, they almost looked like they were young lovers, two college kids who had had too much to drink and passed out on a living room chair at a party. For a moment, I imagined myself as being much older than them. I was the old person dying, and they were the young lovers, keeping vigil. My body certainly felt like it was ten thousand years old.

What made my life meaningful?

Up until now, I didn't realize how much of my identity had been bound up with the idea that I had a future. Humans aren't just animals with memories; we are creatures who plan. The idea of having a future is just as integral as the fact that we have a past.

It's not until you're dying that you realize that who you are right now is intrinsically bound up with who you were and who you want to be. Without a future to imagine, I didn't know who I was anymore.

Just a few months ago, I'd been a teenager looking forward to her senior year. And now, I was a person living moment to moment, attached to a dying animal. For the first time in my life, I felt like I was living entirely in the present, and now the present seemed to expand before me, to widen, to deepen, in ways I didn't realize were possible.

The doctor had asked me what mattered to me. What made my life meaningful. I tried to think, but my mind drew a blank.

On my toughest days, I'd always loved keeping a journal and writing. When nothing seemed to make sense, I could crawl into bed with a pen and the blank page and somehow find a way to make sense of it. While I'd never had a crisis in my life of the magnitude of a terminal diagnosis, a few years earlier, when I'd just started middle school, and before I'd met Tay, I remembered feeling alone and sad. During lunch time, I'd take my journal and a book to the field behind the school, and I'd sit there alone and read, and write, trying to make sense of things.

I had read *Siddhartha* under the canopy of a big oak tree and wondered if he was right about attachment being the cause of suffering. Would being less attached to my life and my concept of a self, release me from suffering? Something felt off about this.

I had read *Romeo and Juliet*, out under the oak behind the school as well. I remember getting caught in a rainstorm, right before the moment Romeo would walk in on Juliet, who had taken the sleeping potion the apothecary had given her, and think she was dead. I slammed shut the book, knowing what came next... He thinks she's dead, and he kills himself, and just as he's about to die, she wakes up because the medicine that puts her to sleep wears off. I remember holding the book tight under my arms, running inside, away from the rain, setting my things down in a quiet stairwell, and finishing the book with clenched teeth. Romeo and Juliet's death made me feel sick inside. I'd never felt that way before—the feeling you get when someone makes a mistake, and you know they are making a mistake, and the mistake's consequences are permanent and irreversible. The feeling of watching someone do something like that is not quite like regret or sadness, though. I don't think there's a word for that feeling—the feeling of watching someone throw their whole life away.

Stupid. Stupid. Stupid.

Maybe I could make sense of what life meant to me by making a list of the books that had meant something to me? But when I thought about the books that had meant the most to me, they slipped away from my thoughts, like will-o'-the-wisps. So many of the books meant something because they spoke to life itself, or at least to life lived in the thick of it. When the poet, Arthur Rimbaud wrote about the "systematic derangement of the senses," he was writing about living, and also probably also about doing drugs, the latter of which I had no intention of doing, while the former seemed to slip away from me.

When my parents had told me we were moving to Hawaii, I'd joked with Tay, telling her that maybe I'd join a drum circle of beaded and dread locked hippies and drink magic tea. But did I really want to tell my parents that one of my bucket-list dying wishes was to drink a potion and sit in a drum circle? That sounded insane.

One of my favorite books had been *The Awakening*, by Kate Chopin, a feminist allegory about a woman who chooses to drown herself rather than live within the strictures of Victorian femininity. Rather than raise children and be subservient to her husband, Edna Pontellier chooses to swim out to sea and disappear. When I'd read the book, her suicide felt like a radical act. It was an act of protest.

But now, her suicide seemed absurd to me.

Why didn't she just take a train to France or Spain? She could have run away, or taken up art, or killed her husband, or... a thousand other things.

I remember I'd read this poem where the poet imagined a world where time ran in reverse. She imagined starting life out old and becoming young again, her limbs growing stronger rather than weaker, her senses growing sharper rather than dull. She imagined meeting that other possible self in the dead middle of her life, and wondered if she'd already passed that moment, where for just an instant, it didn't matter if time was moving forward or backward. It just was. I had only just turned 18 a few months ago, but now I wondered whether I'd already passed the middle of my life. There was no question about it now. Me and my doppelganger had passed each other years ago, and the whole time I'd been oblivious about it.

Oh, there were so many poems I could think about, too. Donald Justice imagined being able to watch the grave diggers bury his own body. Emily Dickinson wrote about grief with precision, especially the way that grief numbs you long before it really hurts. Dante Alighieri walked through the afterlife, emerging every time to *the sun and the other stars.* And then there were poems I had loved just because of the people who had introduced them to me.

But I didn't want to read. I'd spent my whole childhood reading about people living their lives.

I opened my journal to a blank page.

I want to live my life. What's left of it.

I want to kiss a boy. I want to drink until I'm drunk, and see the stars wheel above me.

But more than all of that, I want my life to have meant something. By which, I guess I meant that I wanted my life to have some kind of purpose.

But what?

I spent the next few days in the hospital. They were giving me palliative medicines to get me stronger, so I'd be able to be released. I started to feel way better, good even.

It was impossible to really believe I was dying. The thought was so terrifying and immense that I just couldn't let myself think it.

Besides, I felt a little better each day, my body, along with the medicine, fighting the sepsis and infection.

The palliative care doctors came at one point, and they brought with them the same impossible existential questions. *Think about what matters to you now; what makes life meaningful.* This, they explained, would inform my care. For example, one of the doctors said, noticing the journal on my lap, if I wanted to write a book before I died, they could give me medicine to help me focus through the pain.

I told them I didn't have plans to write a book anytime soon.

"Well, some people choose to focus on their relationships with the people closest to them. When time is short, many people feel that relationships are the most important thing in life."

I nodded but didn't know what to say. Mom and Dad clung to each other like two people on a sinking boat might cling to a life raft.

Still, I couldn't help but think that the doctor was right about our relationships being the most important thing in a life.

What did I have to show for anything? My closest relationships were to my parents. I didn't have a boyfriend or anything. And my best friend didn't even know I was sick. I figured I should fix that soon, but I didn't want to call her and tell her just yet. Telling her would make it real, and I didn't want it to be real.

Chapter 19

When I was discharged from the hospital, Mom and Dad made it clear that they had other plans. They wanted a second opinion and had scheduled us to fly to O'ahu to talk to the bone marrow doctors.

"I don't understand how those doctors get off giving a young 18-year-old girl a death sentence," Dad muttered in the front seat.

"These doctors in Hilo don't know what they're talking about."

Hearing Mom and Dad talk like this loosened something hard and scary inside me. What if the doctors were wrong? Doctors were wrong about things all the time. What did doctors in Hilo know about rare cases of leukemia? Hilo was a town built on a lava field, and every fifty years a river of lava burned the whole place down. These country doctors knew nothing. Mom and Dad were going to take me a to real doctor.

I could feel Mom's rage simmering hot from the front seat. Who were these Hilo doctors to tell her to just sit back and watch her daughter die? Palliative care, ha. Hospice!

Mom and Dad wouldn't use the language in front of me, but I could feel the energy of it.

Fuck those Hilo doctors.

So, we went to the airport to see the *real* doctors. The doctors at the Tier 1 medical center in Honolulu.

But after we had gone home and packed quick travel bags, and driven to the airport, and gotten through TSA, and finally settled into our seats for the quick hour-long flight to Honolulu, I couldn't help but feel an old sense of dread return. Mom and Dad were indignant, but they weren't inside my body. They couldn't feel what I felt.

Deep down, I knew that they were deceiving themselves. Something terrible was happening to my blood and my bones. Its urgency and importance made itself unavoidable with the jolts of pain that shot through my bones or made my muscles spasm without warning. And even though Mom and Dad sat close enough to me to touch, I realized that I alone knew what was happening inside my body, I alone was aware of the seriousness of it. It made me feel lonelier than I'd ever felt in my life.

I could try to explain it to Mom and Dad, but I knew it would just make them sad. As the plane's wheels left the runway, as we left the city of Hilo behind us, soaring above the clouds, the ocean below us like an idea, my parents still had hope.

And I didn't want to take away their hope.

Mom and Dad booked us a room at a nice hotel in the heart of Waikiki. We could see the ocean and Diamond Head from our room. From the lanai, I could hear the captains of the catamarans blow their conch shells, watch the people sunbathing on the beach, and see the black tubes of the snorkelers as they swam endless circles around a patch of dark reef in the middle of a stunning turquoise ocean. I was too tired to go out to dinner, so Mom and Dad ordered takeout, and we watched the sunset. I had no appetite but tried to eat a few bites because I didn't want to worry Mom.

When the sun set, the sky filled with stars, and men in white shirts lit the tiki torches down below, and the whole scene—the stars flickering on the ocean waves, and the torches turning the water the color of lava where it crashed into the shore—was so magical and beautiful that it almost made me cry.

Of course, I couldn't let myself cry, because that would make Mom and Dad sad. And they looked so hopeful and happy. I decided they deserved this. One happy night where they could still have hope.

But when Mom and Dad turned off the lights and the hotel room went pitch black, the dark thoughts spun in my head like a tempest. In the depth of my soul, I knew I was dying, and I knew I'd have to face it, but the more I tried to understand it and believe it, the more absurd the whole thing seemed.

Of course, I'd always known that eventually everyone dies, but it's one thing to know that we all die in the abstract, and another thing to know that *I* was dying, and not just in some abstract remote future—but soon.

How was it possible?

To die. For all this—to become nothing. All my memories, and dreams, and love, and feelings, to just disappear, to go nowhere, or if somewhere, where?

It just couldn't be real.

I grasped for something real—the soft hotel sheets rubbing against my legs and arms. The pillow that felt like a cloud under my head. The smell of the hotel room—like plumeria. Everything soft and gentle and beautiful. And then I'd feel a stabbing pain shoot through my head like a knife cutting through my skull, and the thought of death would return.

No amount of luxury or comfort or expense could stop the pain, the endless waves of pain.

I turned on my phone and scrolled. A girl recited a poem under an oak tree. A woman protested a war, holding a sign on an empty street corner. A politician gave a speech that made half the country happy and the other half angry. A girl with my diagnosis opened her closet, revealing her hat collection. I saw an advertisement for a resort in Mexico that offered intuitive healing approaches. It seemed that already the algorithm knew I was dying, knew I was grasping for any shred of hope. I kept scrolling, scrolling, but no matter what I saw, I couldn't forget it—forget that I was dying, forget that all of this would soon be nothing, and I'd be gone.

I stared out the window at the blue light of the moon on the ocean and the beautiful, sumptuous curtain swaying in our hotel room. This room must have cost my parents a fortune. The meetings with the doctors tomorrow and the tests they would do must have cost my parents a fortune. I knew that insurance surely wouldn't have covered it. The Hilo doctors had told us that it was pointless.

Pointless. Pointless. It was all pointless. I stared at the white pillowcase, the closest thing to my head, and noticed a stray thread dangling loose. It was just a small imperfection in the pillowcase, but it must have been worth a fortune, and now it was all coming undone, unraveling before my very eyes.

I wanted to throw the pillow and pillowcase across the room. I wanted to be anywhere but right here. I didn't want to die.

The next day, we took a cab to the Tier 1 hospital, and Mom and Dad accompanied me from test to test. A nurse drew tube after tube of blood to test my white blood cell counts, but I didn't need test results to know it was bad. The look she gave me when she drew the blood out of my veins said it all. I wasn't a doctor or a nurse, but I knew that whatever it was she was pulling out of my veins didn't look like blood at all. The blood was more clear than red, more gooey than flowy.

Mom and Dad accompanied me to the rooms where they scanned my whole body. The rooms where they took X-rays of my chest, and where they did a sonogram of my chest.

We ate lunch in a big white cafeteria, where doctors and red-eyed families ate burgers and chicken sandwiches and ice cream sandwiches in silence. I tried to eat even though I felt nauseous, and when I had to vomit up the little I had eaten, I hid how sick I was, lying, telling my parents I just needed to go to the bathroom.

Over the toilet, I heaved and heaved.

I didn't need a doctor to tell me I was dying, but at the end of the day, a nurse led me to an examination room where I was, for the tenth time, asked to take off my clothes and put on the backless examination gown. I sat on the examination table, shivering, with the crinkly white paper beneath my skin, crackling every time I shifted my body.

The doctor walked in and turned on the computer in the room. I could tell he was stalling. His eyes looked tired and sad. I knew he didn't want to say what he had to say, and he didn't know how to say it.

Again, the same old words.

Gravely ill.

Bone marrow transplant would kill me.

Metastasis and spread.

Incurable.

"We can offer palliative care. Hospice. Find ways to ease the pain..."

The ride back to the hotel room, we didn't talk. Mom and Dad didn't want to talk about death, and I didn't either. Dad booked our flights back to Hilo for the morning.

I didn't sleep all night. The gnawing pain was accompanied by a dark terror—the sense that maybe the only novel thing I had to look forward to was death.

And pain. Pain and more pain, ended only by what? Death. I felt like a body caught in a violent shore break, the waves thrashing me repeatedly on the sand, no escape from the cycle—just the knowledge that the next wave would come, and then one after that, until death claimed me at last.

No. No. No. No.

And in the morning, I was too sick to eat and didn't pretend I could.

As we walked through the airport to our terminal, I couldn't help but think about how every single person in the airport would someday die. Each person, who had not been asked whether he or she wanted to be alive, was here, alive—some eating sandwiches, others sipping expensive overpriced lattes, others using the scrap of time between flights to send out an urgent email, others napping—each would someday leave this world. For some, death was an abstract concept. For people like me, it was closer, clearer, more terrifying, and palpable.

I felt the panic again. The sense that I was on the other side of it—of life, as if I was already being unstitched from the seams of the world.

I used to be scared when I'd fly, but as I fastened my seat belt, I felt nothing. If the plane went down, at least we'd all go down together. But if we landed safely in Hilo, then it would be me who would have to die alone.

I felt selfish thinking the thoughts I was thinking, but then again, did we even really have control over what we thought? Thoughts came and went. The only choice we had was whether to attend to them or to let them go.

Let them go.

The airport bustled with life. Modern life. Sanitized. Sterile.

Everywhere I looked, there were things to buy—magazines, books, bags of chips, coffees, beers, wines, t-shirts with the name of the places we were and had been. Everywhere I looked, I could see the excess of it, a people who had become disconnected from the earth, and the limits of their own bodies, who had been trained to seek meaning and comfort in material things. Everywhere, the durability of things insisted themselves upon the senses, mementos designed to make a moment in time permanent—turtle figurines, the magnets with photos of the sunset, little spoons with the word Hawaii written in rainbows.

My parents, who now had all the money in the world, couldn't save me, and everywhere I looked I saw things, things, things. All the things my parents could buy: brand new cars, big screen televisions, vacation homes, a barbecue grill, a brand new refrigerator.

Whatever pleasure I would have taken in my formal life to buy a coffee and a t-shirt, or a magazine, was gone.

Everything around me stank of more, more, more, while my body asserted itself and retreated into its pain. The pain was a bell that rang through every fiber of my being. It said, now, now, now.

Back in my room, which didn't feel like my room, I felt like an animal trapped in a cage. My body was feeling marginally better, but my mind acutely remembered what it had felt like to be sick and helpless. The result was that I spent more days in bed than I probably should have. I told myself I needed to rest, when I probably had enough energy to go out.

One day, I'd finally had enough. I decided to try for a walk to the beach.

I dragged my aching body out of bed and threw on a pair of shorts and the first t-shirt I could find.

The walk took longer than it ever had, but it felt good to feel the sun on my shoulders. It was a weekday, and the beach was deserted. Just me, the gulls, and the sound of the ocean.

I sat down and shut my eyes, trying to imagine what it would feel like if I could 'just be here now,' but thoughts about mortality and sadness would crowd in, taking me away from the sound of the ocean or the feeling of the warmth on my skin.

When I opened my eyes, I swear I almost had a heart attack.

Chapter 20

Gabriel sat there, wearing the same ugly heavy jacket he'd worn when we ran into one another on the beach, the same ugly jacket he'd worn the night he took me to Mauna Kea. Nothing seemed to have changed. His stare was as intense as ever, and his posture was strange, his head hunched over, as if he was still struggling to carry the weight on his back.

"What are you doing here?" I said, realizing immediately that my words came out more like an accusation than an *I'm happy to see you* vibe.

"I didn't get to say goodbye."

"What?"

We sat in silence. He looked incredibly sad.

"I don't want to say goodbye," I said, defiant. "Can we just try again?"

He bit his lip and looked down at his feet.

"You're not going to make this easy for me, are you?" he said, sighing.

I tried to hide my smile.

"Okay," he said sighing. "You got me. Let's stick to lower elevations, this time. There's this place called the City of Refuge near Captain Cook and Kona. I want to take you there. This Saturday morning. How does 7:30 sound?" his eyes were earnest, eager; he leaned forward toward me. I felt an intense urge to touch him, a craving.

I could see the thought cross his mind. He sensed it—my craving. He stepped away from the doorway, almost as if to protect himself.

7:30 sounded ridiculously early to me, especially given that I slept basically 18 hours a day these days, but I nodded.

"I'll bring extra-large coffees," he said, and then whirled around to leave without saying goodbye. He backed away from me and then slipped around me without a sound. I could tell it was difficult for him to be near me, but I wondered if it was difficult for him in the same way it was for me. He seemed to be fighting with himself, resisting an urge...

To do what?

As he walked away, I turned around to see him go. It looked like he was carrying an extra-large camper's backpack under his jacket, but who on earth would go around doing something like that?

I didn't want to admit how much I liked him, and how curious I was about what was going on with him.

The next day, I had an appointment with palliative care. It was nice to be able to go to a doctor's appointment that wasn't in the hospital. The palliative care clinic was in this big strip mall in Kona, flanked by a poke shop and a vape store. The waiting room looked like it could have been any other dentist's office, with a fish tank in the corner and a table full of magazines. That is to say—it could have been any other dentist's office except for the fact that the two older people sitting in the plastic chairs looked skeletal and pale. They looked like people who were dying, and I wondered if I looked like I was dying, too.

It's easy to see changes in other people, but harder to see the changes in yourself.

The nurse called one of the patients in for their appointment, and I tried not to stare at the man who remained. His eyes were sunken, with black circles, and his arms and legs were impossibly thin. When he coughed, his whole body rattled, and he hunched over in his seat. Mom kept glancing over to him, her eyes full of worry, the kind of face she seemed to give me all the time these days.

The tinted office door swung open. I expected another skeletal old person to walk through the door, but instead, it was a boy. Well, not a boy exactly. It was a guy my age, maybe a little younger. He looked native Hawaiian, his skin copper-gold, his hair thick and jet black, his eyes auburn and bright. He was lanky, but his arms were muscular and strong. He looked like he would have been a surfer or a wrestler–if not for how emaciated he looked. He was followed into the waiting room by a pretty woman in a red dress, with dark hair, and high cheekbones. His eyes caught mine, and he smiled at me, plunking himself in the chairs directly opposite from me. His mom sat next to him.

"Hi, I'm Elijah, and I have cancer everywhere. Well, it started as liver cancer, but now it's everywhere–in my bones and brain and lungs. I have lung cancer, and I've never smoked a day in my life," he said, with a smile.

I was shocked at how forthright he was, shocked at how much courage he had. I wouldn't have had the courage to introduce myself to him, much less announce my diagnosis so openly.

"I'm Maya. I have... I don't know, some rare kind of leukemia. It's everywhere, too."

"Is this your first appointment with palliative care?"

"Yes."

"Figures. I think they intentionally schedule the young cancer patients together in the hopes that we'll become friends. It's not like there are a lot of support groups or anything on Big Island. Get ready for them to give you a lecture about the importance of community and interpersonal relationships as you navigate 'living with your disease.'"

I laughed. I liked Elijah already.

"How old are you?" I asked.

"18. I guess I look younger, but believe me when I say, that before I lost the weight and muscle mass, I was a stunner. Had half the girls in high school (and some of the guys) trying to date me."

Elijah's Mom's face flushed, she laughed, and then rolled her eyes, but I could tell he wasn't lying. I could imagine a world where Elijah weighed 50 pounds heavier, didn't have cancer, and had a fawning following.

"They're going to give you a list of books to read, and a little workbook to help you figure out what matters to you now that you're going to kick the bucket, but honestly, Maya, none of that matters. Death is not a homework assignment. If you want to read the books, read the books. If you want to do the writing assignments, do the writing assignments. But all that matters is what you want to do."

I nodded.

The way he spoke so openly about death scared me a little, but it was also freeing. Mom and I had not had a single conversation that admitted the gravity of my situation, but here was this kid—a stranger, laying it all out so plainly.

It was—refreshing.

I didn't want to ask the question that formed in my mind, but his courage had the effect of emboldening me, too.

"So, what matters to you?"

He nodded. I could tell he liked the question but was struggling to put the answer into words. I couldn't blame him; didn't we all struggle with the question of what matters regardless of where we are in our journey toward mortality?

"Terminal diagnosis isn't an epiphany. Pain doesn't illuminate; it erases things. I've spent a lot of time grieving my imagined future. Pain obscures things too. It's hard to think about meaning when you can barely get up to use the restroom most days."

"Tell me about it," I said.

"I've decided that maybe *meaning* is too loaded a word to ask a patient to consider at this late stage. So, instead, I've chosen to think about it like this... Right now—today—as in, this very moment—given my resources and my weaknesses—I like to stop and think--what is important to me? It simplifies things a little and forces me to stay present. If I get tangled up in all that meaning shit, then I start getting tangled up in a future I might not have. And that makes me sad as hell. But if I just stop and ask myself what's important right now, I can kind of make more sense of it. So, like, right now, what's important to me is getting on some stronger painkillers, and maybe that medicine that makes you comfortable with feeling like you can't breathe, so I can maybe go to this party a bunch of my friends are going to on Sunday. I mean, but besides that, today, I kind of just want to have a burger and then take a nap."

I liked his practicality.

"I've never been to a real party."

"Oh, really? Well, then you should come, too. It would be nice to have another cancer kid there, so I won't be the only one getting the pity faces and the weird stares."

I'd only been in the land of the visibly noticeably sick for weeks, but already I'd noticed the faces of pity reserved for me, and then even more so, for my mother. There were some perks. When Mom and I went shopping the other day, we got discounts, and a guy even gave me a free ice cream.

Still.

I looked over at Mom, who nodded.

"I'm in," I said.

Unlike Gabriel, Elijah had a phone. I gave him my number, and he texted me the name of a beach, followed by the date and time. The party didn't conflict with my date with Gabriel, and if things went well on our date, nothing prevented me from inviting Gabriel to the party, too. If I was, in fact, dying, as everyone seemed to suggest, I could take liberties with what I wanted.

I could decide what was important to me now.

Elijah kept glancing up at me and smiling, but before things got too awkward, I was saved by the nurse who called my name.

Elijah nailed the first appointment. The palliative care doctor, an older man with big bushy eyebrows, but kind eyes, gave me a list of books I could read, "but only if I wanted or if I was curious." He also gave me a little packet with worksheets to help me work through what mattered to me now that I was probably going to die, but he warned me that the worksheets had been written with older people in mind.

"I mean, not old old, but for people in their forties."

"So, you mean people with kids and real jobs, and life insurance."

He laughed.

"Yes. What I mean is, don't waste time on irrelevant questions."

"Got it."

"People often confuse palliative care with hospice. We send people to hospice when we think they have less than six months to live. Palliative care is not just for terminal illness. It's for all kinds of chronic illnesses. We do palliative care for all kinds of patients. Patients on dialysis who are waiting for a liver transplant can receive palliative care. People with heart conditions. What I'm trying to tell you is that my only job here is to improve your quality of life. I want you to have the best possible day right now. If you are starting to have symptoms that impact your quality of life, my job is to help you manage them. That includes symptoms like anxiety and depression. Have you been feeling any of that?"

I appreciated how he'd woven mental health concerns into physical concerns so seamlessly. Of course, I was anxious. Who wouldn't be? I wasn't sure if I was depressed. Being so tired that you sleep all day has the effect of feeling like a kind of depression. And some days I woke so sick I almost half-wished I was dead already.

"I guess, I'm a little anxious."

"Of course. Anyone would be. Is it affecting your quality of life?"

"I mean, I'm not waking up with panic attacks."

He nodded. "Okay. Well, we'll table that for now. But if you do experience more anxiety, there are things we can do to help you."

"Like psychedelics?" I blurted out. I couldn't believe myself. Maybe cancer had completely killed my filter.

He seemed taken aback. Mom's jaw dropped open, and I wanted to take my hand and push her mouth shut.

"Well as a matter of fact, there have been studies indicating that psychedelic treatments can help people work through the existential angst they experience with a terminal diagnosis. Ketamine is legal in Hawaii, but psilocybin is not. You are 18 though, and still healthy enough, so traveling to a state where psychedelic therapy is an option would not be out of the question. Is that something you'd like to explore? The existential angst?"

I didn't know what to say.

"Maybe we should table that for now," I said, seeing that Mom was getting upset.

The doctor nodded.

Mom looked relieved.

I left the office with several prescriptions for several different types of painkillers. Some stronger than others. The doctor explained that the stronger ones were better used at night for breakthrough pain because they would make me feel foggy. The less strong ones were for the daytime, or when I wanted to be out and about.

"But you can always carry around the stronger ones if you experience breakthrough pain," the doctors had explained, reassuringly, though the idea of "breakthrough pain" was hardly reassuring at all.

On the car ride home, I couldn't stop thinking about what breakthrough pain would feel like. I'd been incredibly achy and tired for weeks, and the chemo had been hell, but my daily pain so far had been fairly manageable. At least, when I wasn't actively in the hospital, I felt like it was all manageable. It would be nice to have something stronger to take at night. Sometimes the pain was strong enough to wake me up. But I wouldn't necessarily call that breakthrough pain.

The idea that the pain would or could get worse scared me.

Maybe I should have asked the doctor about ways to manage my anxiety.

I pushed the thoughts away.

I didn't want to think about it.

Mom and I stopped at the pharmacy and she asked me if I needed a pill right away. I figured I might as well.

The pill was like a revelation, a rush of euphoria, followed by the biggest feeling of lethargy. I wanted to sleep. I rested my head on the window and drifted off, the world rushing by, unnoticed.

Saturday couldn't come fast enough.

Alone in my house with my parents with nothing to do but watch them hover over me or be hovered over, I started to feel suffocated, like my world was narrowing down to rooms where I'd forever be sick, to a bed where I'd sleep all day and still wake exhausted. The only thing keeping me going was the prospect of having a good weekend. The date with Gabriel, and the party with Elijah.

I flipped through the workbook. Both Elijah and the doctor had been right. Most of the questions were tailored to older people who were about to die, not someone who was 18 years old.

Questions like "What is your greatest accomplishment in life?" or "What lessons have you learned in life that you'd like to impart to the next generation" seemed almost mocking. I hadn't even graduated from high school.

Other questions felt like heavy rocks thrown into the pit of my stomach: "What experiences in my life have brought me the greatest joy?" "What are my core values?" "With the time you have remaining and your current medical reality, how would you like to spend the rest of your life?"

The questions about relationships made me queasy.

"Who are the people most important to me, and have I expressed my love and appreciation for them?" "How do I want my family and loved ones to remember me after I'm gone?"

And then there was a whole section on *Fears, Death, and Spirituality*. That was the final straw. I put the packet down and didn't even bother reading the questions. I wasn't ready.

Death wasn't an assignment.

But living felt like one sometimes.

I struggled to sleep on Friday night. My heart was pounding so hard that I tossed and turned in my bed, unable to get comfortable. I eventually gave in and took the pain pill, even though the adrenaline of looking forward to seeing Gabriel made everything hurt less, and I probably didn't need it. I eventually fell asleep.

I opened my eyes on a familiar beach. The ocean rumbled over volcanic rock, and in the distance, I could see the rainforest. I understood in a vague way that I was dreaming. As I walked toward the ocean, I realized that there was a boy sitting right by the water's edge, facing the ocean, his back turned to me. He wasn't wearing a shirt, and I could make out every muscle in his back. It wasn't until he turned around to face me that I realized it was Elijah. He looked healthy and strong.

He smiled and beckoned me to sit next to him, so I did.

"We don't have very long here," he said, looking out to sea.\

"Oh?"

"You'll eventually have to choose," he said, not taking his eyes off the water.

It took a while to make sense of what was happening. First, it looked like a coconut floating in the ocean. But then

I realized that it was the top of someone's head, and then a face; it wasn't until the eyes opened that I knew who it was.

Gabriel. He walked out of the water. Shirtless, his body glowed marble-white, like the Greek statues I'd seen at the Metropolitan Museum of Art back in middle school, when my parents had taken me to visit New York City. But there was something different about him. He wasn't hunched over as he walked. Two large wings, unfurled behind him, and he looked like an angel in a painting.

Elijah stood up and grabbed my hand.

"Do you want to keep living?"

"What kind of question is that?"

"Run away with me," Elijah said, glancing at Gabriel. His voice was urgent, scared.

I froze, now distinctly aware that I was dreaming, and that I had a choice. Elijah's eyes darted to the rainforest. He wanted to take me there. I imagined us running to a waterfall I had heard could be seen about a mile up the trail. I'd been too sick to do the hike, but in the dream world, my body felt strong and capable. Or I could stay right here on the beach and wait for Gabriel. I got the sense that if I jumped high enough, I'd be able to fly. I could jump up high enough to break through the atmosphere, see the stars unblurred by the ozone. Or maybe Gabriel could wrap me in his arms and take me there himself.

That's when I heard sirens. Some emergency...

I jolted awake to the sound of my alarm clock. The sun had risen, and the light shone bright through my window, hurting my eyes. It was 6:30. I dragged myself out of bed, and in a half-asleep state, struggled to make sense of what I would wear and what I would need to bring with me for this date, or whatever it was.

I decided to wear my bathing suit under a baggy T-shirt, and a pair of shorts. I brought a bottle of water and made sure to bring both the stronger and the weaker of my pain pills. Better to be ready for anything, when anything could happen.

After I packed my bag, I checked my phone. 6:45. I still had some time.

I decided to do a quick Google search. I typed *angels who carry away the dying*. I felt absurd typing the words, but the thought had been put in my head by my crazy dream.

I found a website called the Encyclopedia of Angels and clicked on the link.

The first sentence I saw, I read aloud.

"Angels who carry away the dead are known as psychopomps..."

I read quickly, my heart pounding as my eyes passed over the images, some peaceful and benign, others demonic-looking and downright terrifying.

According to the Encyclopedia of Angels there were different types of figures who guided souls to the afterlife depending on which religious tradition you looked at. In Judaism, there was the angel Azrael. Azrael traditionally took the form of a grim reaper, a robed, hooded figure with dark wings. But in some traditions, Azrael was a terrifying immense and demonic-looking thing with four faces, and a thousand eyes and slithery tongues. The website included some artistic depictions of this terrifying form. I quickly scrolled past them. I didn't ever want to encounter anything like that in my dreaming or living life. I was already having weird enough dreams and didn't need to make things any worse than they were already.

In other traditions, Azrael was a shapeshifter, appearing beautiful if you had lived a good life, but also capable of taking on terrifying forms if you'd lived a bad life. He could also be androgynous, embodying both masculine and feminine energies. This last description reminded me of Gabriel, especially given that his eyes reminded me of that girl in the National Geographic photograph. Still, I felt a little absurd comparing the descriptions to Gabriel to these angels, but there were also things about him that didn't add up. Could the hunch in his back just be wings?

In Islam, the "angel of death" was Malak al-Maut. He was also a shapeshifter, appearing beautiful to the righteous and taking a terrifying form to sinners. According to the Prophet Abraham, Malak al-Maut was a sight so horrific, just being in its presence could make you go unconscious. Its head touched the sky, its body emitted flames, its face was obscured in darkness. It sounded like a creature straight out of hell.

In Christianity, there was the archangel, Michael, that appeared before the dying as a beautiful warrior angel carrying scales.

Even the Hindus have figures known as Yamadutas, messengers of death and agents of Yama, whose job was to escort souls to the netherworld. The Yamadutas sometimes came in the form of terrifying boars, with sharp teeth and bestial forms.

I turned off my phone.

Of course, the whole exercise was absurd. Gabriel was no angel. He was just another sick kid like me, like Elijah. Or maybe he worked at the hospital. I realized I didn't really know anything about him.

But then, there were other things. The way he seemed to appear always when I was the sickest. The way he seemed illuminated at times as if from within. The way my pain seemed to dissolve whenever he touched me. And the biggest thing, the lump in his back that he seemed determined to hide from me at all costs. Could they be wings?

His otherworldly beauty.

For a moment, I allowed myself to really consider the possibility. What if Gabriel was something else, something not entirely human, not entirely of this world?

It would make sense. I was dying after all.

The thing that terrified me the most was not that it could be true, but rather what it would mean if it was true.

I shook the thoughts away. Maybe the cancer was in my brain now, too? I should ask my doctors for a brain scan soon.

He was waiting in the idling Jeep outside at 7 a.m. sharp. The moment his green eyes flickered my way, all the things I'd read slipped off into the background.

Who ever heard of an angel who drove a fiery red Jeep?

Chapter 21

I opened the passenger side door, and he leaned over to give me his hand. His grip was firm. It made my heart flutter.

"Good morning," he said, "How are you?"

I told him I was okay, but his eyes searched my face for signs of another answer.

"I couldn't really sleep," I admitted.

He smiled.

It felt good to be beside him again. It felt like coming home, like peace, like happiness itself. I realized that if he would stay beside me until the day I died (which was likely to be sooner rather than later), that I could probably die happy. I caught my own thoughts, mid-thought, and felt my face go red for thinking these things. Was having a crush on someone all it took to turn me into a teenage girl cliché?

We drove up toward Volcano, my ears popping as the elevation climbed. The trees changed around us. Down near Hilo, the trees were tall pines, but up higher, the trees grew shorter, and squat, and then seemed to disappear entirely as we crossed landscapes that had been completely obliterated by lava, the earth turned to rock—coils of rock like black snakes, smooth petrified rivers of lava that had cooled and turned black.

We drove in silence much of the way. I could feel the closeness of his body, and I quietly wished he'd take my hand. The urge to take his hand was so strong I had to sit on my hands to stop the craving.

Even though I wanted to ask him normal questions, I found my mind kept drifting back to the crazy ones. Things like, "are you an angel, Gabriel?" And, "If you are, what kind of angel are you?" I wondered if he could transform into a more terrifying form, and the thought gave me goosebumps. The idea that Gabriel could become dangerous scared me, but I'll have to admit, it also thrilled me a little. I'd always been the girl to want to go on the scariest theme park rides.

I knew this line of questioning would be insane, so I kept my mouth shut.

When we neared the national park, Gabriel asked me if I wanted to drive through.

"We're in no rush..."

He turned into the park, and we drove down a road that took us through dense forest, which broke unexpectedly into one of the most desolate, blasted landscapes I'd ever seen. A landscape fretted with cinder cones and rock that had once been red and flowing, that had now cooled into something stiff and petrified, like a dead body.

The earth is a dead body, I thought, and almost said it aloud, but stopped myself because I didn't want Gabriel to think I was too weird. He drove skillfully, navigating the road's curves as if he'd driven them a thousand times before. I wasn't sure if it was motion sickness or the longing or my sickness itself that made my stomach flutter.

We crested a hill, and then the landscape opened into an impossible vista, like nothing I'd ever seen before. The road was perched on the side of a mountain that went all the way down to the sea, and for a moment it didn't feel like we were riding in a car but had taken residence in some kind of flying machine that soared impossibly over the landscape.

"This is, like, the most beautiful thing I've ever seen in my life."

Gabriel smiled again. Even though he'd said practically nothing since I'd gotten into the car, every now and then he'd smile and look over at me. He didn't have to say a word, but I could tell he was happy I was in the car with him. At times, it almost seemed as if he could read my mind. Like, when I was thinking about the scary angels, I could swear he chuckled to himself. And when I thought about how I could probably die happy if he stayed right by my side, I could swear I saw his face redden. But maybe I was imagining it.

We reached the bottom of the mountain way faster than I thought I would. The road dropped in elevation so fast that my ears were clicking and a little achy when we got to the bottom, like being on a plane.

The road ended at a little parking lot and a trail that led to a sea cliff. We walked it together, his body so close to mine, our hands almost touching. If longing could kill a person...

If he wanted to take my hand, I'd let him, but I knew that neither of us were brave enough to make the first move.

We stood at the railing in silence for a while, staring at the ocean boiling 200 feet below us.

I turned to look at him, but the wind blew the hair into my face.

He brushed my hair out of my eyes, and for a moment I thought he would take my face in his hands and kiss me. My body tensed up, a sudden fear that I didn't know resided within me. He noticed it and turned back to face the ocean.

We walked back to the car as if nothing had happened.

"Time to go to the City of Refuge," he said.

The City of Refuge was on the Kona side of the island, near a place called Captain Cook. Captain Cook was a great snorkeling spot, and I almost half-hoped we'd also go there.

When my parents and I had first visited Hawaii, we had gone to Captain Cook with rented snorkels and fins at the recommendation of one of our "Hawaiian experience guides."

The coral is very shallow near the shore, but then it drops off precipitously into a staggering and fear-inducing wine-dark deep. It's a place where a lot of sea life tends to gather, including whales in the winter season. We hadn't been visiting in winter, so we hadn't seen any whales.

But we did see a bunch of tropical fish and a few sea turtles. I also saw two spectacular stingrays there. They flew effortlessly underwater, rising from the depths of the sea cliff, their vast wings flickering over the colorful coral. They soared over the coral like birds and then disappeared back into the depths from which they had come. I remembered being in complete awe before them.

The site was also where Captain Cook had first landed and brought disease and conquest to the Hawaiian Islands. The world underwater teemed with life, but the above-water world seemed quiet and a little somber.

"So, what's this place, this City of Refuge?"

"Its Hawaiian name is *Pu'uhonua o Honaunau*, and it is one of the most sacred places in all of Hawaii, protected by Lono, the Hawaiian god of fertility, peace, and healing."

"You're taking me to a place of healing?"

"Yes, but it was more than that. It was a place where a person could access higher planes of consciousness. It was a place where a person could seek forgiveness. In ancient times in Hawaii, if someone broke the sacred laws, the punishment was death. Yet, there was one exception. If a person could evade their captors and reach the City of Refuge, they were granted immediate clemency and protection. The City of Refuge was a sacred place, a place of peace."

I wondered if the City of Refuge also worked for the dying. Was a dying person protected from the angels of death at the City of Refuge? Is this why he had chosen to take me here? Or was there another reason? Was he taking me there to seek forgiveness? Or to ask for it? And if so, for what? As far as I knew I hadn't broken any sacred laws.

"So, the sick go to the City of Refuge for healing."

"Yes, they made a pilgrimage there, too. For healing. For wholeness. But that's not why I'm taking you there."

I feel a chill, but I try to stay calm.

"I imagine a lot of people ended up there," I asked, trying to keep my voice steady.

"Actually, no. The City of Refuge was an incredibly difficult place to reach, almost impossible. It was surrounded by armies of fierce warriors. In ancient times, Hawaii was an island at war with itself. Warring chiefs fought over territory and resources, and warriors surrounded the City of Refuge, to protect this sacred place. Dangerous jungles surrounded the city. Fields of sharp and rugged lava surrounded it, too. If a person seeking refuge made it to the ocean, they'd still have to navigate rugged sea cliffs, wild roiling seas, and a tall wall made of lava rock that protected the city. There was only one way to enter the City of Refuge, and that was by water. People would have to swim for miles over rough and rugged seas. These were not empty oceans. There were sharks and jellyfish, and sharp spiny sea urchins on the rocks."

"So not so many people made it, then?"

"Only the fiercest warriors make it."

"Oh."

We drive down off the volcano. The road opens to views of the stunning Kona Coast. The wide ocean before us, vast and shaded by distant clouds in places.

"Good thing that today we have roads and parking lots," he says, with a chuckle.

We drove a straight road through the scrub brush. We'd dropped in elevation so quickly, I hadn't noticed it. I got the sense that the ocean was close.

"A person who arrives at the City of Refuge begins a process of healing guided by the Kahuna, a spiritual expert whose job is to help the warrior transition from a place of war to a place of peace. It isn't easy to stop fighting when that's all that you're used to doing."

I don't know what to say to all that. For weeks, I'd been fighting for my life. The thought of being able to drop the load and stop sounded wonderful.

Gabriel went on, "There's this idea that the physical body and the spiritual body are deeply interconnected. In Hawaiian spirituality, the breath wasn't just respiration, but a channel that connected the spirit to consciousness and the divinity in all things. There was this Zen monk who once said that when we breathe in, the universe exhales, and when we breathe out, that's the universe taking a breath in. When we breathe in, we breathe in the trees and the forest. We breathe in the clouds and the exhaust of the ocean. We take it all into our lungs, and in the breath, become unified with our consciousness and our living being. We are never divided from everything. The body holds many different types of energies. The physical healing of the body accompanied the healing of the mental energies as well."

I almost laughed. Around Gabriel, I wasn't so sure about my mental energies.

But when it came to everyday life, my mental energies were doing just fine, thank you. Even my own doctors said I was handling my diagnosis with bravery, courage, and a level of stoicism they were not accustomed to seeing. These diagnoses also bothered me. Couldn't they see that I was still in denial, still numb, still not fully processing the gravity of my situation?

"So, you think that taking me to the City of Refuge is going to heal me or something?"

Gabriel smiled and said nothing, not taking his eyes off the road.

My first glimpse of the City of Refuge was a big parking lot. Gabriel helped me out of the Jeep. He knew I was weak, my body ached, and getting down from the height of the seats wasn't easy. His hands felt strong in mine. I secretly wished he'd keep holding them when my two feet hit the asphalt, but he let me go as soon as he could see I was steady enough on my feet.

We walked across the asphalt in silence.

After passing through an open-air hallway adjacent to the visitors' center, the path opened to a series of ancient-looking buildings, rock structures, and ceremonial spaces.

We walked slowly, Gabriel checking his own pace to keep up with me.

Gabriel led the way.

He explained that he was taking me to the most sacred place.

We walked slowly through the ceremonial grounds, passing a sheltered space that held a beautiful canoe, and passing other little houses made of palm fronds and wood.

When we arrived, it looked important. It was a house like the others, but this one was flanked by majestic tikis, with a fence all around it.

"The *Hale o Keawe* temple," he said, his voice a whisper.

"What's that?"

"It once housed the bones of the ali'i."

I nodded, not understanding.

"In Hawaiian spirituality, the ali'i, or the kings, held great mana, or power, in their bodies. In the Hawaiian cosmology, mana is most present in the parts of the body that are slowest to decay—our fingernails, our hair, our bones. The bones of the ali'i were sacred and contained great mana. It's not just the land," he explained. "It's the bones of the chiefs that gave this place its mana, its spiritual power."

I nodded.

He sat down beside the fence and shut his eyes, and I sat down next to him, but didn't shut mine.

I've always found myself weirded out in sacred spaces. There's this sense of expectation attached to them, and I find myself feeling out into the space and often, disappointed to feel nothing. The City of Refuge was no different. It had a sense of quiet and peace about it, and great beauty. But whatever else I was supposed to have felt, the sense of holiness or sacredness–it was lost on me.

Gabriel could see that I was disappointed. It was hard to explain to him, but I tried.

"When you go to places like this. Churches, or sacred sites, do you ever feel disappointed?"

He shook his head and gave me a confused look.

"I feel like I'm supposed to feel something here, but I don't feel anything. I mean, this is beautiful, of course. But my body aches. Where is the promised healing? I just don't feel it."

Gabriel didn't say a word, for a while, but then he spoke.

"I didn't bring you here to ask for healing."

"Then why did you bring me here?"

"To ask for forgiveness," he whispered.

"For what?" I said, feeling the anger return, my old friend.

"For this," he said, pointing to himself and then to me. "For us."

"Why?"

"Because it's wrong," he said.

"Why is it wrong?" I demanded.

He stood up and offered me his hand.

I felt a jolt of electricity pass through my body; all pain dissolved with his touch. He gave me an intense and knowing look, but his face held another expression—fear, worry, or was it sadness? I couldn't tell. Once I was standing up, he released my hand, and the old ache of being a separate body longing for his body returned.

"The journey out of the City of Refuge is much like the journey in. Full of pain and danger. But the person is transformed."

I didn't want to say anything, but I didn't really feel transformed.

We got in the car and drove back across the island. Away from the City of Refuge, away from the Kona Coast, with its reefs teeming with stingrays soaring over submerged cities of coral. I didn't feel transformed or forgiven.

The further away we got from the City of Refuge, the sadder I felt. This was new. With the chaos of the diagnosis, I'd been angry and scared, but never sad.

Now, a deep cloud seemed to cover everything. A literal blanket of clouds hung low over the town of Volcano.

The higher altitude had a chill that it hadn't had on our way over.

Slow tears fell down my cheeks.

Gabriel nodded.

"Grief is also healing," he said, and for the first time, he took my hand, not to help me stand up, but just because he wanted to. I felt a thrill pass through my body.

He looked away, embarrassed, almost as if he could tell what I was thinking.

Chapter 22

He didn't let go of my hand until we reached the driveway to my house. We sat there in silence for what felt like forever. I didn't want to move, and I could tell he didn't want to let me go.

"You should go," he said, finally, his voice a little sad. "They've been worried about you."

They, being my parents. I realized that in my haste, I hadn't told my Mom where I was going, just that I had plans. I hadn't told her I planned to leave the house so early, and she had been asleep when I left that morning. I didn't want to have to deal with the scrutiny. But now, I knew I'd have to deal with the fallout.

"There's a party tomorrow in Puna. A friend of mine invited me to go. You can come, too, if you want?"

He let go of my hand, and a faraway look seemed to pass over his face, as if he could somehow read my mind.

"Maya, I don't want to interfere. I've already interfered too much."

"I don't understand," I said, searching his eyes for answers. "What the hell do you mean."

"Remember what I said about free will earlier? And determinism?"

My mind whirled. I remembered. Free will--the idea that each person had the ability to make their own choices and to guide their destiny. And determinism—the idea that everything was destiny, everything fated to be one way or the other.

"Yes. Everything is destiny, or we have choices," I said, annoyed.

"There are certain things that are meant to be. Certain things are just... predetermined. Like your cancer. It sucks, but it existed as a potentiality, a mutation in your body from the day you were born. But within that framework, each person can make choices. Choices are the whole point of all of this. You and I... we're just not part of the plan, okay? It's not our time to meet. You should have never seen me, and I should have left you alone. I did the wrong thing, and I keep trying to fix it, but I keep making it worse. There are things that still need to happen to you, and choices you still must make."

"But what if I choose you?"

"That is not permitted," he says, his face growing terribly sad.

"Well, you say you keep trying to fix it. Maybe you can fix it at the party tomorrow?"

"I can't go tomorrow. I already have somewhere I need to be..."

I wanted to ask him where he needed to be, but the way his voice faded when he said it made me feel that wherever he needed to be tomorrow was not somewhere he wanted to be.

What did he mean about interfering?

"But if I have time and can do it without interfering, I'll try to make it," he said, breaking my train of thought. "Puna? I think I know where you'll be. The big drum circle with the healers and the ecstatic dancing?"

"I guess," I said, not realizing that Elijah had invited me to something so woo-woo.

"I'll try, okay..."

I wanted to know where he had to be so urgently and what his deal was about interfering but got the sense that by asking, I'd open a door between us that couldn't be so easily shut. I bit my lip instead.

I didn't move. I half wanted him to lean over and kiss me, or at least take my hand again, but he didn't move either.

"I'd like to see you again," he said.

"Me too," I said, too quickly.

His eyes seemed to go somewhere far away then. He was there with me in the car, but also not there with me.

"It's hard to explain, Maya. I have to go away for a little while, but I'll be back soon, okay?"

I nodded, not really understanding.

"Well, you know where to find me," I said, unable to hide the disappointment in my voice.

I opened the car door, but he moved more swiftly, leaving the driver's seat, making his way to my side. He offered me his hand again, and I took it eagerly. It felt so good to hold his hand. Everything else seemed to slip away—even the pain.

But he held it only for a moment, only long enough to offer his support, and then it was just me again, standing alone on my front lawn.

"I'll see you soon," he said, his eyes intense and sad.

I didn't move until he backed out of my driveway and didn't take my eyes off him until the Jeep disappeared down the road.

Mom was very angry with me.

"I didn't know where you were or if you were okay. I was so *worried.* Maya, you could have been passed out in the jungle for all I knew. You are so sick..."

"I was *fine*, Mom. I was just out with a friend."

Mom wasn't buying it.

"That boy you met in palliative care?" Mom said, unable to contain her joy. In addition to all her worries about her daughter dying, she also had the additional worry that her daughter would die friendless and isolated, and it was all her fault because she'd moved me away from all my friends.

I decided it would be better if I didn't let her down.

"As a matter of fact. He invited me to that party tomorrow. I'll be seeing him then."

It wasn't exactly a lie.

Mom nodded and gave me a big hug.

Old Mom would have grounded me for leaving the way I did and worrying her.

But one of the perks of having cancer is that you don't have time to be grounded...

I was exhausted from the day, and asked Mom if I could just go up to bed to rest. Mom brought me a glass of orange juice, and I took my pain pill.

All the hand-holding and adrenaline had had the effect of masking my exhaustion and pain, but back at home, the pain returned, and the exhaustion arrived like an entity that had been following me all day, waiting to shake my body back into submission.

I groaned as I crawled into bed and pulled my bedsheets up to my neck. I was so tired, I didn't even bother getting out of my clothes from the day.

I thought about the party and what it might be like, and wondered if Gabriel would be able to get away from whatever responsibility he didn't want to have so that he could join me.

My brain spun in circles, remembering how it had felt when Gabriel had taken my hand, how it had felt to sit with him at the City of Refuge.

Maybe the mana of the place was working on me, after all. I did feel a little better, a little more peaceful. But it also might have been just the thrill of Gabriel, the feeling of being hopelessly...I didn't want to think it.

Hopelessly... in love.

I slipped into unconsciousness, smiling.

Chapter 23

I slept straight through the night and woke to a blaring headache accompanied by the blaring sun coming in through the window.

I hadn't bothered to set my alarm because the party was at sunset, but I got the feeling that I'd slept through the day long enough that I'd have to get my body moving if I planned to make it to the beach before dark. My legs felt like two pieces of meat attached to my hip. Moving them over the side of the bed took all my strength. I felt nauseous as I rose.

I probably needed to eat something, drink some water, maybe take some pain medicine. I started with the pain medicine and some water, and as I brushed my teeth, I thought about the City of Refuge. There was something about the place that stuck with me, even today. I wondered what it would be like to have an uninterrupted sense of connection to a place, to the land, to the bones of the ancestors. *Mana* felt like the right word to describe it. The closest I'd felt to anything like that was when Gabriel had taken my hand in the car.

I took a shower, and when I returned to my room, my body wrapped in a towel, I noticed the workbook that the doctors of palliative care had given me. The old questions of meaning still lingered on my bedside dresser, unanswered and heavy, but I felt like yesterday I'd come closer to something.

If I was going to die, I wanted to die having known love. And not just love of my parents or love of my best friend. I wanted real love. Romeo and Juliet-style love.

Make out in the back of the car all night kind of love.

Add that to my bucket list.

Mom lent me the family Prius to drive to the beach party.

Elijah had texted me earlier that day, while I was sleeping, asking if I minded giving him a ride, and I said, *sure*. He'd texted me on and off since we'd exchanged numbers, mostly pictures of pretty sunsets and funny memes. I had a weird sense that maybe he had feelings for me and was trying to make this a date, but I pushed the thought out of my mind.

I'd deal with that later, if it came up.

Elijah lived in Hilo with his extended family in a large wooden house not far from the ocean. The house looked like it could have been built in the days of the sugar cane plantations. The jungle had grown up around it, but the land around the house gave off the feeling of having been disturbed or hurt.

There was a big pile of coconut husks at the end of a driveway almost as tall as the house. Next to the pile of coconut husks were several parked Tacomas in various states of repair and decay. One was propped up on a jack, and though the truck itself might have once been white, it was covered in boils of rust that gave it the feeling of a person who had leprosy or really bad eczema. The other two looked dusty and mud-stained from construction work. The one closest to the house had a clean blue paint job and outsized rubber tires.

Elijah was waiting for me on the front porch steps,. sitting. He didn't look like a person who could stay standing for extended periods.

"Welcome to the Kekoa family compound," he said, with a wave of his hand, as he got into my car.

As we drove to the beach, Elijah explained to me that he lived with his mother, father, three older brothers, two of their wives, their children, and his grandmother. Two of his older brothers worked in construction and shared the dusty Tacoma. The brother who was closest to him in age was doing community college and was the owner of the leprous Tacoma. He explained that when the truck wasn't running, his dad often had to drive his brother to his classes. His brother was studying psychology and education and was hoping to work for the Department of Education as a school counselor. His dad worked in construction, and he and his Tacoma were out on a job on the Kona side of the island that night.

"What about that shiny new Tacoma, with the big ass tires?" I asked.

Elijah smiled. "That one's mine," he said, his face going red. "It was my wish. And my brothers are soooo jealous. The wish people had to get me a special permit for the tires," he said laughing.

Apparently, jacked-up Tacomas with big ass tires were a whole thing in Hawaii. Elijah tried to explain it to me, but when he saw the incredulous look I gave him, he dropped it.

"Wait, if you have that fancy nice Tacoma, why did you ask me to drive you?"

"Well, I wanted to ride with you, and your mom gave me overprotective Mom vibes. I figured she'd be more likely to let us ride together if you were driving. Plus, this is a black sand beach. I didn't want to get my truck dirty."

I laughed at the absurdity of the whole thing, convinced that Elijah probably thought this was a date and I'd have to find a way to let him down gently. The fact that he had used his one wish for a truck with big tires made me feel kind of sad for him. I mean, I didn't know what I'd use my one wish on, if I had one, but a brand-new truck was not it. Boys could be weird, though. I felt myself getting judgmental and immediately felt bad about it.

As we drove to the beach, Elijah explained that his family name—*Kekoa*—meant warrior, which he found hilarious because people were always calling cancer kids warriors.

"Do you know of any literal warriors in your family?"

"Naw, not anymore. None of my brothers wants to join the military. The last warriors in my family probably fought for King Kamehameha or something, but family lore is a little hazy, and no one wrote anything down back then. My grandfather worked the sugar cane plantations, when that was a thing. But Mom thinks I got my cancer because of the pesticides."

"The pesticides?"

"Yeah, believe it or not, after the farmers moved their sugar cane operations to Florida, and then to Brazil, the Caribbean, and India, Hawaii's biggest agricultural product became seeds. We used to grow all the seeds here."

"All the seeds?"

"Yeah, all the seeds for corn and stuff. Hawaii is so far away from any of the farms in the Midwest that they can do their genetic engineering without any risk that the seeds will blow to some field and take over. They also can test out their pesticides here, too. The farmers here also use a ton of pesticides because of the climate."

"Ah, so your mom thinks you got cancer because of the pesticides?"

"Yeah, but it's hard to prove. People get cancer all the time who don't live near farms spraying pesticides. Mom and I lived near some farms for a while with my grandma, when she and Dad were going through a thing. Her Mom lives on Hawaiian homelands. Anyway, right next to my school, there was this big field, and every morning the farmers would spray the fields. The spray would sometimes rain down on us during recess. Some of the kids would get bad headaches, or nosebleeds, or they'd get dizzy during recess. I never really got any of those symptoms. But here I am, so who knows?"

"I can't believe they let people spray that shit near schools."

"Yeah, you wouldn't believe what happens in Hawaii if you knew," he said, his voice growing dark. "The state finally passed laws requiring the companies to disclose which pesticides they are using, and to create a buffer between their fields and any schools, thankfully."

"That's crazy. And kind of infuriating."

"Yeah, people get this vision of Hawaii as this pure, untouched virgin land, but they don't realize that the trace pesticides are everywhere–in the soil, and in the water. The days of sugar cane wrecked the land. And don't get me started on the military and their leaking underground vats of oil... If you're a local, you know not to drink the tap water," he says, with a laugh.

"I'll let my parents know."

"Oh yeah. You better. It's so sad because in Hawaiian culture, water is life, water is wealth, water is healing. But the water is sick. The people are sick."

I didn't know what to say to all that. It felt so sad and like there weren't any easy solutions for the people most affected.

"Is there anything that can be done about it?"

"People are trying. There's a big movement to protect the water. I don't know if I want to devote my limited time to it, though, however worthy it might be."

I nodded. The narrowing of one's individual timeline required such ruthlessness. I'd already felt it in my own small ways between deciding whether to call Tay or read before bed.

More often these days, I chose to read or daydream about Gabriel—the gulf between Tay and I growing as wide as the Pacific between us.

The light seemed to brighten as we made our way closer to the beach. I'd Googled the place where the party was taking place before leaving home. It was a black sand beach that also had some hot springs near it.

"So, when faced with the fact of large corporations and the military industrial complex poisoning your water, you've just decided to party," I say, playfully.

Elijah laughs.

"Wow, you say the shit no one says out loud, don't you?"

Now I'm laughing.

"Well, is it true or untrue?" I say.

"True. But I like to think of it as using my time wisely. You can't heal others or the world without first healing yourself, after all. You know what they say, *put your gas mask on before putting it on the passenger beside you.* Either way, I think these are more than parties. You'll see. This isn't just some high school party with a big beer keg. This one is organized by various healers in the community. I'm of the school that we need to heal our collective spirit before we can heal anything else. I mean, we're not going to get people to stop poisoning the water if their ultimate intention is the profit motive. Intentions matter."

"Wait, so you didn't invite me to a big kegger?" I said, pretending to be disappointed, but honestly a little relieved.

"I mean, if you're asking, there's beer... if that's what's important to you," he said.

I felt my face go red. I didn't want to be *that girl.* The party girl. I didn't want him to think that my only intention in going to the party was because I wanted to get wasted, but if I was entirely honest, I'd never been drunk before, and didn't want to go to my death bed having only had the sip of beer, my Dad let me have last New Year's Eve.

I bit my lip. I wanted to ask him more about what this party was about, but I'd find out for myself soon enough. We pulled into a bustling parking lot.

As I'd half-expected, there were a lot of college-age people with dread locks wearing colorfully patterned prints that looked like they'd been imported directly from Thailand or India. Watching them made me feel wistful, like observing a possible life I might have lived if I wasn't trapped in my timeline.

There were a lot of regular-looking kids like me and Elijah, Hawaiian kids, military kids, kids who looked like they could have lived in the suburbs of Portland just like me.

I lost track of Elijah as I wandered around the beach, making sure not to the step on the scattered drums, singing bowls, yoga mats, colorful beach blankets, occasional bongs, and yes, keg.

I took note of all of it, but really, I was scanning the crowd to see if Gabriel had been able to make it to the party. I know he hadn't given me any promises, but deep down I'd been hoping he would come. But as I searched the crowd for any sign of him, I felt the waves of disappointment slither down my spine, settling into my stomach where it spasmed. Gabriel was a striking person, tall, noticeable. I would have been able to find him quickly in a crowd. I hadn't expected his absence to have such an effect on me, a mix of anticipation, disappointment, and a little anger. He had promised me nothing, but I still felt stood up.

I realized that Elijah had been walking beside me the whole time, and I hoped he couldn't see the disappointment on my face. I pushed back the hot tears that wanted desperately to come out. My face hurt from trying to hide the feelings of desolation that coursed through my body.

I let Elijah lead the way through the growing crowd, wiping the tears out of my eyes when I was safely out of his sight.

We found our way to a big blue blanket someone had spread on the outside of the general commotion. A heavy-set Hawaiian boy sat on one of the corners of the blanket, strumming a ukulele, while staring off into space. A thin girl with brown skin, thick hair had laid herself down on another corner beside a big green bong and a black speaker that quietly played reggae music as her arms swung above her body to the beat. A couple of cute-looking Hawaiian boys sat on the black sand beside the blanket, talking animatedly, but I only caught snippets of their conversation. Either they were talking about a video game or actual hunting, but it was hard to tell.

"Hi, guys," Elijah said. "This is my new friend Maya. Please be nice to her," he said, muttering the last part under his breath. Then he introduced me to his friends one by one. The heavy-set boy's name was Isaiah. One of the cute Hawaiian boys was named Jed, short for Jedidiah. The girl's name was Ruth. The other Hawaiian boy's name was Keoni.

They all wanted to know how long I'd been on the island and if I was here on vacation or if I'd moved for good, but Elijah mercifully extracted me from the interrogations.

"What's with all the Bible names?" I whispered to Elijah as he pulled a blanket of his own from his bookbag. I wasn't feeling very social, given Gabriel's no-show, and figured I wouldn't have to talk as much if I just sat with Elijah.

"Oh, a lot of our parents are Mormon or really super Christian. I mean, you know this place has more missionaries than cockroaches?"

I nodded as Elijah went on, "My parents are Catholic. Jed's parents are Mormon. Ruth's parents are Mormon, too. But Keoni's parents are pure kanaka."

"Kanaka?"

"Yeah, Kanaka Maoli. Hawaiian. His mom teaches hula at the Heiau with Auntie Nalani."

I had no idea what he was talking about, but had the sense that it was very important.

I tried to distract myself from the pangs of disappointment and sadness by taking in the scene around me, but everyone looked the same in different ways. There were the dread locked Rastas with their colorful clothes. When they walked past our blanket, they brought with them the strong smell of pot. There were transplants like me, that dressed like any other person from the suburbs would dress in Hawaii. The girls wore sun dresses or shorts, and the guys wore board shorts, and everyone looked wide-eyed and in awe of all the beauty. There were the Hawaiian kids, who wore T-shirts with logos from local brands I'd never heard of before. Some of them carried ukuleles, and others carried leis, and gourds covered with kukui nuts.

With the smell of pot in the air, I felt a little buzz with every deep breath I took in. I'd never smoked, and I didn't want to smoke, especially with Elijah there and his bad lungs, but I set my head back on the blanket, and shut my eyes, feeling the warmth of the sun on my skin. The air felt cool and refreshing. No matter how hot it seemed to get in Hawaii, the air always got cool at night. The contrast felt delicious.

When I opened my eyes, everyone seemed bathed in a red tint. The sun was setting. Some of the Hawaiian kids had brought tikis and were hammering them into the sand. Some of the dreadlocked kids danced in the center of the crowd, even though there was no music playing at all yet.

"So, what does one do in a thing like this?" I said, finally breaking the silence between me and Elijah. I could tell he was watching me take it all in and had mercifully given me space to do so.

"What do you mean?"

"I mean. What do people do at a party?"

His eyes narrowed with shock, and he put his hand on his heart, as if grabbing a pair of invisible pearls. "Are you actually going to tell me a pretty girl like you has never been to a party before?"

When Elijah had introduced me to his friends as his "friend," I'd felt a wash of relief, like I wasn't going to have to dodge any awkward googly eyes later in the evening. But when he said "pretty girl" just now, he said it quietly, in a flirty way.

I decided to try to ignore it.

"My friends in Portland were all kind of nerdy, more focused on studying than parties. I guess you could say that this was one of my bucket list things." I knew that using the plural for friends was a bit of a lie, but I didn't want Elijah to think I had been a loser back in Portland.

"Well then. We are going to make this one worth it," he said, calling Jed over from his seat on the communal blanket.

"Jed, my friend Maya has never been to a party before. Get this girl a beer!"

Jed's eyes went wide. "I guess they don't have parties in cold, rainy Portland?" he said, unzipping a black bookbag that sat in the middle of the group. He pulled out two frosty bottles, handing one to Elijah and the other to me.

Elijah pulled out his house keys. He had a bottle opener on the keychain.

"Drink responsibly," Jed said, with a laugh, as Elijah popped open the bottles.

The beer tasted awful on the first sip, but Elijah didn't stop at the first sip so I didn't either. With the tiki torches finally lit, and the sun almost fully set, a warm buzz filled my body, probably confounded by the pain pills I'd taken earlier.

I could have happily sat there on Elijah's blanket all night, buzzing out to the beer, but Elijah wasn't having it. Slowly, as if moving through great pain, he shuffled himself to his feet, grabbing my hand for balance.

"Come with me. It's time to consult the oracle."

"The oracle?" I said, confused, remembering hazy movies I'd seen where heroes or heroines consulted the Oracle at Delphi to learn their future. From what I remember, it didn't always seem to end well.

He could see my confusion.

"I know some kids who do the I-Ching at these things. We should do it together before they get too much of a crowd," he said, offering me his hand. I took it, knowing that he'd probably read more into it than just me really needing the help to stand up. Despite the strong pain pill and the beer, my body ached something awful, and just trying to stand up left me breathless. Standing up, I felt a little dizzy and then a little scared. What if I passed out here like I'd passed out on the mountain with Gabriel?

I pushed the thought out of my head. The beach was at sea level, so the chances of me going dizzy from lack of oxygen were less likely. Deep down, I worried that maybe my body was getting weaker, but I pushed this thought away, too.

Still, as Elijah led me through the crowd, I couldn't stop thinking about how much my head hurt and how in the past couple of days, even the stronger pain pills had been unable to touch most of the pain. I took a deep breath in, breathing in the dense smell of pot and palo santo, and told myself that there was no point in thinking about things I couldn't change. I had a doctor's appointment on Tuesday and could address all that then. Right now, I was at a party, and Gabriel or no Gabriel, I intended to have fun.

The I-Ching lady sat at a table with a red tablecloth, some coins, and a big, dog-eared book.

"You first," Elijah said. "Want privacy?"

I nodded, and Elijah wandered away, but not so far away that he couldn't glance over at me from time to time. Every time our eyes met, his face turned red, and he looked away shyly. I hated this. I'd have to find a way to let him down gently. But how do you tell a dying kid you don't like them, that way? Ugh. These thoughts I also pushed out of my mind.

The lady's name was Elenor, and she looked like one of the older people at the party. She could have been thirty.

"What brings you to the divining table today?" she said, her voice somber and mysterious.

"I don't know..."

She nodded, and began speaking, "The I-Ching, or the Book of Changes, is an ancient practice of Chinese divination that goes back 3000 years. There are 64 hexagrams, or paths. Divination comes from the word, *divine*. What is important to remember is that when we consult an oracle or perform divination, we are entering into dialogue with the divine. It's important that you set a clear intention, that you ask a clear question before you consult the oracle, before you throw the coins."

Everyone—from the doctors at palliative care to this woo-woo I-Ching lady seemed to want me to clarify my intentions but I didn't know. What if, beyond maybe wanting to get kissed, and wanting to go to a real party, I didn't know what I wanted?

But then, as if the divine were answering the blankness within me, the question materialized in my head.

Will I kiss Gabriel? Does Gabriel like me?

I felt my face go red with the thought. Had I really become such a cliché teenager as to be asking psychics about my crush?

"Well, okay then," I-Ching lady said out loud, even though I'd said nothing to her. Maybe she *was* a psychic. "Got your question?"

"Yes," I said.

She gave me the coins to toss.

And then she arranged the hexagram on the table.

She smiled.

"Hexagram 56. The wanderer."

She opened her book and read from it.

"The lava is catastrophic to the city, but not to the mountain. The wise person waits for clarity before acting. Keep moving forward."

The beer buzz was really making my head spin, but I didn't need the I-Ching lady to explain it to me. I thought about how Gabriel had been with me at the volcano. The landscape is eternal. Its own changing doesn't matter. Change only matters to people.

"You are a stranger here?" she asked.

I nodded, figuring that she meant that I was a new arrival. Basically, no better than a tourist.

"You are attracted to exotic things and people. That has led you here. But you won't be here for long."

She was right about that, so right I almost laughed.

"Look," she said, growing very serious, staring down at her book. "You don't know the customs here. It's easy to cross a line you can't see. You're like a foreigner in a foreign country. Pay attention to things. Listen more than you speak. If you're going to do anything, do it with care and consideration."

It felt like a warning.

"That wasn't your real question, though," she said, her voice growing darker, even more serious. "No. No. This isn't right. There's another question beneath this question. The real question."

She paused.

I didn't know what she was talking about, but at the same time, I did.

Was I really dying? And if I was dying, what should I be doing with my remaining time on this planet?

She nodded. She somehow seemed to know intuitively when I'd locked in on a question.

She gave me the coins to toss again.

A look of deep worry crossed her face.

"Hexagram 29. Dangerously Deep."

I waited for her to go on, but the look of worry didn't leave her face, and she looked up to study mine a second time.

"Water flows to the sea, despite all obstacles. You will show others the way."

She didn't say a word. Her face had grown terribly pale. She looked sick, like she might throw up. She glanced over at Elijah, and I could see her taking him in, his thinness, his paleness, then turning to look at my pale face, my frail body.

Oh God, she knows I'm dying.

Chapter 24

I walked away from the table in a daze.

"Oh no," Elijah said, half-laughing. "Did she read you the death hexagram?"

"What's the death hexagram?"

"The one that comes up when people are dying. She always gets that scared face. The one about the water flowing to the sea?"

I nodded.

Elijah laughed, like he thought it was the funniest thing I'd said all night. It made me angry. He stopped laughing when he saw that I wasn't laughing with him.

"Oh," he said, and then grew very silent.

"You haven't accepted your diagnosis, have you?"

I shook my head, "Of course, I've accepted my diagnosis. We all know we're going to die. I just know it's going to happen to me sooner than most people."

"You know what helped me accept my diagnosis?" Elijah said, his voice dropping, dripping with mystery like I-Ching lady.

"Oh God. I don't know. What helped you accept your diagnosis?"

"You need the tea!" he said, whirling around, scanning the party for something I couldn't see.

"The tea?"

“Yes. Psychedelic therapy,” he said.

“Palliative care?” I asked.

“Oh, what did palliative care say?” he said, his voice sounding sarcastic.

“They told me that they’d have to see if I was healthy enough to travel to Portland, where the therapy is legal. I mean, I’m 18. I could try it.”

“Oh. My. God. Fuck palliative care,” Elijah said, slapping his head. “I know a guy, Maya. Not sure if you want to do them in this setting though... We will see.”

He led me through the crowd to a place where a woman in a flowing white dress, wearing a crown of flowers on her head, sat in the center of a ring of white singing bowls. She played the bowls with shut eyes, seemingly unaware of the people around her, her body swaying to the energies.

I found my body swaying as well, lifted and moved by sound.

Elijah took my hand and led me to a half-circle of meditation cushions set facing the beach. A man with a round drum pounded a regular rhythm as Elijah and I sat with closed eyes, listening to the rhythm of the drum intermixed with the rhythm of the ocean waves breaking on the shore. In palliative care the doctors had mentioned something called mindfulness meditation and said it could help me with the pain and anxiety, and as I sat in the semi-circle of meditators, listening to the drum, and focusing on my breath, it wouldn’t be entirely wrong to say that something arose from the act that was perhaps distinct from the act, a presence of peace that hadn't been there before.

A guy arrived with a big speaker on wheels and with it came the music. Native American chants mixed with EDM beats. A mass of bodies made their way to the center of the party, writhing ecstatically. Some bodies moved in tune with the music, and others moved to their own rhythm. At some point in the commotion, I lost Elijah—or Elijah lost me. I had no intention of joining the dancers, so I made my way back to where we'd rolled out the blankets and where his friends sat, each in their own worlds.

Isaiah was still playing the ukulele. When he saw me return, he gave me a little nod and continued playing. Ruth's was still lying next to the bong with closed eyes. Wherever she was, it appeared she had disappeared even deeper into it. Keoni and Jed were gone.

I relished the moment of peace. In a corner of the party, some girls were taking off their clothes to go skinny dipping in the ocean. The moon above the sea was bright and blue, forming a silver path that went all the way to the horizon. With the moon out, their bare skin looked pale blue, and you could see the shape of them as they ran over the black sand. As I watched them run into the water, I couldn't help but feel a little jealous. Part of me wanted to join them, but I didn't think I had it in me to take off my clothes, to bare myself to strangers like that. It wasn't that I didn't like my body. It's just that I didn't always feel comfortable in it, and definitely not comfortable enough to show it to other people.

Elijah returned and touched my shoulder. He plunked himself down next to me on the beach towel, his breath strained. He was holding a little wooden cup in his hand. He presented it to me.

I looked down inside the cup and saw a bunch of brown, withered things that looked like they had been shaved off a tree, like roots pulled up from the earth.

"What's this?"

Elijah smiled playfully.

"Really?" I said.

"Yep."

He was trying so hard to get me to like him. At some point, I'd have to break the news, but maybe not tonight. Maybe by the time I had to tell him, Gabriel and I would be dating. That would make everything so much easier.

Still, I wasn't about to throw away an act of kindness or let a dying wish go so easily.

"You can eat them whole, or I can find us some hot water, and you can drink it as a tea."

I almost grabbed the woody slivers and put them in my mouth, but then thought better of it. I got sick easily.

"Maybe try it as a tea?"

Elijah nodded and helped me to my feet. We walked through the crowd, carrying the cup like a sacred chalice, and made our way to a place near the parking lot where a girl had set up a table. She was selling muffins and brownies, and kombucha, and local beers, and she also had a big kettle on a hot plate with boiling water.

"Annie, do you think you could fill me up?" Elijah asked, with a smile.

The girl, who was dancing as she handed muffins with one hand and took money with the other, smiled and said, "help yourself."

I watched as Elijah poured the steaming hot water into the little wooden cup and handed it to me. His hand trembled as he poured.

Then, we walked back to our little perch on the periphery of the party.

I waited for the tea to steep and the water to cool, and then, with a pounding heart, began to drink the tea.

Chapter 25

If you'd asked me then exactly what I'd expected to happen, I wouldn't have been able to tell you. A group of people had started to build a bonfire on the beach and if a dragon had emerged from the flames, I wouldn't have been surprised. But no dragon emerged.

"Have you gotten any closer to answering those big existential questions from the workbook?" Elija asked.

"Not really," I said, looking up at the sky, expecting the stars to shift or something. "What about you?"

"Same," he said, inching closer to me on the blanket.

I could tell he was trying to be romantic. I didn't want romance. I wanted... well, I didn't know what I wanted. I wanted Gabriel to swoop in and take me in his arms like he'd done up on the mountain to warm me when I'd been cold. The truth was that I didn't want to die having never been kissed, but it's not like I could tell Elijah that. He'd only see that as an invitation to kiss me.

Even so, I had to admit the whole thing was pretty romantic. Isaiah's ukulele music, the moonlight, the stars, the pounding drums, the chanting, the sound of the distant waves and the flickering torches.

Fortunately, at least at that moment, Elijah was behaving himself.

And whatever romance we might have had was interrupted with his talk of dying...

"I don't want to die in pain. And I don't want to end up being hooked up to machines for months and months, a hole in my neck to breathe through, tubes for feeding, tubes for shitting. None of that. I just want my parents to let me go. Let me finish my unmediated dying, thank you very much."

When Elijah started talking about death, I noticed a shift in the way the flickering torches moved. They seemed to have a halo around them—to have dimension about them that they hadn't had before. I blinked. The dimensionality of the fire remained. I looked up into the sky and realized an intricate pattern inlaid in the sky, like a rose window I'd once seen in St. Peter's Cathedral in New York City.

"I think something's happening," I whispered.

"Oh, good."

Elijah got quiet then, letting me disappear into the patterns and tunnels that mysteriously formed in the sky, labyrinths of light, deep, intricate spirals that grew more intricate as I felt my body moving through them.

"What do you see?" Elijah asked.

"I see..."

I couldn't really explain what I was seeing. A cathedral of light that opened to infinity. A galaxy of stars being born and dying, that dissolved into a room full of jack-in-the-boxes, jester faces attached to springs. This made me laugh. But also made me a little scared.

"I see... light... and clowns."

Elijah laughed, but his laugh fractured into a million sonic pieces, and even though I knew he was sitting right beside me, he disappeared.

I looked up at the sky, and the stars themselves all seemed to come apart at once.

"Disaster..." I said.

From a distant tunnel in another universe, I heard a voice asking me what I meant by disaster, but I couldn't reach back into that universe anymore. I was somewhere else, and words could no longer come out of my mouth. When I did manage to eke out a word or a sound, it shattered in the ether into a million echoes.

All these weird thoughts came to me at once.

Aster means star in Latin. The real meaning of *Disaster* is shattering star, a star coming apart at its seams. What did it mean to have a body coming apart at its seams? Was this what it meant? I stared at my hand, and my hands became the hands of a very old woman. And then, I watched the skin dissolve, revealing my bones.

I shut my eyes tighter and pressed my face to the earth. My eyes grew roots, and bioluminescence flickered around thin filaments of mushroom mycelium that grew between the roots, connecting every tree to every other tree, connecting the trees to the earth and water, and connecting me to all of it. I saw my own connection to the roots and to the soil. And I felt the pain of the soil, the pain of a plant pulled up by its roots, the pain of the mycelium when a shovel cut through it, and my whole body writhed with it.

I was the disaster. I was the shattering star.

I felt myself fall apart into a thousand pieces. And then I woke up in my dying body, unable quite yet to let go. To inhabit that moment felt impossible.

I can't possibly be really dying right now, right here? Where are my parents?

But a voice from deep within me said, *why not right now; why not right here?*

It was in that moment that I realized that all moments existed on top of each other, all at once. The moment of my birth alongside the moment of my dying and all the moments in between. And even though they existed, and their existence was incontrovertible, it became clear that the time had come to release my attachment to my own specificity.

I had been holding on so tightly to myself, and the holding was what hurt.

So, I let go of it all.

And I went somewhere else.

I don't know where that was, just that it was peaceful. No eye had heard, no ear has seen, no tongue has perceived, no heart beats there in its labor. Words are blunt scalpels that try to pierce into the mystery of that place. They cut into the truth, destroying it.

And then, just like that, I returned.

Back in my body, the stars pulsing above me, intact again. Elijah sitting vigil beside me, his body gently swaying to the music.

I found myself silently weeping with gratitude. What a miracle to get to be myself for a little while longer, how precious.

To have inhabited the moment of my dying made the miracle that I hadn't reached that moment yet feel even more profound.

I sat up and laughed and cried, and Elijah asked me if I was okay and I said yes. I asked him if he'd walk with me to the ocean, the intact ocean, with the moon whole and glowing above it.

Elijah helped me to my feet. For once, nothing in my body hurt. I knew this would only be temporary. That the pain would return, but I was grateful for the respite.

The warm water lapped my feet, and instinctively I found myself pulling off my clothes. I didn't care if Elijah saw me naked. I didn't care who saw me. I wanted to jump into the water as myself, to be cleansed.

The ocean water was warmer than the air, and I felt like every negative thought and all the negative energy I'd ever carried in my body was being carried away by the sea. I screamed into the darkness, the roar of the ocean drowning out my screams. And I laughed, the ocean drowning out my laughter. Elijah watched me closely from the beach. I could tell he was worried I'd slip underwater, never to be seen again, but I could also tell that he didn't want to interrupt my process.

I eventually crawled out of the water, my limbs tingling.

For a while, I just lay on the black sand beach, unable to move. My body breathing itself. Occasionally laughing.

"That was something," I said. "That was something."

My body started to shiver. The cool night air hitting my skin, cooling me from within. Elijah got up to get me a blanket, and I sat for what felt like forever staring up into the stars, shivering.

That's when I felt a strong hand pull me into an upright sitting position. I half expected to see Elijah when I opened my eyes, but gasped when I realized it was Gabriel's penetrating green eyes looking down at me.

"Are you okay?"

I nodded, still shivering.

I couldn't take my eyes off his face, my teeth chattering something awful. He was removing the big black ugly jacket he wore, the big ugly jacket that covered his back, and hid whatever he'd been hiding back there. Beneath the jacket, he was wearing a tight black, short-sleeve shirt. It fit him snugly, emphasizing his muscular chest. My eyes hungrily took him in—his gorgeous face, his stunning body.

He wrapped the jacket around me, holding me tight in his strong arms. I felt my body instantly go warm.

His jacket smelled like earth and palo santo, more like a church smell than cologne.

He watched me sink into the jacket and sink into him, my body growing still as it warmed up. It was then that I realized I was naked, and I grew incredibly embarrassed.

"Oh my God, I need my clothes.... Where are my clothes?" I said, wrapping the jacket tighter around my body to hide my breasts and my legs.

Gabriel laughed. "They're right here. But you might want to give yourself a moment to warm up before you put them back on."

I stopped feeling so self-conscious about being naked in front of Gabriel. I could see him trying not to stare at my body, and I liked it. He looked more nervous than I was.

He stood turned facing me, his back hidden from view, our faces just inches apart.

I felt the incredible urge to kiss him, my lips craving his lips, craving all of him.

He must have felt it, too.

Cautiously, I reached up to stroke his cheek, cool from the night air.

He closed his eyes and sighed.

"Is that okay?" I asked.

"It feels so good," he whispered, but then he pulled away. "But we can't do this."

I realized I could almost make something out in the blue-tinged moonlight, something coming from his back.

"Are you going to finally let me see?" I asked.

He shook his head, no.

Maybe it was the tea, or maybe it was just how warm and good it felt to be wrapped in his arms, but I felt myself feeling suddenly bolder.

"Take off your shirt," I commanded.

He laughed. "Hells no."

"Don't make me take it off for you," the glare in my eyes made it clear to him that I wasn't delivering an idle threat.

He stepped further back, his green eyes wide with shock. I immediately regretted threatening him.

"I'm sorry. I'm sorry. But I do have an idea of what you might be."

"Oh?" he said, not drawing closer. I felt myself starting to shiver again. He noticed and drew closer to me, rubbing my shoulders with his strong hands.

"Well. Somehow, every time I seem to have a medical crisis, you seem to be there. Like, when I first started to get sick, I saw you in my backyard for the first time..."

He laughed. "Are you sure that you weren't seeing the menehune?"

This made me laugh. The menehune were mythical Hawaiian little people who appeared after dark, emerging from the forests to construct temples and sea walls. Basically, they were Hawaiian gnomes or elves.

"You know quite well it wasn't the menehune. And then, the first time I had to go to the clinic, you were there. And then, in the hospital, when I thought I was dying–you show up..."

He leaned closer, waiting for me to finish my thought.

"When I asked you on our first date what you did, you said you help people with transitions..."

When I said the word *date,* he smiled and then tried to suppress the smile.

"But you also disappear at weird times, too. Like when I'm stronger, or when there are doctors or my parents are around. Which is kind of weird."

He looked away when I mentioned his disappearances. Like he was ashamed. Or perhaps my words had come out as more accusatory. It did make me sad when he wasn't around.

"You can trust me with it, with whatever's going on with you. I can take it. I mean, my best friend here is basically dying of lung cancer."

"I'm not dying," he said, abruptly.

"I know," I said, not adding*, because you're not alive,* but wanting to.

But it was almost like he could hear my thoughts.

"This is way more difficult than I thought it would be," he said, putting his hand over his eyes. "I'm real. Just not..."

I couldn't believe what I was hearing.

"...just not in the way that you think. I mean, I'm real, if that's what you're asking."

"Of course you're real," I said, leaning into the warmth of his body, breathing in the smell of palo santo, thyme, and church smells in his jacket.

I started to wonder if I was imagining all this. Maybe it was the tea? It couldn't be.

Gabriel felt too real for all that. All of this was too real to be a hallucination or a dream.

In the distance, I could still hear the party, though it was clearly late, and the party had wound down. Laughter. The music had been turned down. The lights of the torches flickered on Gabriel's handsome face. I felt the urge to kiss him, but stopped myself.

"I am here to look after you, to help you eventually, when you...," he said, stoking my cheek again. "But here I am, even though I shouldn't be."

My eyes narrowed.

"So you were *sent*?"

He looked away.

"I mean," he said, course correcting. "I see what you're going through. It's hard. I've just been watching out for you, is all."

"So, you've been stalking me?" I said, my tone more playful than accusatory.

"Well...no, not quite."

"Then what?"

"Are you ready to go home? It's late, Maya," he said, changing the subject.

"I guess..." I said.

He handed me my clothes and then stood up, not turning his back to me. I wanted so badly to see his back, to finally make sense of it.

I slowly pulled on my shorts, taking glancing looks over toward him to see if he was looking, but he kept his face turned away, toward the party.

As I pulled on my shirt, a gust of wind blew. It was so strong I thought it would knock me off my feet. The wind knocked over one of the speakers and with a loud bang the party went silent.

The sound startled Gabriel. He turned his back to face the party, and that's when I saw it for the first time—his back, facing me. Underneath his shirt, I could make out the complex outline of a shape.

It couldn't be.

But it was.

Wings.

Two large, folded wings.

Chapter 26

He opened the door of his Jeep, offering me his hand to help me into the car, careful to keep his back turned. I climbed into the passenger seat and smiled. I didn't say a word. Was I still hallucinating? Had I really seen what I thought I'd seen? It had to be the tea.

I hoped he'd walk in front of the car so I'd be able to get a better glimpse of him, but he walked behind the Jeep, and when I turned my body to get a better look, the seats and the trunk blocked my view.

He pulled himself into the driver's seat. Without his jacket on, I could get a better look at his back. Delicate ridges. Yes, just like wings. I wondered if he felt exposed without his jacket on. Realizing that he was probably giving me a better view of his secret, he quickly turned his body away from me, sitting in the driver's seat all twisted up. He turned on the engine, rolled up the windows, and turned the heater up high. Without Gabriel's arms around me, I'd started to shiver again, even with his heavy jacket on. But the car warmed up quickly.

"Do you want your jacket back?" I asked when I realized that he had no intention of shifting his body into the center of the seat into a more comfortable position.

"No, I'm okay," he said, not taking his eyes off the road as he pulled out of the parking space. The headlights cut through the darkness, illuminating a heavily pot holed road in front of us.

"You're not going to tell me, are you?" I said, sighing with defeat.

"Tell you what?" he said, not taking his green eyes off the road.

"Oh, come on," I said, growing exasperated. "You show up whenever I get really sick. You don't seem to come around when I have other people around me. You make me feel really good..."

He smiled when I said the last thing.

"Well, what do you think?" he said. I wasn't sure if he knew I'd seen his back yet, but surely he had to know that I could see him more clearly with just his black shirt on.

I felt my body go cold even though we were sitting in a warm car. I didn't want to say what I thought out loud, but maybe it was the tea or the beer, or that fact that all the evidence seemed to point in just one direction.

"I think..." I said.

"You think," he said, not taking his eyes off the road.

"Well, I had this dream, I said. And in the dream, I saw you. I saw all of you."

"Like me naked?" he said, his voice playful.

"No. But you, without your shirt."

His face reddened.

"And when I woke up, I had this idea about what you might be. And I did some research. But look, what I'm trying to say, is that I don't really care what you are."

For the first time, he took his eyes off the road, staring at me with an intensity I'd never seen before, with a longing.

"You don't care?" he said, turning back to the road, his body shifting ever so slightly toward me.

"No. I don't care. I know you're here to take me when my time comes. And I'm okay with that."

He exhaled, a long, slow breath that seemed to last forever.

"So, what do you think I am?" he said, his voice softening.

"I saw your wings. In my dream, and..." I stopped. I could see his body tense up.

"Keep going," he whispered.

"And I saw them through your shirt earlier. When the speaker crashed at the party."

He didn't take his eyes off the road.

I didn't want to say the word *angel,* but the unspoken word lingered between us, heavy, like a stone.

"When will you take me?" I said, finally forcing myself to ask the question I didn't want to ask.

I half-expected him to avoid the question, to change the subject, but he glanced my way for a moment, opened his mouth as if to say something, and then stopped, but then opened his mouth again, and this time spoke.

"When you're ready," he said, biting his lower lip.

Now, I wasn't sure what we were talking about.

"All I know is that we shouldn't be doing this. This is not the protocol," he whispered.

"The protocol? What's the protocol?"

He bit his lower lip.

"Well, you can't dangle that in front of me and then not say anything," I said.

"When you're ready, my job is to be there—to help you transition. Until then, I'm supposed to watch over you. But I shouldn't be interacting you like this."

"So, you're here to help me die," I whisper, but then feel the anger return. "But you did interact with me. You did," I almost shout.

"Yes. I did. And I've been trying to figure out how to fix that problem."

"What if it's not a problem that needs to be fixed?" I asked.

He bit his lip, and a troubled look crossed his face.

I had so many things I wanted to ask him, but it was too late. We were home. He shut off the car and walked around it, this time up front. This time, with the glow of his headlights, I could see him distinctly. Two wings, tightly packed into his snug shirt, but they seemed to be straining against the fabric, trying to unfurl.

I hadn't imagined it.

I wasn't hallucinating it.

Gabriel was an angel.

I had so many questions at that moment. Like, how was it possible that Mom was able to see him when he had come to pick me up from that date? And if he was here to "take me," as he had said, why didn't he just take me earlier? Why was I still here? Or why was he still here?

He gave me his hand and helped me out of the car. Our eyes locked for a long time; his intense green stare seemed to penetrate straight to my soul.

I wanted to reach out and touch him, but I was scared my hand might go straight through him. I could tell he wanted me to stay, but also was begging me to leave.

"I have so many questions," I said, finally.

"I know," he said, glancing down at the road below us. "And I promise, they'll be answered eventually. But not tonight, okay? Can I just stand here for a moment and look at you?"

"Yes," I said, my voice trembling.

His eyes looked hungry as he took me in, first at my face, and then my body. I felt my bones turn to marshmallow inside me. Delicious and a little gooey.

His body seemed to tremble for a moment, and for the first time, I saw what looked like two elbows rising behind his shoulders. The wings, straining against his shirt. If they opened any more, they would rip the shirt open.

He looked away, and the wings folded back down and disappeared. His torso, like that of a linebacker, hid them well.

"Is this hard for you?"

"Yes," he said, finally.

"Do you want to take me now?"

"Yes," he admitted, not looking up from the ground.

"What if I wanted you to take me now?" I whispered, my body melting just saying the words.

His face changed, his gentle smile twisted into a scowl.

"You don't know what you're talking about, Maya. You should go now. Just go home, okay?" he said, turning his face away from me, as if I was made of blinding white light.

"Okay," I said, confused, unable to hide my heartbreak.

"Please just go," he said, shielding his intense green eyes with his hand, as if my body were a bright, hot flame that would burn him or blind him.

I could feel the tears coming, hot and embarrassing.

"Please, no," he said. "Don't do that."

I wanted to stop crying, but I couldn't stop. I found myself choking on my own sobs.

"I just... don't want to interfere with your life. What I mean is, I'm not supposed to interfere. When I saw you in the clinic, the first time, I was shocked because I had an appointment with someone else."

"A doctor's appointment?"

"No. Someone else was dying that day. I'm not scheduled to see you for a while..."

My mind spun with questions. So many questions.

"When are you scheduled to see me?" I asked, growing frightened.

"I can't tell you. That would interfere with... this process," he said, gesturing at me.

"What process?"

"Your life."

"But then why did you take me to the top of Mauna Kea that night?"

"We are permitted to intercede in limited circumstances. Sometimes, when we are sent to help people cross, our presence can affect others who are keeping vigil over the dead. Usually, we have to worry about wives, husbands, nurses, people doing CPR. They tend to overhear the conversations I have with the person I've been sent to take. Of course, they only hear the dying person's side of the conversation; my voice never crosses the veil... but even this can be problematic. Usually, these are easy fixes. I'll ask the person to say their mother's name so that their wife or husband thinks they're just seeing ghosts or something. But your case is more... complicated. I've never had someone I wasn't sent to take see me. And I wasn't expecting you to be able to see me at the clinic that day."

"So, most people can't see you?"

"No. Only the ones who are closer to the veil, those who are actively dying. You must have been sicker that day, closer to the veil."

"Then why can I see you now?"

"Because I'm trying to fix what I've messed up."

"It's not working," I said.

"Look, my job is to help you cross when it's your time. But right now, I've been sent to fix the ways I've already interfered with your life. I was permitted to cross the veil for a single day to take you to Mauna Kea because I was hoping you'd think I was a near-death experience or something. I was hoping to rid you of your fixation."

"You were hoping to rid me of my fixation?" I said, feeling my heart start to pound with anger.

"Yes, your fixation," he said.

"My fixation on what?"

"On me," he said, sighing.

"So that's why you took me to Mauna Kea, to get me to stop thinking about you? That sounds like the dumbest idea I've ever heard."

He looked down in shame.

"Yes. It's all gone wrong. I'm new at this, young in a metaphorical sense. I've never helped someone like you. You're so much younger than the others. So much more... beautiful," he turned away with embarrassment. "I was sent to the hospital to take someone else, a little girl. I couldn't help myself. I had to see you, to talk to you. I knew it was wrong. But love is the most powerful force in the universe, you know?"

I felt my ears go warm.

"When I saw you were at the caldera, the place where earth itself is created, your pull... it was too powerful. I couldn't resist. And you were so sick that day... I wanted so badly to take you, to ease you of your pain. You're not like the others I've helped cross over. I didn't know what to do."

"The others?"

He slowly backed away from me, and for the first time ever, I saw fear in his eyes. I almost looked behind me to see if there was a shadow or a monster behind me, but I sensed that the fear came from something inside him, or, maybe something inside me.

"The others I've helped transition," he whispered. "But I can't explain. This is not for you to know," he said. "But this is my last chance. I've already done too much damage. This is the last time I'll be permitted to see you for a long time."

"No. I don't care. I don't think it's wrong. I'm glad you showed yourself to me when you did."

He shook his head, like I was a small child or too stupid to understand what I was saying.

"I just don't want to interfere with your *time*. It's precious, Maya. After tonight, you know that, don't you?"

I nodded, remembering what it had felt like to let myself go to that other place, that place where who I was didn't matter, that place where words made no sense, and what it had felt to return, to be myself again, to be in my body, in my specificity as a person. He was right. I wouldn't have been able to put it into words if he asked me, but my specificity *mattered*. It mattered in a profound way, the profundity of which escaped my grasp now, and at any moment I tried to hold onto it.

"Well, it's a little too late for that," I said, gesturing to him, to the marvelousness of him.

He shook his head and said, "No. That's not true," a low growl, just under his breath.

I didn't move from my spot.

"I want to see you again," I said, feeling myself say the words, butterflies in my pelvis and throat.

He looked away again.

"I've already taken so much from you..." he said. "I'll see you again. When it's time. When it's time, we'll have all the time in the world, okay?"

"Is tomorrow time?" I said, unable to hide the panic from my voice.

He looked away, not saying a word.

He stepped in closer and pulled his jacket off me. I took a deep breath, breathing in the smell of palo santo and the churchiness. I didn't want to forget that smell.

He took it back and slipped back into it. I could see his body relax with the extra coverage. He must have felt exposed in that shirt, with his wings so visible like that.

Before I could turn to go, he said my name, the sound of my name in his voice, melted me.

"Maya?" he said, softer this time, as if relishing the sound of my name in his mouth, "Promise me something?"

"What?" I said, worried about what he would ask me.

"If you get a chance to kiss Elijah, do it."

"What?" I said, my stomach dropping to my feet in disappointment.

"You deserve to be kissed, before...."

My face scrambled.

I wanted to say, but I want to kiss you, not Elijah, and he could see me struggling, fighting myself. Yet, seeing me struggle like that seemed to satisfy something inside him.

"I don't want to kiss Elijah," I finally managed to splutter out, biting my lip so as not to say the other stuff. I was mad, so mad that I couldn't hide my anger.

But when I said I didn't want to kiss Elijah, I saw relief cross his face, and I realized that given that I'd gone with Elijah to the party, maybe he had thought I had been on a date with him, or something.

"You know what, never mind," he said.

"Never mind what?"

"Everything. Just forget about it," he said.

I didn't know what he meant.

I nodded.

I walked away slowly, not wanting to leave him. But I could feel an energy coming from him, pushing me away, pushing me home.

As I walked to my front door, I glanced back and saw that he had already slipped back into the driver's seat, his intense eyes never leaving me, as I kept walking to my front door, stopping every few steps to look back and smile. Every time I glanced back, he smiled, and then I smiled, and we did this slow dance until I reached my front door.

I didn't want to open my front door, but I heard the engine rev behind me, and watched the Jeep back away from my driveway, until it disappeared into the darkness of the unlit road, two red taillights glowing in the dark like haunting demonic eyes.

I turned back to face my front door, put my key in the lock, and pulled it open.

That's when all hell broke loose.

Chapter 27

Even though it must have been well past midnight, the lights in the house were all on. I was confused. I hadn't expected Mom and Dad to wait up for me.

Dad stood in the middle of the living room. He'd been pacing. When he saw me open the door, he released a little gasp. He had a look of anger, terror, and relief on his face--like he'd just seen a ghost. I've never seen him give me that look before, a look like I'd just punched him in the stomach and at the same time given him a hug. Mom had been sitting on the couch, but when she saw me walk through the door, she started to sob audibly.

But what did it for me was Elijah.

He was there too, sitting on the couch beside Mom, his eyes swollen, like he'd been crying.

"What the hell?" I said.

"Where did you go? One minute you were there, and then, you were gone..." he said, his voice trembling.

"What do you mean? Gabriel gave me a ride home."

"Who is Gabriel?" Mom said, her face twisting from relief to worry.

"Who is Gabriel?" Elijah said, his voice sounding angry and not a little hurt.

My head spun. I didn't know what to say. Gabriel, the angel... Gabriel the guy who had taken me on a date that ended with me being in the hospital. Gabriel, who had taken me to the City of Refuge, where we had stood under the temple waiting for God, but I'd felt nothing.

Nothing I could say would make sense. I decided that I'd have to spin my story.

"I... I got a ride home....from a friend..."

Elijah's eyes narrowed. I could tell he could tell I was lying, but Mom and Dad seemed to be buying it.

"Maya," Mom said, her voice slow and clear, but pierced with pain. "We were so worried. Elijah was worried."

"After we had that beer, you just disappeared..." Elijah said.

My body softened with relief. For a moment, I thought he had told my parents about the tea. It was bad enough that I had cancer. I didn't want to die due to parenticide.

Over the course of the next hour, as everyone's anger settled down, I was finally able to piece together what happened. Apparently, not long after I'd had the tea, I disappeared. Elijah was gracious enough to omit the part where I drank the tea when he told my parents the story. In his account, after I had the beer with him, I'd wandered off, and he couldn't find me.

My head was all wrong. What was true? What wasn't true?

I had jumped into the water, right?

Elijah wasn't lying about not seeing me, though. He had searched the party, asking everyone if they'd seen a girl with a pink beanie, blue shorts, and a white shirt, but I could have been about anyone, and no one could find me.

"You didn't see me sitting on the beach with Gabriel? I thought you waved to me..."

"No," Elijah said. "After the beer, I couldn't find you anywhere. Isaiah had to break into your car so I could get your home address from your car registration. Isaiah gave me a ride here, and I told your parents what happened.

As the course of Elijah's evening became clear to me, I grew increasingly frightened and confused. If he hadn't seen me with Gabriel like I thought he had, maybe I *had* hallucinated the whole thing.

But then again, if I had hallucinated the whole thing, how did I get home?

Gabriel had driven me home.

Eventually, I managed to settle on a story about the night that satisfied Mom and Dad. After the beer, I'd wandered to the beach, where I'd met Gabriel. We must have gone for a walk or something and lost track of Elijah. When I got back, Elijah was gone, and I wasn't feeling well, so Gabriel offered to give me a ride home.

When Mom and Dad were sufficiently satisfied with my story and convinced that I hadn't been recruited into human trafficking in the few hours Elijah had lost track of me, Dad offered to give Elijah a ride home.

"We're all tired," he said.

But as he walked out the door, he said ominously, "We'll discuss tomorrow how we are going to make sure something like this never happens again."

That gave me chills. If they forbid me from seeing Gabriel, I would die. I had to stifle a laugh at the irony of the thought.

With Elijah and Dad gone, Mom just sighed and shook her head.

"We were so worried, Maya... If anything ever happened to you, I would..." but with the thought, she stifled a loud sob.

"Mom, I think we all just need some rest. I'm sorry. I didn't mean to worry anyone. It was just a big misunderstanding."

I make my way up the stairs with effort, my body aching with each step.

The pain had returned, radiating from my bones through my whole body, a pulsing throb that increased with motion. Already, I could feel the exhaustion clouding my brain, drawing a heavy blanket over my ability to think clearly about what had happened. I thought about taking a shower, but the thought of taking off my clothes, and being cold, and climbing in and out of the tub sounded too exhausting. I walked to my room and collapsed in my bed, with my clothes still on.

I thought about Gabriel and felt immediately warm.

Whatever had happened at the party, whatever Gabriel was, a man, demon, angel, figment of my imagination, or hallucination, I was certain about one thing–I was completely and absolutely in love with him.

Chapter 28

When I woke in the morning, with more distance and time between me and whatever had happened at that party, I couldn't help but feel like I'd hallucinated the whole thing. Gabriel had told me he wouldn't be at the party, and the idea of a man with the wings of an angel—or a demon driving me home sounded insane in the light of day.

Of one thing I could be sure—someone had brought me home. But beyond that, it could have been anyone, or anything.

And yet, I could still feel his body warm against mine, still feel the weight and strength of his arms warming me. I could still smell him, that palo santo churchy smell.

I leaned over to check my phone, knowing that I'd have no messages from Gabriel. Instead, I had a bunch of unread messages, all from Elijah.

My heart sank.

Where did you really go last night?

I was so worried about you...

Who is Gabriel?

I'm sorry I worried your parents like that. I was really scared.

If you're not grounded, would you want to grab lunch in town?

My brain felt foggy as I read the texts. The more I thought about Gabriel, the more I felt like I must have imagined the whole thing. Or hallucinated it.

Yet even though my memory of the night before felt hazy, other parts of me felt cleared out, and other memories felt clear and solid. Gabriel's Jeep. The smell of Gabriel's clothes when he had pulled me close.

I hadn't realized it, but all along I'd been carrying a weight inside me. It hadn't felt too heavy in the early days of my illness, just a nagging anxiety that I dragged along with me. But after my diagnosis, it had become heavier, harder, like a stone I pushed to the top of a hill all day, only to have it roll down to the bottom in the morning again.

It was the weight of fear and anxiety, and anger, but after the tea, I felt cleansed. The fear and anxiety and anger were still there, but they felt lighter, more manageable, smaller, and more human-sized.

Dying was and wasn't okay, and I could live in that ambiguity.

While I sat there staring at my phone, it started ringing.

It was Elijah.

I answered.

"Hi," he said, his voice sounding small and hurt. It made me sad. I hadn't meant to hurt him.

"Hi," I said, and then quickly. "I'm sorry about last night."

"Yeah, here I was hoping my grand romantic gesture was going to win you over, and you ended up disappearing and going home with another guy."

"Ouch," I said.

"True? Or untrue?"

"I mean, did you really think something was going to happen between us last night?"

He laughed. "I mean, not last night, but maybe someday... I'd like to not die a virgin and it's not like a guy like me gets too many chances."

"You're a virgin?"

He laughed. "It's a hard life beating away all the women whose only dream in life is to date a dying man."

"I mean, you'll be surprised..." I said, laughing.

"I like *you*," he said, emphasizing the word *you*, as in, me.

I didn't know what to say. If it weren't for Gabriel, I might have almost fallen for him, too. We did have quite a bit in common. In another world, another timeline, I might have swooned about his grand gesture of the tea, and his invitation for coffee, and his attentive texts, and his morning phone calls. But deep down I wished it was Gabriel who had been calling me and texting me.

He broke the awkward silence. "Well, what do you say to a very platonic cup of coffee in Hilo, then?"

I laughed.

"We need to talk about integrating your journey in a meaningful way. It's a very important part of the process. I won't make any moves. I promise."

"Okay," I said. "But only if I'm not grounded, and only if you promise to keep it platonic."

Elijah laughed. "One of the perks of having a terminal illness is that your parents know that time is precious. They're not going to ground you. Watch."

I got off the phone and told him we'd hammer out the details after I managed to get some breakfast into my body.

As I walked down the stairs, I figured, *why not meet with Elijah for a very platonic cup of coffee--who could possibly get hurt?*

Elijah was right. Mom and Dad weren't grounding me. Dad was annoyed that he had had to take an Uber all the way to the black sand beach to retrieve my car from the parking lot, and he was even more annoyed that when he had arrived at the black sand beach and found the car, the window was broken because Elijah had had to break into the car. But he tried to hide his annoyance for my sake. In between the annoyance, I could also glimpse a subtle sense of amusement in my Dad's face.

I think all this time my parents had been half-waiting for me to enter my "rebellious teenager phase" where I'd finally go on dates, and stay out late, and sneak away to beer parties, but when it had just not happened, I think they'd secretly been a little worried that I was going through some kind of developmental delay. And honestly, in Portland, I hadn't had any interest in "growing up." I mean, deep down I wanted a boyfriend and fantasized about what it would like to be kissed when I read books about it, but mostly I was content hanging out with Tay at the mall and spending most nights reading in my room. Knowing I was dying had changed me, though. All those things I figured I could put off until college could no longer wait. Between Dad's obvious annoyance, I could sense another emotion, awe, relief, even a little joy in seeing me become my own person.

All that left unsaid, Dad made it clear and very much said that in the future, he did want me letting them know exactly where I was going, who I was going there with, when I planned to return home, and which transportation modality or modalities I planned to use in the process. This felt like a reasonable request.

I decided to use that opportunity to let them know that Elijah had asked me out for coffee in Hilo. Mom's face brightened. I could tell she really liked Elijah. He had, after all, had the sense to get my address and contact them as soon as I'd gone missing.

And even though I'd been mad at Elijah last night about the whole thing, in the light of the morning, it did come across as a reasonable move. He must have been scared that I'd jumped into the ocean or something.

"You can go, but only if I drive you. I have errands to do in town, anyway," Mom said.

I texted Elijah to let him know.

He texted back immediately.

Coffee Shop. Eleven?

He sent me a pin and I forwarded it to Mom, then dragged my tired body upstairs to shower, medicine, and clothe myself.

Chapter 29

It was a cute little coffee shop, decorated with pink roses. Everything was pink and rose-themed. The coffee tables had little vases, each with one pink rose in it. Bouquets of pink roses overflowed from the counter, crowding out the display cases of muffins and pink cupcakes.

Elijah sat at a table under a trellis of roses, nursing a white mug of steaming coffee when I walked in. The ambiance was at once incredibly romantic and incredibly platonic. It was a girls' coffee shop. There were t-shirts with the word *slay* on them. I felt comfortable immediately.

I ordered my coffee and plunked myself down in the empty seat Elijah had saved for me.

He stared at me with eager eyes, and I almost felt a flutter in my stomach, but quickly looked down at my latte to break whatever spell he was trying to cast on me. I didn't like that it was kind of working.

"Integration time?" he asked, pulling out a decomposition book.

"Integration time?" I asked, looking at the notebook with curiosity and a little worry.

"I got you this notebook so you can write things down as they come to you. It helps to write about the experience, for the purpose of processing everything."

I nodded.

Elijah pulled some creased sheets from his bookbag.

“I did this a while ago, but there were some parts of it that really helped. There’s this idea that in every person, there are these domains of experience: mind, body, and spirit. These experiences can have the effect of changing your relationship to these domains. We also go into the experience with intentions, either explicit or implicit. I mean, my own intention was to make sense of my own dying and to come to peace with it.”

He paused and gazed in my direction. His dark eyes were eager and intense. I felt the flutter in my stomach again, and drank a sip of coffee, trying to shake it away.

“I think my intentions were the same,” I said, cautiously.

“Did the experience respond to your intention in any way?”

I didn’t know how to respond to this. If Elijah were to ask me how I felt about my own dying, I’d probably say that I felt more at peace with it after last night. But if he asked me if the experience had helped me make any sense of my dying, then no. If anything, it had made me more confused. If Gabriel was just a hallucination—which I knew he was not—then what role did he have in my dying? And even if he wasn’t a hallucination, what was I to make of those wings and the angelic qualities I’d witnessed?

And Gabriel had seemed very concerned about me living out my last days in the best way possible. He’d even suggested that I kiss Elijah.

"That's hard to articulate. So many things happened, Elijah. I don't even really know which things were real or which were imagined—or hallucinated."

"Oh, Maya. Everything is real. Everything you encounter in that realm is real."

I'd felt in my soul the truth of those words but hearing him say it aloud helped me feel less crazy, less alone.

"Everything I've read said that we really should try to avoid classifying experiences as 'good' or 'bad' but if you focus on the overall emotions or quality of your experience, was there any feeling you take away from it?"

This felt easy.

"Love. Gratitude. Oh, deep gratitude that I get even a little more time to be me."

Elijah didn't take his eyes off my eyes.

He nodded. It was weird because I could feel his love emanating from him, an intensity I couldn't shake by just taking a sip of coffee or looking away.

In that moment, I decided to just accept it. It didn't feel bad.

His love had the quality of just being, of not needing reciprocation.

Elijah could sense the shift between us, and it made him smile. He took a long, deep breath. It could have been a breath to get his composure, but it could also have been because he was struggling to breathe.

"You know, when I first got my diagnosis, I was like, 14 years old," he said. "The whole world stopped for me and my family. Suddenly, everything revolved around the hospital and treatments and life expectancies, and all this—cancer shit. But outside our little cancer bubble, the world continued just as it had before. Like, the whole stupid world didn't give a shit. Like...my friends went to junior prom, and everyone was obsessed with who was going with whom and who was wearing what, while I was just sitting there... dying. It felt so fucking unfair, Maya. I was so mad."

I nodded. "Yes. It makes me mad a lot of the time, too. It's so damn unfair."

He went on, "Before I got diagnosed, I had a girlfriend. But then, I had all these doctors' appointments and chemo, and she dumped me. You want to know why?"

"Why?"

"Because she knew I wouldn't be able to go to the junior prom, and she didn't want to miss out on it."

"Wow," I said, my jaw dropping, and then I inexplicably felt the urge to laugh. I mean, I didn't want to laugh, but the selfishness and ridiculousness of it was so egregious that one could only laugh. It was also a bit absurd.

Elijah's face twisted into shock when he saw me hide the laugh, but then, suddenly, he was laughing too.

"I mean, Maya. I was dying. The doctors had told me that the cancer was terminal. I had mets all over my body. When they took me into the body scan, my body lit up like a picture from the Hubble. Galaxies of cancer in my lungs, lymph nodes, and brain. And she was... worried about a dance!" he laughed again, but then he bit his lip, and the laughter turned into a stifled sob. "I was so fucking lonely," he said, his voice cracking.

He went on, holding back sobs, "Most of my friends didn't know what to say to me anymore. It was like... I was in this glass bubble, and everyone was outside it. And the exhaustion and the pain, it just left no room for anyone else's feelings or anyone else, period. I wanted to be the bigger person and have consideration for her experience, but at the end of the day, I only had room for me, for my own suffering."

I nodded. I understood.

I didn't know what to do. I took his hand and squeezed it. I hoped he knew it was just a platonic gesture, but in that moment, it didn't seem to matter what it meant or didn't mean.

Compassion. Human connection. That mattered.

"I have a confession to make," I said.

"Oh?" he said. He looked up hopefully.

"I haven't told my best friend about my diagnosis. I mean, she's on the mainland. We haven't even done a video call since I lost my hair."

"What?!" his mouth went wide, a big, round O.

"It's just what you've been saying. I know that saying something will change everything, and I don't want anything to change."

"But what if it's a good change? I mean, you haven't even given your best friend a chance to show up for you."

"Yeah, but you said so yourself. People went away when they found out."

"Yes," he said, looking down into his cup of coffee as if there were perhaps answers there. Of course, there were no answers there. It was just coffee.

"But," he added, "some people, like Isaiah, and Jed, and Keoni, and Ruth. They showed up in ways I never thought possible. You can't close yourself to love, Maya. You're just going to die before you die if you do that. Love is the whole point of life. Love is the only intelligent response to all of this suffering."

I liked that idea. I looked around at all the roses and pushed back the tears.

"Yeah, love is the only intelligent response to all of this, isn't it?" I said.

"Yeah," he said. "I mean, I still feel pretty cheated. I want to grow up, go to college, try to pursue an impossible dream of being an artist, or a writer, or an actor, and experience failure. Is that crazy? I want to experience failure."

"You want to have the chance to fail?"

"Yeah, like, the chance to fail at something I love. Or... I don't know, being in love, and being rejected. That's a gift, too," he looked at me meaningfully, and then down at his coffee again.

"I mean, if you had time, if you could grow up and go to college, and do all the things, what dream would want to pursue—other than getting a brand-new Tacoma with big ass tires?"

This made him laugh out loud. But then his eyes got a faraway look to them.

"I always wanted to try to be a writer. To write something important, something meaningful, something that would change the world. But more than that—I'd like to not be a virgin when I die."

This made me laugh.

"Well, I don't know how much I can help you with the last one, but what's stopping you from writing? I mean, there are tons of writers who wrote amazing books right before they died, books that mattered because they were written by someone staring mortality in the eye."

Elijah teared up a little and said, "This was supposed to be your integration. Not mine."

I stared down at my coffee. The silence felt heavy.

"What would your dream be?" he asked.

I paused and thought for a long time. All I could think about was Gabriel. Maybe if I'd had time to go to college and explore my interests and try out different hobbies, maybe I'd eventually have a dream of my own. Right now, I just didn't want to die having never been kissed. I decided not to mention that because I didn't want Elijah to see it as an invitation to turn our platonic coffee date into a date date.

“I don’t know,” I said. “I’d like to die knowing who I am.”

“You don’t feel like you know who you are?”

“No,” I said, looking down at my half-finished latte. I didn’t.

“But you said that the overwhelming feeling of the tea was this gratitude to be you, so I feel like your essential self knows itself, even if your rational self doesn’t.”

I’d never thought of it like that before.

“Do you ever sometimes feel like you’re only half alive?” I asked.

“What do you mean? The pain?”

“No. The pain makes me feel more alive, and in a strange way more connected. I find myself reading about kids dying in distant wars or starving to death because they can’t get enough food, and I find myself feeling strangely connected to them. It’s not that. It’s this feeling I get after I’ve spent a whole afternoon on TikTok. When my mom snaps me out of it and calls me to dinner, I get this feeling, like I just woke up, only I was awake the whole time.”

“Do you spend a lot of time on TikTok?”

“More than I’d like. I’d rather, you know, go snorkeling with the stingrays or something.” Elijah perked up. “Would you want to do that with me sometime? Snorkel with the stingrays? They have a tour where they take you out to the reef at night, and they illuminate the reef..."

"I've heard of it," I said. "I'd like to do that."

I immediately regretted saying *yes.* I didn't want him to get his hopes up thinking it was a date or anything, but then again, I really did want to see the stingrays at night. Maybe if I hadn't met Gabriel first, I would have developed a crush on Elijah. He was very crushable. He also was the kind of person I felt like I could talk to for hours, like a best friend.

Elijah was trying hard to not give me puppy-dog eyes.

I decided that I'd need to be brave.

"Is it okay if we just be best friends, Elijah?" I asked.

He nodded, not looking disappointed at all.

"My Mom always told me that whatever I do with my life, if I ever get married, I better make sure I marry my best friend," he said, smirking.

"Please stop," I said.

He put his hand on his heart and looked down at his feet.

"Okay. I promise. No more flirting. I'll be completely platonic from here on out. I just..." he said, staring past me, clearly embarrassed but struggling to get the words out.

"Just?" I said, urging him forward. "I don't have much time left, Elijah," I said, tapping on the table.

This made him laugh. "I just. Is it me? I mean, is it something about me? Is there anything I could—like—change?"

In my head I'd always assumed that he knew my perspective on things. It had never occurred to me that he'd take my soft rejections *personally.*

"Oh God, no," I said. "I met someone when I moved here. And I've kinda fallen for him. If it weren't for him, you and I would totally be together."

This made Elijah smile, a big, wide, toothy grin.

"Who is this mystery man who has stolen your heart so I can kill him?"

This made me laugh so hard I almost snorted the coffee through my nose.

"Well, I saw him yesterday, during my... experience."

"No. No. No. No. No," Elijah said, burying his head in his hands. "You are not telling me, Maya, that the only thing blocking me from dying a virgin is a guy you hallucinated after drinking the magic tea?"

"I did not hallucinate him," I say, feeling my chest grow hot with anger. "I met him when I first moved here. We've been on a couple of dates. Well, I guess you can call them dates. I invited him to the party and didn't think he was going to come, but then I ran into him. That's why I went missing. He drove me home. Last time I checked, hallucinations cannot drive."

This explanation both satisfied and disappointed Elijah. His eyes got a faraway look to them, and then he looked at his feet for a long time, and then I thought he was going to pass out because his breathing became labored, and then I worried he might be about to cry.

I knew this whole thing was a mistake.

But he seemed to compose himself at the last minute.

"I'd much rather be your friend than nothing at all," he said finally.

I felt relieved when he said it. It was nice talking to him, and I didn't want to lose a potentially good friend for a guy who probably didn't even want to date me, and for a guy who might still possibly be a figment of my imagination. I'd conveniently omitted all the uncertainty I had about Gabriel. Hadn't he said he would see me today? Did he mean tonight? What if he came by my house and I wasn't there? Screw that. A girl couldn't just sit around all day waiting for a guy to maybe show up.

"I'd rather be your friend, too," I said, also relieved that we'd gotten past the awkwardness.

My phone buzzed. Mom was done with her errands, and she wanted to know if I needed more time.

"Text me later," Elijah asked. "We're not done with your integration yet. It looks like your experience might have brought up some unresolved emotions?"

"They are not unresolved, just unreciprocated."

“Oh, that’s intriguing as hell,” he said.

Chapter 30

The car ride home, I thought about Elijah and how he'd said that he'd rather be my friend rather than nothing at all.

I wasn't sure I'd be able to do the same with Gabriel. I didn't just want to be Gabriel's friend, and I didn't think I could endure the torture of a platonic relationship with him if that had been what he wanted.

Deep down, I worried that the kind thing to do would be to keep my distance from Elijah, at least for a little while, to let his feelings settle. But selfishly, I wanted to be around him. I liked myself better when I was around him. He understood what I was going through in a way no one else could. He was funny. And kind.

And yet, I couldn't stop thinking about Gabriel. Would he return as he had promised, and if so, when? I wish he had a phone so I could at least call or text him. Or at the very least, some kind of social media presence I could follow.

When we got home, I told Mom I was tired, so I went up to bed. Wrapped in my blanket, with my stack of books, and my phone, I felt cozy and safe, but also full of body aches. I took a pain pill and quickly fell asleep.

When I woke, it was dark outside, the day having passed without my participation in it, as so many days now passed. I could see the flickering of the tiki torches from my window, and I could swear I smelled BBQ.

I struggled to pull off the covers, aching to stand up straight from the pain, but managed to see Dad at the grill, with Mom beside him. They looked happy, their lives going on without me.

It felt like I could glimpse, for a moment, what their lives had been before I was born, and what their lives might be after I died. Seeing them happy like that made me happy. I knew I could go downstairs and join them, but the thought of taking a whole flight of stairs by myself made me nauseous. Better to just stay in bed. I wondered if Gabriel had come knocking at the door at any point during the day, but Dad had been home all day, and I was pretty sure he would have let me know if I'd had any visitors. At the very least, he would have had some questions.

I crawled back into bed with my pillows and my phone.

Elijah had texted me while I was sleeping.

Thanks for going out for that very platonic cup of coffee. I like spending time with you. It makes me feel more alive, if that makes any sense. I guess I mean... it makes me feel more human...

Then another text, he'd sent about an hour after the first.

If your boyfriend stands you up, Isaiah, Ruth, and I are going to the movies in Hilo tonight. Let me know if you want to come. I can pick you up in my wish truck.

I wanted to respond to the first text to let him know the feeling was mutual, that I was also glad we had hung out, but I also didn't want to give him the wrong idea. About the second text, I wasn't so sure. It reeked of double date to me, and I was still hoping Gabriel would show up.

I wrote something back, and then deleted it, and then wrote again, and then deleted it again. Before I could try to write something else, I could see the little dots indicating Elijah was writing. I stopped writing. This made the three little dots stop for a minute and then start up again. Elijah texted me before I could think of anything to say.

Sorry. I know this is going to sound weird, but I've been checking my phone ever since I sent you that last text. For the whole afternoon I thought you had just decided to ghost me. But when I saw you responding, I got really excited that you weren't ghosting me, so I started writing something, but then I realized that you could probably see that I was writing and I realized that that would probably look really weird, so I stopped writing, but then I realized that you probably saw me stop writing, so then I decided to write this. I completely understand if you never want to speak to me ever again.

This made me laugh out loud. I was also a little mad about his text suggesting that Gabriel would ghost me, but it was getting late, and he still hadn't come by.

I texted Elijah back.

I'm not ghosting you. I would have the decency to let you know if I needed some space. I think I'm going to pass on the movie. It sounds suspiciously like a double date. I'm still up for seeing the stingrays sometime, though. As a matter of fact, I'm seeing Gabriel tonight...

The last sentence was more wishful thinking than hopeful thinking, but I was still stung from Elijah suggesting that Gabriel would stand me up.

It's not a double date, but... Isaiah does have a little crush on Ruth to be honest, but he's too scared to tell her. He doesn't want to ruin the friendship. I keep trying to get him to tell her, but he's scared, and given that he's not dying, he feels like he has time....

I type back quickly.

What a coward! Well, maybe you could use your friendship with me as proof that revealing one's feelings doesn't have to ruin a friendship?

I see the three little dots going. Then stop. Then start again. Elijah responds.

So, you're coming to the movie then?

Ugh. I type back.

Seeing Gabriel tonight.

I immediately regret lying after I hit send. His response comes quickly, too quickly. I can tell he's trying to be happy for me.

Oh yeah. That. Have fun. Tell me how it goes...

I put my phone face down on my bedside table and shut my eyes. I start to wonder if I'm being stupid waiting for Gabriel. It's not like I have all the time in the world to wait, and the idea of going on a platonic movie date with Elijah sounds kind of fun.

A huge gust of wind blows, and for a moment, I feel like it might blow my window open or shatter the glass.

Downstairs, I can hear Mom laughing at something Dad has said.

I think about what Elijah told me about telling Tay. About how I should give her a chance to show up. I pick up my phone to text her, but then put it back.

Coward.

I pick up my phone again and start typing. I send the text without re-reading it.

Hey Tay. Let me know when you have time to talk. I have something to tell you.

Not tonight.

Then I put my phone on silent and put my phone face down on my nightstand.

I'll tell her, but not tonight.

Chapter 31

Gabriel never showed up, of course. I stayed up as late as I could. But eventually the pain in my bones grew so intense that I relented and took a pain pill. Even so, I was so angry at Gabriel that even without the pain in my body, I couldn't sleep. I took two sleeping pills and was grateful when I finally slipped into unconsciousness.

I woke confused and sad. Confused about why I was so sad. Confused about why my body hurt so much. Sometimes I woke up forgetting how sick I was, forgetting that I was dying, and then the ache in my bones would help me remember.

I knew I should go downstairs and eat, but now a new pain competed with the physical pain for attention.

The longing. The grief. The sense that Gabriel wouldn't be back for a long time, if at all.

I spent the next week depressed, waiting for Gabriel to come as he had promised, but finding in his place a vast emptiness that nothing could fill. I took more pain pills during the day and found myself enjoying the soft morphine-induced gloaming at night, that space between day and night, sleeping and waking. The medicines not only shut off my body's brain signals, but they also shut down my mind, clearing away the clouds of sadness, and fear, leaving me alone with a distance from everything that I welcomed.

I eventually managed to get Tay on a Zoom call, and I can still remember how her face twisted into shock and horror when she saw that I was bald, and then how embarrassed she became when she realized that I wasn't going for the intentional Sinead O'Connor look. She was polite, asked me lots of questions, and I gave her straightforward answers. Told her the doctors had said I was incurable. Whatever gulf had already been forming between us became a Grand Canyon. She got off the phone more quickly than I expected she would. And while she still occasionally sent me text messages and funny memes, she didn't call me again after that.

I had given her a chance to show up for me.

I hadn't expected her to be one of the people to disappear.

In the days when I wasn't sleeping, I watched episode after episode of *Six Feet Under*. One episode would end, and I'd let the next one start without moving from my semi-reclining position on the couch. At the beginning of each episode, a person dies. Usually, it's someone unrelated to the main characters who run a funeral home and whose job it is to come into close contact with death and grieving, but sometimes one of the central characters would die, a reminder that death arrives eventually for us all, and even more alarmingly, it visits those closest to us when we least expect it.

Sometimes the people who died were young, their lives snatched away from them, and those they loved unexpectedly. In these moments, I often found myself crying uncontrollably in front of the television. It was cathartic to grieve at these funerals of the young, even if the funerals were fictional. In watching the parents walk up to an open casket, or weep inconsolably on a funeral home couch, I caught a glimpse of my parents' future and my own death and could grieve the one topic my parents didn't seem to want to discuss.

Mom and Dad didn't want to talk about my dying. And Tay seemed more interested in sending me GIFs of cats in sweaters. I know it was her way of trying to be there with me, her way of finding words for the anguish that I knew she didn't know how to articulate, but it still hurt as one day passed, and then another, and another, without her giving me a single phone call.

But Gabriel's absence hurt the most.

Mom was especially concerned. In the afternoons, she'd ask me if I wanted to get away from the TV for a while to take a walk or go for a drive, but I was usually too tired by then to leave my perch on the couch or peel myself away from the latest development on *Six Feet Under*. Besides, with my egg-white bald head, painted eyebrows, and with my new sick-thin figure that made me look like a walking skeleton, everywhere I went, I could feel the second glances and worried stares.

My sickness was its own announcement, and I wanted the peace of anonymity.

It felt safer on my couch, where I could cry in peace and not have to worry about getting nauseous while walking through the mall. Since my diagnosis, I'd already found myself more than once retching into public garbage cans, my whole body heaving and trembling, legs weak. Vomiting never felt good, but nothing felt worse than vomiting in public, where people could stop and stare.

"Do you have any plans to meet up with Elijah again?" Mom asked, casually, every morning.

But no, and no.

Elijah texted me throughout the day, and we usually spoke on the phone after I first woke up, when I still felt like myself. I was grateful. He knew better than to send me funny memes. The morning after Gabriel didn't visit me as he had promised, Elijah mercifully didn't ask me how my date went. I think he could sense the disappointment in my voice.

Instead, he texted me to announce that I had officially inspired him to start working on a book.

It would be his final testament to the world, a project centered around his own dying, but more specifically around the process of dying when you are so damn young. He wanted it to serve as a kind of guide for other kids like us, others who had been robbed of their lives before they'd even had a chance to live it.

Even though Elijah had become quite busy, writing every good waking hour he had, he still made time to text me throughout the day, and call me in the morning when he knew I was likely to have awoken from my pain medicine coma.

I told him about how the phone call with Tay had gone, and he told me that when you live in Hawaii for many years, you get used to people coming into your life and leaving it. Apparently, a lot of people move to Hawaii with the same idea that it's this perfect paradise where people spend all day on the beach.

"After a few years, they realize that they can't spend every waking hour at the beach, that groceries here cost more than rent in some places, and that local people who have grown tired of giving their hearts to people who move away don't want to invest time in people likely to leave in a couple of years anyway. It can be very difficult to build community. And community is what ultimately makes life worth living. Either way, they run out of money or get bored, and they move back to wherever they came from."

He went on, "When I was younger, I'd often be the one to befriend the new kids. But by the time I'd entered sixth grade, I'd already lost three best friends to the mainland. I decided I'd stay closer to the kids who had been born here, the ones more likely to stay, the ones less likely to break my heart. But even they sometimes broke my heart, too. It's so expensive that even the locals get priced out of paradise."

"I thought you said I should open myself up to a broken heart. Give people a chance to show up?"

"That's not what I meant at all," he said. "If you've already let someone in, you've already made the investment in them. Might as well give them the opportunity to show up. But I've learned that my heartbreak has made me more discerning. Some people enter your life, and you know in your gut right away that they're going to break your heart. It's always safest to just walk away."

"Like me?" I asked.

"No. I've always had a good feeling about you. I even broke my rule about befriending transplants."

I laughed, but as I hung up the phone, I worried that he had gotten it all wrong about me.

I would leave him like all his other best friends had. One way or another, I would break his heart.

"We need to make plans about seeing the stingrays," Elijah said one morning. It was over a week since I'd seen him, and I knew he was eager to see me again, but didn't want any offer to hang out to come across as anything but platonic.

"Yes," I said. "But maybe we should try something that requires less exertion first, like maybe a movie?"

"I know a place that has a good coffee shop near it. We could talk about your continued integration and my book."

We made plans to meet the next day.

The coffee shop was in the mall, near the movie theatre, and the whole place gave off conflicting smells—movie-theatre popcorn on one end and coffee on the other. I didn't know whether to perk up or relax.

Elijah sat at a table tucked into a corner, where he and I would be less likely to draw attention to ourselves. The sick kids.

Elijah looked considerably sicker, and I wondered if I did, too. I bought myself a latte and sunk down into the soft chair in front of him.

Elijah looked paler and skinnier since I last saw him. If babies change and grow by the day and week—one week staring off into space and barely able to sit up, and the next saying first words and crawling around—Elijah seemed to be decaying at a similar rate. Not even two weeks had passed, and he looked less like a teenager and more like a small child.

"How are things going with Gabriel?"

On the phone, he'd avoided the topic, but in person, he was bolder.

"I don't want to talk about Gabriel."

Elijah wrestled with himself. I could tell he had a lot of questions.

"It's okay. I don't care," I said, taking a long sip of my latte.

"But you do care. It's obvious," he said, taking a long sip of his coffee to hide a half-smile.

"Yeah, I do care," I admitted. "My mom thinks I'm depressed—about the cancer."

This made Elijah laugh.

"What about the other stuff, though? All this focus on Gabriel feels like a distraction from the other questions."

This made me angry. "But what if it's not a distraction? What if love, human connection, and relationships are all we have in the end? I keep getting the sense that relationships are the things that give human life meaning. Like, if I was an ant or a bird, maybe I would be focused on other things, like building an ant pile or making a nest. But I'm a human. What if love is the only intelligent response to all this?"

Elijah stayed very quiet, staring at me for a long time.

"What about hermits?" he said, finally.

"Hermits?"

"You know, monks who live in caves. What about them?" he asked.

"What about them?" I said, growing annoyed.

"First, let me say that I think you're right about relationships being the most important thing. But not everyone gets relationships. Some people are just lonely. Or too broken. Or too hurt. And for those people, I think they find meaning in creating something or pursuing something that gives them a sense of meaning, like religion. Or hermeticism."

"How's your book going?" I asked.

Elijah finally let himself fully smile. "I can't explain it, really. Sometimes you sit down to write something, and the sentences just fight you the whole way. It's *labor*. That's how most writing has been for me. But this project. The project of my dying, it doesn't feel like work at all. I sit down, and the words seem to write themselves. I sometimes don't know where they come from. The characters feel like entities, spirits who have visited me to send me a very important message...."

"And that message is?"

"Oh," Elijah says. He gives me a look like I just poked him hard in the side. "That's harder to articulate. I can say this. When I'm writing, I feel completely human. It's the first time I've ever really felt that way."

I went silent and got very sad. If I thought about my life, I couldn't think of a single thing I did that made me feel completely human, besides waiting for Gabriel to return and watching *Six Feet Under.*

And even though Elijah looked sicker than ever, it was clear from his eyes that something had awoken in his spirit. He looked like a person who had something to live for.

Elijah could see me thinking hard, and he gave me time to think.

"What makes you feel most alive?" he asked, cautiously.

The few times I'd been with Gabriel came immediately to mind, but I got the sense that Elijah wasn't talking about those. And either way, given how long Gabriel had been AWOL, it didn't seem likely that I'd ever see him again, or that I had any control over whether I'd see him again or not.

"You know," I said, smiling. "Reading. Reading makes me feel most alive."

Elijah smiled even wider and clapped giddily. "So, the thing I'm creating that makes me feel most alive is the thing you experience that makes you feel most alive? How perfect is that?"

He was right. It was perfect.

Chapter 32

We watched a movie about a woman who worked as a housemaid for a psychopath.

Afterward, Elijah asked me if I wanted to go to the bookstore with him.

I wandered through the fiction section, but in the weeks after my diagnosis, fiction had started to feel a little pointless and like a waste of time. I wanted to read books about real people, facing their real deaths. I wanted real answers, not presumed ones.

I found myself in the religion section, surrounded by Bibles, books written by monks, and nuns, and meditation teachers. I felt overwhelmed, surrounded by a thousand possible answers, each slightly different, each untrustworthy in its way. But my eye caught the white spine of a book called *The Zen Struggle with Death.* I pulled it out and read the back flap.

After years of Zen training, David Lindstrom was diagnosed with late-stage pancreatic cancer. Rather than quit the monastery and return to his sick bed, David decides to continue to pursue his calling with grace and faith. This is his story.

On a whim, I decided to buy the book. I'd always wanted to learn more about Zen meditation practice, and I wondered if David Lindstrom had some nugget of wisdom that would make this whole thing slightly less painful.

As we wandered the aisles, I found the old feelings of anger returning. Not just for me and my own mortality, but for David.

This was all so unfair. Surely, there was more meaning to my life than reading a bunch of books? And surely, Elijah's life mattered more than some book he was writing that no one would probably read.

I sat down in the metaphysics corner, fighting myself until Elijah found me.

"What's wrong, Maya?"

"Sometimes I feel like I have this entity inside me."

Elijah eyed me curiously. It wasn't helped by the fact that I had decided to sit in a place surrounded by Tarot cards and books about crystal healing.

I realized where we were, and course-corrected. "I mean, the anger has this power over me that it feels like an entity. It feels like it has a life—no, a spirit of its own. Sometimes I have to literally peel myself away from it, and it's so hard. It's like a weight, or a magnet, drawing me in."

Elijah nodded. "Anger is a normal part of the grieving process..."

"Yes, but this feels different. I've been angry. This anger is powerful. Elijah, it's bad enough that this illness is slowly destroying my body. I don't want it to destroy my spirit."

With much difficulty, Elijah got down on the floor next to me. It was hard for him to move that way. I could see it. But despite his breathlessness, he got down on his knees beside me and wrapped his arms around my shoulders. In his arms, I felt something loosen within me. The sobs came unexpectedly. I tried to fight them at first, but the grief was also an entity. Or perhaps, the grief was anger's true form transformed. I don't know how long I sat there sobbing in Elijah's arms.

What I do know is that I felt better afterward.

No matter what Elijah told me about purpose and meaning, one thing I knew was true—in the end, our relationships would be all that really mattered.

After all, when it came down to it, it's not like I was reaching for a book at that moment.

Back at home, in the comfort of my bed, surrounded by soft pillows and my books, I found myself unable to stop thinking about Elijah and what had happened at the bookstore. I felt this pull toward Elijah, toward his kindness, and toward how connected we were, toward how comfortable I felt around him, and toward the sense I had that he understood everything I was going through and had the patience to walk with me through my uncertainty. But there was also a sense of repulsion there, too. Elijah was very sick. And whenever I let myself get even the slightest bit close to him, I felt Gabriel's shadow, pulling me away, pulling me to wherever it was we had been the night of the party—if that was even a real place.

It overwhelmed me, but going in circles wasn't going to solve anything.

I pulled out David Lindstrom's book and started reading *The Zen Struggle with Death.*

David Lindstrom had a lot to say about the illusion of the ego. Whenever he'd find himself facing the fear of death, he'd stop and ask himself, "What is the part of me that dies?"

He had this idea that awareness was somehow bigger than death, and viewed death as a natural transformation, like the water in a river flowing to the ocean, or a wave crashing on the beach. The wave doesn't disappear, he explained. It just goes back to being the ocean it was all along. The purpose of death was to instill a sense of urgency in the living to live each moment fully. All that mattered was the present moment, each one, unfolding.

Look at how easily you let each moment arise and go in your own life, he wrote. *Just now, you've experienced a kind of death. In our daily lives, we seldom cling to any given moment. It arises and passes. The moment of our dying is no different. The moment of our dying* will be *no different.*

This didn't feel right. David Lindstrom hadn't considered the problem of pain.

I pulled my blanket up to my chin and considered letting myself inhabit the moment fully, but the moment only brought the full awareness of how much in pain I was. In the safety of my bed, I felt free to feel the pain, free to be inside my body, attending to its demands. But at the same time, I didn't want to be there.

Being in my body had become more demanding lately and being out in the world always felt like having a kind of divided attention, my body's demands pulling me inside, away from people and the world, and the world's demands—Mom and Dad's endless worry, Elijah's attempts to help me wrench the last bit of meaning from my mostly meaningless life, and Gabriel's absence. Between the outside world and the inner world, the pain always eventually seemed to win.

I Googled David Lindstrom. Apparently, despite his late-stage cancer diagnosis, he was still alive and well and running a Zen Dojo somewhere in Southern California. I Googled the name of the Dojo and realized that it had a contact form.

I'd never really written to a writer before, but I had questions about David's approach, and the questions were urgent.

> Subject: Seeking Spiritual Guidance
>
> Dear Mr. Lindstrom,
>
> I'm writing, because like you, I have been diagnosed with terminal cancer. I am impressed by your stoic approach to death. The idea of living moment by moment sounds right to me. And your idea that awareness somehow lives on is somewhat comforting.
>
> My question is this. When every single moment hurts so much, when every single

moment is utter and complete excruciating pain, how do you continue to live in the moment? You talk about death being a natural part of nature, but I can't get past the fact that nature is so fucking cruel. I think about that orca momma floating around the Pacific, grieving, dragging around the corpse of her calf. What kind of world is this? And in a world with so much sorrow, do you ever fear that expansive awareness might not be some kind of utter and exquisite torture? The idea of awareness being so wide as to hold the whole world's grief, the whole world's pain—it sounds incredibly overwhelming.

I'd love to hear your thoughts.

Sincerely,

Maya West

Writing the one email was exhilarating, and it opened something up in me. I realized Mom had been reading these brother John books. Brother John was a Christian monk. He had written a bunch of books about dying and suffering, and I decided I would write to that monastery, too. If I was going to seek the Zen Buddhist perspective, I might as well also seek the Christian one, too.

I Googled the monk's name and found his monastery quickly. Just like the Zen monastery, the Christian one also had a contact form.

Subject: Seeking Spiritual Guidance

Dear Brother John,

I am writing because I am an 18-year-old girl who has been diagnosed with terminal cancer, and I was wondering a little about how my mother will manage to get on after I die. I saw her reading your books, and I was wondering if you have any insight about why an omnipotent and good God would kill little children?

I'm not just asking about myself. I'm also asking about children starving in war zones and the fact that teenagers and little kids die in horrific car accidents all the time, and the fact that there are thousands of other kids with cancer just like me, suffering in a hundred hospitals around the world.

What sense do you make of this? How do you maintain your faith in the face of this horror?

Sincerely,

Maya West

I fell asleep thinking about what Brother John and David Lindstrom's responses might be. I fell asleep feeling vaguely comforted. If prayer was meant for the person praying, in my half-awake, half-asleep state, I felt something like an answer arrive in the quiet.

I checked my email in the morning, like I always checked my email every morning, and found myself shocked to have received a quick response from Brother John's monastery.

> Good Evening,
>
> Brother John is very busy at the moment, working on his writing, which requires his complete and uninterrupted attention. As a result, Brother John is currently unable to respond to any correspondence.
>
> In the meantime, if you or your mother needs spiritual guidance, we welcome you to the monastery. Spiritual guidance is for those at the monastery.
>
> Sincerely,
>
> Brother Chris

I closed my computer and shut my eyes. I didn't know why I wanted to cry so badly. I'd cried a lot since my diagnosis, but the tears I felt welling up behind my eyes were more urgent tears. They had the force of anger behind them.

The idea of Mom going to a Brother John retreat at his monastery brought me some measure of comfort, but something about the wording of the letter made me incredibly sad and angry.

Spiritual guidance is for those at the monastery.

I called Elijah immediately and explained the situation to him, choking back sobs. I knew his family was Catholic. Maybe he'd be able to offer some insight.

Instead, all he could say was "wow."

"Wow?"

"I mean," Elijah spluttered. "It seems like Brother John seems to think his monastery has some kind of monopoly on spiritual guidance."

I could count on Elijah the writer to put my impossible-to-articulate feelings into the right words.

The anger rose in me again.

"I never want to step foot in a monastery as long as I live," I said. "Why can't a tree provide me with spiritual guidance? Why can't a river or a stone? Spiritual guidance is for everyone, not just for those who have the money and time to go to a damn monastery!" I said, feeling the anger mixed up with my warm tears.

"But maybe we should play devil's advocate for a moment? You see Brother John's letter as a rejection. But what if it's something else also?"

"What else could it be? I asked for spiritual guidance and I got nothing. It's a rejection."

Except even as I said those words I knew they weren't entirely true. After I had written the letter to Brother John, I had sat in bed afterward for a very long time and felt a peace come over me unlike anything I'd ever felt. The guidance had already been there, in a weird way. And I'd even told myself then that it didn't really matter whether Brother John answered or not. Still, I didn't want Elijah to be right.

"Okay, Elijah. What else do you think it is?"

"I understand why you would see Brother John's letter as a kind of rejection. But what if it's something else also?"

"What else could it be? I asked Brother John for spiritual guidance and got nothing. It's a rejection."

"Maybe. But it's also an invitation."

"One I don't have the time to accept," I shot back.

"Do you have breath in your lungs?"

"Yeah."

"Then you still have time to accept it."

"Well, maybe I don't want to," I said softly.

"Totally valid choice," he said, smiling.

"I see what you just did there," I said, laughing now.

"What?"

"You turned this whole thing that I thought was a rejection into an invitation and a choice."

Elijah nodded, and said, "You have to figure out what you want, Maya. And this is part of it. No one is going to blame you for not wanting to spend your last days in a nunnery."

I laughed. But the conversation made me think. How many other times in my life had I misinterpreted the situation? It felt as if Elijah had put up a mirror to my own mirror, revealing a new way to see things. How many other times in my life had I mistaken someone's kindness for meanness, someone's invitation for a rejection? And it made me think about Gabriel. What if his leaving me wasn't rejection but a kind of mercy?

Maybe Elijah was right. Maybe I'd hallucinated the whole thing.

I told Elijah I needed to go get some breakfast and medicine to still my pounding head. The crying had made the headache that always pulsed in the background of my life ten thousand times worse.

A week later, I received another email, this time from a monk at David Lindstrom's monastery. Two months earlier, David Lindstrom had succumbed to his cancer, surrounded by loved ones and the peace of his own awareness.

I was also surrounded by loved ones, but I worried about the impact I was having on them. Mom had stopped doing anything for herself to become my full-time caregiver. In the weeks before we'd moved to Hawaii, she had talked about learning how to scuba dive and maybe taking hula classes. When she'd been a student in college, she'd wanted to be an actress, and before we moved, she talked about auditioning for roles at the little Hilo playhouse. But even since I got sick, all of that was on hold. Mom still hadn't learned to Scuba dive, hadn't signed up for a single hula class, and hadn't signed up for any roles at the little Hilo playhouse.

Dad often went for long drives and would return home with red, swollen eyes. He had been training for a marathon before my diagnosis, but now he barely ran, much less did anything but mope about the house.

While Mom and Dad had enough money to cover hospital bills and treatments, I often wondered what they would have done if all this had hit us before our good fortune. They certainly wouldn't have been able to afford any of it.

Tay texted me videos of dancing puppies, but I could tell she didn't know how to deal with it, how to deal with the immensity of what I was going through.

No one knew how to deal with it.

Except Elijah.

Elijah was getting sicker.

He hadn't asked me if I wanted to hang out in over a week.

I had given up on ever seeing Gabriel again.

I figured I had a choice. I could spend the rest of my days avoiding people because one person who might not even be a person had decided to disappear on me, or I could reach out to the people who were there.

I told Elijah my parents were being weird and asked if he wanted to get coffee.

"How are your parents being weird?"

"Dad has this new habit where he comes into my room after I've gone to bed and if I'm awake, he'll go on this long monologue about how much he loves me. Sometimes I can't take it, so I pretend I'm asleep, but if he thinks I'm asleep, I can feel him standing there, *staring* at me."

"Oh yeah. That's entirely normal. My Mom takes pictures of me when she thinks I'm not looking," Elijah said, coughing and catching his breath. "It's like they're curating the photos for the funeral program while I'm still alive."

I laughed. Elijah somehow found a way to put into words the terrible things I felt and thought but couldn't quite articulate.

We met for coffee. Elijah looked even smaller this time, his body swallowed by the plush coffee shop chair.

"How's the writing going?" I asked.

"Slow. Everything hurts. I can only write for about a good hour every morning, before my brain turns to mush and the pain gets all my attention."

I nodded. I understood the feeling. How, after a full night's sleep, my body had just enough energy to get me a shower, a breakfast, and barely just enough time to do one thing that mattered. Sometimes I'd just lie on the lanai and feel the sun on my skin, other times, I felt an urgency to figure things out, and I'd try to read one of the books I'd bought about dying, but after an hour or so, my vision would grow blurred or crossed, and I'd lose the thread.

"How do you know what to write?" I asked.

"I don't know," Elijah whispered, staring down at his coffee. "I write about the things no one wants to talk about."

The next morning, as I drank my orange juice, Elijah texted me.

Something had shifted between us, but I couldn't quite name what exactly it was.

He said it was time we made plans to see the stingrays.

I told him that maybe we should try something less strenuous, like a short hike to a waterfall.

I don't think I have time for a hike, Maya. We need to make plans about the stingrays now—or not at all. I don't know how many good days I have left...

I didn't ask for details. I didn't want to ask for details. It was true. Yesterday, Elijah had looked way sicker than he had ever looked before.

Okay. This weekend, then. Do you want to or me to drive?

Elijah wrote back quickly, as if he was indeed running out of time.

I'll drive. We can get dinner before... I'll book us the tickets. So excited!

I didn't want to be excited, but I was excited. I'd never gone snorkeling at night, and even though I'd seen a stingray once, this place was known for its plethora of stingrays. I couldn't imagine what that would feel like, to be surrounded underwater by two dozen large flying creatures.

I smiled at the thought of sending Brother John a picture of me and Elijah surrounded by stingrays. I would write under the picture...

"Spiritual guidance is available for everyone, anywhere."

I dreamt that I was dying. I couldn't breathe. I woke up coughing, and my coughing woke up Mom and she cuddled with me in my bed for an hour, just holding and rocking me until I fell asleep. I could tell she wanted to cry, but somehow managed to stay strong for my sake.

When I woke up, she was still in bed with me.

I knew that she didn't want me to die, just as much as I didn't want to die. These two unspoken truths formed a wall between us, the unspeakable and the unbearable, pressed against the unfathomable and the unimaginable. I wondered if this was what Elijah managed to write about.

When Mom told her friends back at home what was going on, I could hear many of them say, "I don't have the words," but the truth was not that they didn't have the words, but that the only true words left were so unspeakable as to be downright cruel.

Sometimes the only thing left to do is to state the facts.

Someone had to let my mother know I was dying so that she could learn how to radically accept the fact.

The doctors often spoke evasively to her, as if the palliative care was just a game we were playing while the doctors came up with the real treatment, even though we all knew we were out of treatment options.

I watched Mom sleep. For the first time in all this mess it occurred to me that there might be something harder than my own dying.

Mom would have to go on living without me after this.

How would she go on living?

That thought scared me more than my own dying.

Chapter 33

On Saturday morning, shortly after I had breakfast with Mom and Dad, Elijah pulled up to my driveway with his big shiny new Tacoma. If I'm entirely accurate, I heard his Tacoma before I saw it. I'd just taken my last sip of orange juice when I heard the horn honking outside.

"That's Elijah," I said, working my way to my feet through the pain.

"You have your phone?" Mom asked. She always asked me now. She never wanted a repeat of what had happened at the party that night.

"Yes. I have my phone."

"Okay," she said, taking Dad's hand. "Text me when you get to Kona, and text me when the tour's over so I know you're okay, and text me..."

"When we're on our way home," I said, annoyed, but I got it. If I had a daughter who seemed to have a medical emergency every few weeks, I'd want a text message every hour to know she was still alive. Dad tried to hide his face, but as I made my way to the door, I could swear he was wiping away tears.

I don't want to do this today.

That was the thought that entered my mind. Going to see the stingrays with Elijah was a happy thing. I was having a good day. I felt reasonably well. I didn't want to be sad today, and as much as I loved Mom and Dad, I couldn't protect them from their pain.

I gave them both a quick hug and walked out the front door, into a bright and beautiful morning, where Elijah waited for me, in his brand-new truck.

Behind the wheel, Elijah didn't look as sick. It looked like he was having a good day, too.

The road through Volcano, to the Kona side of the island had become familiar to me now. I knew that when the trees grew smaller on account of the elevation that my ears would pop—and they did. I could see Elijah struggling to breathe as we drove the stretch of miles at the top of the mountain, the caldera not even a mile from us. We decided not to stop. The volcano had gone dormant; there was no lava to see.

I looked forward to the other side, to the part where the land seemed to open, revealing an airplane's eye view of the ocean. The side of the mountain was dotted with coffee farms, and even from a distance I could see the shiny red berries. When Mom and Dad and I had come here for vacation—another life, really—we had walked through a coffee farm and had been served steaming hot cups of coffee on a little patio overlooking the mountains, the coffee farm, and the distant sea below. Mom had kept saying over and over that it reminded her of Italy or France, but I had been to neither, and now I would never, so the Kona coffee farms would have to be enough.

Elijah occasionally glanced at me, and it reminded me of how it had been to be riding in the car with Gabriel. Except, I felt safer with Elijah. There were no secrets between us.

We had time before dinner. A lot of time, in fact. Elijah asked me if I wanted to go to one of the coffee farms. I said yes, but that I didn't want to walk around. The ache in my body had returned when we'd hit the higher elevation road, and I didn't feel like I had the energy to do a whole walking tour just to look at a bunch of coffee plants. I could already feel myself battling with the pain that urged me inward, away from the wide world outside with all its beauty and fascination. I would not let the pain win. Not today.

Elijah didn't have to say a word. He coughed and caught his breath, and I knew he understood.

We went to the same little coffee farm where Dad, Mom, and I had done the tour, except this time, Elijah and I just sat on the patio, two cups of coffee between us, and the whole ocean below us.

The coffee was incredibly strong. Even with a bunch of half-and-half poured in, it still tasted just like black coffee.

I winced with each sip from the bitterness. The barista arrived with a plate of chocolate scones. After the bitterness of the coffee, the scones tasted like heaven.

"The sweetness is sweeter after the bitter," Elijah said, raising his glass.

We clinked our glasses together.

"But I don't like that as an apology for suffering," I said. "Yes, the world always feels lighter after we've come through the tunnel of a great pain, but I still don't like to think of that as an excuse for the necessity of pain."

Elijah stared at me for a long time.

"That's beautiful. And I agree," he said. "Do you mind if I write it down?"

He pulled out a little notebook he had started carrying around ever since he started writing his book.

"How's the book going?"

"Almost done. I've decided it's going to be a short book. I feel like books about mortality should be short."

"That's amazing!" I said.

"Actually, not," he said, looking down at his feet.

"Why?"

"When it's over, it's over. And I don't want it to be over. Writing it has given my life meaning. And without the act of writing it, I don't know if I'll feel the same about my life, or if I'll feel the same sense of meaning."

"You can always write other things," I offered.

He looked away, then, his eyes on the distant horizon. The ocean was particularly blue today. The sky even bluer. It was difficult to discern the line between water and sky.

"I don't have time to write other things, Maya," he said, his voice sad, but his tone firm.

I let myself look at his body. He looked even thinner today than he had when we'd gone for coffee. Neither of us said anything about it, but I knew he was getting sicker.

“Maybe you can keep a journal that will get published,” I said, not realizing that I was saying something sacrilegious and a little offensive until I said it.

“Like the Diary of Anne Frank?” Elijah said, saying the unsayable, and laughing a little at the absurdity and horror of it.

“I’d rather focus on my relationships…” he said, avoiding my eyes as he said it.

I looked away, avoiding his gaze.

Gabriel felt like a distant memory, like a hallucination even, but even just the thought of him made my heart flutter a little. I pushed it out of my mind.

I’d decided at the start of the day that nothing was going to ruin today.

No matter how much I lost, no matter how horrible things got, I still got to choose how to live right now.

As we sat there on that patio overlooking the ocean, I understood completely that even though suffering wasn’t required for a person to find meaning in life, a person could choose to see their suffering as a kind of assignment that life had given them.

I didn’t like the assignment.

But I wasn’t going to let it ruin what was turning into a perfectly good day.

Elijah and I sat in silence, watching the sunlight play on the water. It was so beautiful. Despite the pain, it was so achingly beautiful.

Elijah wanted to go for a drive.

There was this temple not far beyond Kona, and he wanted to see it. This was not the City of Refuge. I'd told Elijah about it, but he'd just sighed, almost as if he too had gone somewhere hoping to feel something—to find refuge--but had been disappointed to find no solace there—no refuge.

"As I get closer and closer to finishing my book, it becomes clear to me that it's impossible to really find meaning in life from work. By this I mean—meaningful work matters, but it can only carry you so far."

"What takes you all the way?" I asked.

"Love," he said, not taking his eyes off the road. "Love."

The temple was closed, or maybe it had always been closed, always off limits. We stood outside the ancient rock walls and Elijah didn't say a word.

Until he finally did say something.

"What was it I said earlier this week, when that monk's assistant gave you that ridiculous answer?"

I was shocked he couldn't remember. Maybe it was the chemo brain fog, but I worried about other things, like the cancer spreading to his brain.

"Spiritual guidance is for everyone, everywhere," I said. "And you said that I shouldn't see his letter as a rejection, but as an invitation."

"Yes," he whispered. "Let's go get some dinner."

He'd made reservations at a fancy restaurant overlooking the sea, just in time for sunset dinner. The waiter led us to a table overlooking the ocean.

Even though I know it hurt him to do so, he walked around the table and pulled out my seat, his breath cutting short as he pushed the chair in with me in it.

The waiter served us sparkling water, and we sipped the cool drinks while watching the sun slowly inch its way to the sea, turning the sky bright orange, then red. A coolness cut through the heat of the day, which made me shiver. Elijah noticed right away. He slipped out of his jacket, handing it to me over the table. Without his jacket, his body looked frighteningly thin and childlike, like he was slowly withering away to nothing.

"Are you sure you won't be cold?"

"No. Take it. I don't want you to be cold."

The first course was oysters. Pulsing white muscle in a bed of broth so pungent and umami it took my breath away, when I brought it to my lips. Chanterelle mushrooms arranged like a bouquet of flowers in a vase of delicate pastry with feta cheese that somehow wasn't too salty, but wasn't too sweet, either. Salmon with a lemon zest crust so tangy and salty at the same time, I wanted to order a second.

All the while, the setting sun performed pyrotechnics display above the ocean that would have put any fireworks show to shame.

"I want to drink every last drop of sunlight, until there's no sunlight left," Elijah said, taking a bite of a perfectly salted shitake mushroom, shutting his eyes with pleasure.

"These are the best shits I've ever had," I said.

Elijah laughed harder than I'd ever heard him laugh—ever.

"Oh my God, we need to tell the waiter they have the best shits. Please do it, Maya."

"No way!"

"What if it was my dying wish?" he said, getting serious.

"I'd think you'd want to spend your dying wish on something better than that!"

He laughed, nodded but then got very serious, as he eyed my lips.

I knew what he was thinking, and didn't want him to be thinking it, but also kind of enjoyed it at the same time.

The waiter asked us if we wanted dessert, but we were both too full for dessert. Besides, we needed to give our bodies at least a half hour before we got in the water for the night stingray snorkel tour. Elijah and I walked down a sidewalk by the sea, our bodies so close, I could tell he wanted to take my hand.

I let my hand graze his, just enough for him to see that I wanted him to take it, and we walked hand in hand beside the sea, under the flickering tiki torches, not saying a word.

Part of me wanted to joke that our hand holding was entirely platonic, but that would be untrue, and tonight was too beautiful for me to say anything untrue, even as a joke.

Chapter 34

Because of Elijah's breathing problems we were only able to stay in the water for a few minutes, and even then, I could see that he was struggling. His mother had made a special arrangement with the stingray tour people to have a nurse on board, to help him get into the water and out of it. The nurse was also there for me, but Elijah was clearly sicker than me, and her attention was mostly focused on him, making sure he was breathing properly. I imagined if Elijah hadn't been dying, he wouldn't have been allowed on the tour, but the tour guides were extra nice to us, giving us extra snacks and asking us more times than anyone else if our masks fit or if we needed to try another one.

But in the water, it felt like it was just us. In the water, Elijah took my hand without me having to reach out for him.

The stingrays were more beautiful than I'd imagined they would be. They emerged from the darkness of the sea into the big spotlight that the boat made and disappeared back into the darkness of the ocean. And even though they were only with us for a moment, the marvel of their being at all was enough to take my breath away.

It was like being surrounded by angels in a night sky, except I didn't believe in angels anymore, not after that stupid monk had decided that Christians had a monopoly on spiritual guidance.

When we got out of the water, Elijah was very cold and shivering and even though the girl who was our tour guide gave us like five towels, Elijah's teeth didn't stop chattering. I rubbed his arms and face, and legs trying to warm him up, but when we got back to the shore, I could see his lips were blue and his jaw was clenched to hide his chattering teeth. The nurse gave him some medicine, and by the time we got back into the car and turned the heater on full blast, I could finally see that his body had relaxed a bit. Not that his body was warm. His lips were still blue, and he was still shivering a little, but his teeth weren't chattering so badly, and he finally could talk.

When he finally stopped shivering, he spoke.

"I love you, Maya West."

"Elijah..."

"I love you," he was looking at me with earnest, but tired eyes, and I could see how scared he was to be saying what he was saying. "I'm in love with you. And I know you want this to stay platonic. But I just can't die without you knowing. I just can't. I'm in love with you, and my love is so big that it's perfectly content with loving you exactly however you want to be loved."

I didn't know what to say. I didn't say a word. He put his hand on my cheek for a moment, and his hand felt incredibly cold, but I didn't look away or pull away. I just felt full. Full of every possible emotion. Full of delicious food, and beauty, and love that maybe was platonic on my part, but maybe wasn't.

I wasn't sure.

I didn't say a word.

Elijah nodded and then started the car for our long drive back to Hilo.

When we reached Volcano, I asked him if he wanted to stop at the caldera.

"But there's no lava there now," he said.

"I don't care."

He turned into the park, and we drove the long, dark road to the overlook. The air up at the caldera was impossibly cold, but there were so many stars above us, each one like a little piece of shattered ice splintered into the sky. Elijah shivered. Now, I took off the jacket and wrapped him in it. He sighed. I wasn't sure if it was the warmth of the jacket or the gesture that had warmed him, and for a moment, I realized it didn't matter.

We walked along a dark path, using our phones to illuminate the way. Occasionally, the light hit upon a lehua flower, this spidery red flower that grew in Hawaii and seemed to thrive best in the blasted volcanic land around the caldera. When we reached the railing that overlooked the five-hundred-foot drop into the caldera below, we gasped.

The caldera wasn't spewing a dramatic fountain of lava, nor was there a river of lava flowing there, but instead, the ground glowed red, the embers of a brilliant blaze that once was, the rock still holding on to the little glow it still had.

Elijah and I stood over the caldera, side by side, starting at the glowing embers. Because the caldera wasn't bright, we could see the full glory of the Milky Way above us, a white road to the infinite.

"Elijah," I whispered, wondering if we could still be platonic friends if I kissed him, wondering if maybe we could be something better if I did.

The question of the possibility lingered for a moment, and then it wasn't a question, because he was kissing me. He pulled me close. Even though I know Elijah still felt cold, for a moment, we were both warm, wrapped in each other's arms. I felt dizzy but not like I would pass out or have another health episode. For a moment, the stars disappeared, and the smoldering caldera disappeared, and the pain of my body disappeared, and it was just me and Elijah, two dying bodies, holding on to the last of our warmth, surrounded by an impossibly cold universe.

I didn't want the kiss to end, but when I pulled away, Elijah's eyes flickered in the darkness.

"That was very platonic," he said.

I laughed.

Back in the car, with the heater on, we stared into the darkness before us, unsure what to do next.

"Do you think we could just sleep here tonight? I'm so tired, I don't want to drive. There's room in the back seat where we could lie down..."

"Okay," I said, and then we made our way to the backseat, with a lot of effort and pain, but when we were finally there, our bodies were pressed so close together I felt myself go a little breathless.

He had a blanket back there, and he wrapped us in it.

"It almost looks like you planned this," I said, playfully.

He smiled, leaning his body into mine. It felt good to be so close to him, to be pressed together like that.

We started kissing. An infinite kiss that seemed to last forever.

He pulled my shirt up off my body, and normally I would have wanted to hide the port in my chest where the doctors hooked the tubes to give me chemo, but I knew that he had one, too. And then, our bodies twisted together, and for a moment, I couldn't tell where my body ended, and his began, where my pain ended, and his began, where my pleasure ended, and his began...

Afterward, Elijah said he was very tired. I stared at our hands intertwined together, marveling at how naturally they fit together.

"Don't forget to text your Mom. I don't want her to worry..."

I laughed.

"What should I tell her?" I asked.

"Maybe the truth?" he said, a puckish grin on his face.

I wasn't going to die a virgin, and neither was Elijah.

Chapter 35

I told Mom we had decided to camp near the volcano. I expected her to be angry or worried, but Mom's response was shockingly stoic.

Be safe. I love you.

It made me laugh. I wanted to share it with Elijah, but he was already asleep, so I set my head on his chest and thought about the Zen idea about awareness being wider than a single life or a single body, the idea of separation and duality slipping away and becoming one thing...

Elijah and I woke the next morning to a blinding blazing sun. It was still desperately early. The parking lot still empty. Our bodies made the car warm, and I pulled Elijah close to me and kissed his closed eyes, his cheeks, his mouth. He woke up smiling.

"Am I dead?" he asked. "I've totally died."

"No."

We kissed a kiss that didn't end, that didn't want to end, and then managed to extricate ourselves from one another and crawl into the front seat of the car. We were both hurting as we drove home, but I got the sense that Elijah might be hurting a little more.

When we reached my driveway, Elijah took my hand and kissed me lightly on the forehead.

"I'll call you later," he said.

"I love you," I said.

He smiled.

Mom was waiting for me at the kitchen table when I got home. She didn't have anything to say, and I didn't know what to say, but she was smiling. I could tell she was happy I had gotten to have one normal thing.

She offered to make me breakfast, and I sat down and watched her while she moved effortlessly through the kitchen. I envied her a little, the way she moved without pain through the world.

She still hadn't said a word other than asking me if I wanted breakfast, but I found myself both envious of my mother and a little in awe of her. She was losing her only child and yet somehow managed to show up for me every day with this feeling of pure positivity and joy and grace. I mean, yes, sometimes she cried, like on the days we'd gotten the worst and hardest of the news, but other than those days, she was just...there.

The night before had made me feel more courageous.

"How do you do it, Mom?"

"Do what?"

"Not, like, completely collapse into a puddle of worry."

She had been cutting mushrooms and onions with the grace of a dancer, but my question made her stop.

"I... I guess it's just that... and maybe this is denial, but I still have hope."

"Hope?"

"Yeah. Look, in my life, worrying about anything too much hasn't really served me. Any time I've worried about anything, I've always regretted it."

"Why?"

"Because things never turn out exactly how you worry they will. Life always manages to surprise you. So, early on, I realized that there was no point to worrying. And no matter what the doctors say, there's always hope. Who's to say they don't find something between now and whenever that might extend your life? And who's to say that in that time, they don't find a cure?"

"But that's nearly impossible, Mom."

"We talk about nearly impossible things as if they never happen. But if you think about it, you and I are nearly impossible things. Think about all the things that had to go perfectly right for you to be here. Of all the people in the world I could have chosen to marry, I chose your dad. And of all the people in the world he could have chosen to marry, he chose me. And then, of the million possible eggs in my ovaries—one happened to be there just at the right time for—"

"Mom!"

Mom smiled and went on, "—one of like, 40 million sperm that managed against all odds to make it to that egg to produce the exact genetic code that would make you, you. And not just that. The conditions in my womb happened to be just right that day, and they were. In any given month, there's only a few days where the conditions are just right. If you think about it, we are all here, walking around like this is entirely normal, but really, we are these nearly impossible things. These statistically nearly impossible things, that, despite it all, happened to happen. You know what that tells me?"

"What?"

"That nearly impossible things happen all the time. And if they do, why not believe in nearly impossible things happening?"

"I mean, Mom. You do know my cancer is *incurable*, right?"

"Yes. Right now. But every day, doctors are finding new cancer therapies. We don't know how long you are going to live, right?"

"But average survival rates are..."

"Averages. Some people have less time, and others have more. Who is to say that doctors don't come up with a new therapy or even a cure? Every day, doctors are finding these new gene therapies that target specific genes that cause certain types of cancer to be cancer. Who is to say that tomorrow we get a phone call saying that the doctors have found a new gene therapy targeting your specific cancer?"

The whole thing sounded delusional to me, a mother refusing to face the reality that she was losing her daughter. I didn't know what to say.

"Look," Mom said, returning to slicing and dicing an onion. "If it turns out I end up having to grieve, I'll grieve. But there's no use in grieving on a perfectly beautiful day in Hawaii while my daughter is sitting there, clearly falling in love. I don't want to talk about dying. I want to talk about love."

"But what if I want to talk about dying? What if I want to know that you'll be okay?"

Mom stopped cutting again and turned to me. It was the first time I'd said those words aloud. Mom's expression became pensive and then shocked, like it had never occurred to her that I would worry about *her*.

"If you were to die, Maya, nothing would ever be okay again....but your Dad and I would be okay. Does that make sense?"

It did. It didn't.

The very idea of death felt like a paradox. The very idea that parents had to go on living after their kids died—well, there was no single word in the English language for that.

After breakfast, I went upstairs, and took a shower, luxuriating in the warm water. Then, I slipped into pajamas I hadn't worn in a while and crawled into bed. Even though it was bright outside, I was exhausted.

I woke to the sound of Mom hanging up the phone.

"Okay," she said, excitedly. "Yes, okay. I'll tell her."

Mom knocked on the door.

"Tell her what?" I asked through the shut door.

"It was your doctor," she said.

"My doctor?"

"Yes. He's calling because they've found a gene therapy that might be able to target your specific cancer cells."

"What?" I said, unable to believe what I was hearing.

For the first time in weeks, I felt it—a sliver of hope.

For the first time, I let myself imagine a life without the constant dull ache that backgrounded everything. For a moment, I let myself imagine a future that didn't involve my imminent demise. It felt weird to feel hope. Mom embraced me in a big hug, and I let her squeeze me.

"When do we start?" I asked.

"Tomorrow," she said.

"And I'll start to feel better again?"

"The doctor said it might take a few weeks, but if your body responds to the treatment, then yes. You should start to feel better in a few weeks."

Mom left me alone in the room, and I felt a future unspool before me. A future without incessant pain. I could go to college. I would be able to get to know myself, figure out if I had dreams, and once I learned what they were—pursue them.

After Mom gave me another big hug, I walked to the big mirror behind my bedroom door and looked at myself in it. For the first time, I didn't see sick Maya in it. I saw the potential of the old me staring back.

But the feeling was short-lived.

My thoughts went to Elijah.

He was dying.

The second I had the thought, my skin dissolved before my eyes, revealing, where my face had been, a skull. I screamed out for help, but no sound came out. And then I saw two black wings fold over my body, turning everything in the world to pain.

I woke up in my own bed, confused.

Had I dreamt it all—the cure, and the wings? Or had I fainted and if I went downstairs now to ask Mom about it, she'd hug me again and tell me that the appointment tomorrow was still on. My body hurt more than anything.

I didn't know what to believe, but the lingering feeling of having a future, of having a life to live, it didn't go away when I dragged myself out of bed and slowly made my way downstairs.

"Mom?" I said, probing the dark for her. The sun had set, and the house was quiet. "Mom?"

I heard a shuffle from upstairs. Mom had been asleep.

"Maya?" she said, her voice thick with panic.

"I'm okay. I just woke up and was wondering."

I couldn't bring myself to ask the question. In one instant, I knew the answer would either give me a life or take it away.

"Did the doctor call today about gene therapy? Or did I just dream that?"

Mom's face crumpled and I instantly knew my answer.

"Oh, honey," she said. "No. No, he didn't."

She pulled me into a tight embrace, and then, before I could pull myself away, I felt her body heaving beneath me. She was sobbing. Uncontrollably. All her strength and hope withered away, and I sat there in her arms, my body shaking with her grief, holding it.

It was all too much to hold

Chapter 36

Mom gave me some medicine and tucked me back into bed. The pain medicine warmed me and erased some of the scary feelings, and I slipped into a dreamless sleep.

When I woke, the room was bright with the light of the day, and I didn't know how long I'd slept and didn't know if I cared. I checked my phone to see if Elijah had called or texted.

Yesterday was the best day of my entire life.

I smiled and texted back.

I don't have the words for yesterday....

I made my way downstairs. Mom sat at the kitchen table, a faraway look in her eyes.

Something hard and painful formed in my stomach when I saw Mom's face. That was the face she wore when I had been the sickest, the closest to death, the face she got right after I got the worst kind of news.

I didn't need her to tell me to sit down. I sat down, my body aching with each movement.

"Elijah's Mom called me this morning," Mom said.

This confused me. I had steeled myself to hear that the doctors had more bad news for me, but I hadn't expected Elijah to be part of this conversation. Maybe Elijah's Mom told my Mom we'd had sex, but the thought that my mom would sit me down for a serious conversation after that seemed absurd to me. On the day I'd first gotten my period, years earlier, Mom had sat me down to tell me she had made an appointment with the doctor to put me on birth control medicine, and had told me that day, and at least a hundred embarrassing times afterward, that sex was a natural human process, like eating or pooping, and all that mattered about it was that I was ready and wanted to do it. Then she'd go off on this side lecture about how even if I'd said *yes* to a boy, I had the right to change my mind and say *no.* You don't owe anyone your *yes*, and when you give someone your *yes*, they have to keep earning it.

All those thoughts flashed through my mind in a flash, but I knew Mom wasn't here to talk to me about my date with Elijah.

"What does this have to do with Elijah?" I managed to squeak out, my voice growing suddenly small and shaky.

"Elijah's mom called the house this morning. She didn't have your phone number, and she didn't know how to unlock Elijah's phone. So, she looked us up online and found our house number and called it..."

I could tell she was delaying. She didn't want to say what she had to say next.

"There's no easy way to say this, Maya...."

I leaned forward. No easy way to say, what?

"Elijah is in the hospital. The doctors say he doesn't have long to live."

Mom paused, giving me a moment to take in what she had just said.

But all that I could focus on was the last thing she had said. Elijah didn't have long to live, but that meant he was still alive.

"Elijah's alive then? He's okay."

I said the word *okay* less like a statement and more like a question.

"The doctors say that the only next option for him is surgery, but they believe that it's likely he would die on the surgical table, and even if he survives, they worry that if they intubate him to help him breathe, they won't be able to remove the machines."

My head spun. Now I didn't understand a word Mom was saying. Mom could see the confusion and panic in my eyes.

Mom went on slowly, "Maya, Elijah's cancer has spread. It has blocked his intestines. He cannot eat. To unblock it, the doctors would have to perform surgery, but because of the limited capacity of his other organs, the doctors are worried that if they take him into surgery, he won't ever again become strong enough for them to remove the machines to keep him alive safely. Elijah doesn't want to die hooked up to a machine."

I understood.

"So, he just wants to die? He doesn't want to fight? To try?" I said, my voice growing high-pitched and angry at the same time.

"No, Maya. He doesn't want to die. He's dying. He wants to see you before they start giving him stronger pain medicine that might affect his ability to be lucid—to talk to you."

"No," I say. "I just texted him. There's no way any of this is true."

Mom got the faraway look in her eyes again.

"I can drive you to the hospital when you're ready to go. Or, if this is too hard for you, I can call Elijah's mom and..."

"No. No. No. No. No," I say, each no angrier and sadder than the next. "Why didn't you wake me? Why didn't you tell me as soon as Elijah's mom called?"

"She just called five minutes ago. I was processing the news and trying to think about how to tell you," Mom said. And then I could see the small tears forming in the corner of her eyes, and this made me feel very sorry for her. It was bad enough to have a daughter dying from cancer, but another thing to have to tell said daughter that her boyfriend was actively dying.

I had to pull myself together. Not just for Mom, but for Elijah.

As quickly as the pain would allow me to, I went upstairs and got dressed. I decided to wear a pretty white sundress I'd bought in Portland with Mom after she'd told me we were moving to Hawaii. When I'd bought it, I'd imagined all the occasions I might wear it. Dinner out in town with my parents. A school dance. A first date. In a thousand years, it would never have occurred to me that I would wear it to see my boyfriend on his deathbed.

Even though I was usually adamantly opposed to makeup, I pulled out an ancient tube of Chanel lipstick my mother had bought me for my 16th birthday and slowly put it on my lips.

Mom gasped when she saw me, and then she choked back a sob, the only one she'd allowed herself all morning.

"You look so beautiful, Maya," she said, her voice cracking.

I didn't know what to say. We made our way to the car and drove to the hospital in silence. I turned my head toward the window, so Mom wouldn't have to see the tears flowing down my face.

It took us an eternity to navigate the parking garage and find a spot. If dying or being sick is bad enough, hospital parking lots just make it worse.

When we entered the hospital lobby, Mom asked me if I wanted to get Elijah a gift at the gift shop, but what would be the point of that?

We rode the elevator up to his floor. When we got to his hospital door, Mom and I stood in front of it silently, neither of us ready to knock.

Chapter 37

I took a few deep breaths and knocked. I heard the movement of feet and then the door slid open.

The room was brightly lit and full of people. Elijah's Mom and Dad, his two brothers, and other family members I'd never met before. A very old woman wearing a ring of flowers around her head looked like she could be his grandma. Very softly, she chanted in Hawaiian beside Elijah's bed, her eyes closed.

It took my eyes a moment to adjust, to recognize Elijah in the middle of a web of tubes his face covered behind a breathing mask.

"Maya," he said, his eyes lighting up, his voice very soft.

I went to his bed and took his hand, but he gestured me closer, and before I knew it, I had crawled into the bed with him, and he had wrapped his arms around me.

The very old woman who had been chanting, stopped chanting, and looked to the family.

"I think we should give them a moment alone," she said.

Elijah's mom, whose eyes were swollen from crying, nodded. His dad's face brightened inexplicably as he said, "yes, of course, of course," and his brothers chuckled and winked at Elijah from their plastic chairs as they stood up to leave. The other cousins all shuffled out.

The room cleared quickly, and then it was just me and Elijah.

He stared at me for a long time, stroking my face, not saying a word.

"The doctors say that the surgery would probably kill me anyway," he said, his voice straining every word.

"Well, why don't you let them try?"

He sat up in his bed, even though I could tell it took all his energy to do so.

"No," he said, firmly. "I don't want to spend weeks hooked up to machines, waiting for someone to pull the plug on me so I can die. I don't want that. I want to die peacefully."

Every word hurt him to say. He strained for air to say each one.

"I understand," I said, touching his cheek gently. "I understand."

He nodded.

Very slowly, he started to speak.

"It takes so much courage to be a human, Maya. So much courage. Even if the universe may be this unfeeling immense thing that doesn't care what happens to humans, I am grateful to have had the chance to be a human who got to feel something. I want to feel something for just a little while longer, for as long as I can take it."

I got the sense that beyond all this static of pain and fear, there was an essential truth that just existed, waiting for us to become aware of it, waiting for Elijah to join it.

Elijah and I had sometimes circled around the idea of there being a God or an afterlife, or something more than just matter and energy and a bunch of atoms bouncing off one another, but I knew he didn't have any living energy left to discuss any of that now.

"Hurts," he said.

I nodded.

"Why don't we ask them to bring some pain medicine?" I said, grabbing the little button by his bed to hand it to him, but he put his hand on my hand to stop me.

"Not just yet," he said. "I want just a little more lucid time with you. I want to memorize your face," he said, staring into my eyes, looking me over as if he were studying for a final exam.

"I like this dress," he said, touching the hem of my skirt.

I laughed. Ever the flirt.

Elijah winced in pain, and he took three short inhales, struggling to get in a full, deep breath. His face grew very serious.

"I do have a request," he said.

"Elijah, you know we can't have sex with your whole family outside."

Elijah laughed weakly.

"As wonderful and hilarious as that would be, that's not my request. Though it would be nice if we could maybe try second base, or something."

This made me laugh.

But Elijah got serious again, carefully formulating his words because each word hurt him so much.

"I want you to read what I wrote. I wanted to be there when you died, but that's not going to happen, so I'll have to settle for the next best thing."

Now I was crying. It hadn't occurred to me until right now that if Elijah died before me, I'd have to die alone. It hadn't occurred to me that he saw his book as a way of making sure I wouldn't die alone.

"Yes. Okay. Of course," I managed through my tears.

I didn't know what to say after that. He squeezed my hand so tight, like a person who has fallen into the sea might hold on to a hand offered to him from a life raft. He buried his masked face in the crook of my neck and breathed in deeply.

"I love how you smell."

We cuddled together for what felt like an eternity, kissing and holding one another.

But then his face shifted, and he seemed to travel a thousand miles away from me to a place that wasn't this hospital bed in my arms.

"Are you okay?"

"Hurts," he said, through clenched teeth.

I didn't say a word. I knew that offering him the pain medicine meant that he would no longer be lucid, no longer as fully alive as he was right now. I also knew that the pain was becoming unbearable. Soon he would need more pain medicine, so much that he wouldn't be able to be on it and stay awake.

He looked at me for a long time, the studying look. And then we kissed for what felt like forever, my body warm with the warmth of his body.

Eventually, he ran out of breath and had to put the mask back on.

"I love this life," he said. "I love my life."

I nodded.

"But I'm ready," he said.

"Okay. Okay. I love you."

Chapter 38

Everyone gathered around Elijah's bed. With tears, his Mom, Dad and grandma and brothers said *I love you, forever,* and *I'm so proud of you,* and a thousand other little things, some too personal and private to mention here.

They started the pain medicine, and I saw Elijah's face relax for the first time all morning.

The room grew very silent.

Elijah winced and asked for more morphine. His mom called a nurse.

He held my hand tightly, and then his grip loosened, and he slipped into a shallow-breath morphine sleep.

For hours, we sat in the room and watched him breathe. The sun set and the room darkened, and Elijah kept breathing. I slept in the bed with him that night, barely sleeping, listening to his breathing, waking to check that his chest was rising and falling.

It still was.

Morning light filtered through the curtains, and Elijah was still breathing, but his breaths had become irregular, and there would sometimes be long pauses between each breath.

His throat rattled a little with each breath, a soft groaning sound, and we called in a nurse, who cleared his airway and told us that everything was just fine.

Nothing was just fine, but she assured us Elijah wasn't in any pain.

Every now and then, he'd exhale and then not inhale for a long time. And we'd all wait for the silence, or for the next inhale. For hours, with every ounce of effort, he would somehow manage to breathe in.

With the setting sun, the room brightened, a golden light that made everything sharper and clearer for just a moment.

It made me wonder how long a moment lasted. Now and now and now. How long is now? How long does that moment last, when someone is alive, and then they are not?

Elijah took one deep inhale and then exhaled slowly and quietly.

Chapter 39

He didn't breathe back in.

He was there, and then he wasn't.

We sat in the stillness. The stillness wasn't entirely absence.

Elijah was gone.

But he was also somehow everywhere.

At some point, Mom came into the room, and helped me out of the bed, because the nurses needed to do whatever nurses need to do with a person when they die. But I didn't want to let him go, and the whole thing was horrible, watching the nurses pull and cut away the jungle of tubes that had connected him to his medicines, and food, water, air—life. Just when I thought I couldn't take another moment of it, one of the nurses came with a little tub of water and a bunch of white washcloths.

"Do you want to help wash his body?" she asked.

I wasn't sure, but I found myself nodding.

So that's what we did. When there was nothing left to do, me, Elijah's grandma, his mom, his dad, his brothers, and his cousins, all silently dipped the white washcloths into the tub of water, and cleaned his arms, his legs, his face.

That night, I didn't want to go to sleep, because I didn't want to have to experience that moment where I'd wake up and for a moment think Elijah was still alive and then have to remember he was dead and go through the shock of grief all over again.

But eventually Mom convinced me that I had to rest. She gave me a pain pill, which didn't touch the anguish or the grief, but somewhat helped with the ache in my bones.

In the middle of the night, I woke, and for a moment all I could think about was how much I wanted to text Elijah. I had to tell him something important, though I couldn't remember what. But as the room clarified, and my pain came into focus, I remembered.

I had wanted to tell him something about anguish and grief, how it was so much worse than physical pain.

I could tell Mom or Dad, but they weren't Elijah. They wouldn't get it.

I didn't want to go to the funeral. It felt like a preview to my own funeral, and I didn't want to see Elijah's Mom and Dad and brothers look all devastated.

Mom managed to convince me to go, helping me into a black dress she somehow managed to buy between those last days in the hospital and the quiet, sad days that followed, where I just lay in my bed crying, taking the maximum permitted dosage of my pain medicine.

We took a boat out to sea. Elijah's brothers sat near the bow, cradling the urn with his ashes in it. His grandma sat near the stern, quietly chanting to herself. His puffy-eyed dad held his mom's shoulders as she cried.

When the shore was far enough away to feel more like an idea than a real thing, the captain cut the engine. His grandma chanted long flowing chants that filled the boat with words I didn't understand but felt clear in my soul. Beautiful words, grieving words, words of hope and sorrow.

The brothers scattered Elijah's ashes into the sea. His mom and dad scattered flowers into the ocean. His grandma had given me a lei of flowers to wear on my head like a crown. I took it off my head and tore the flowers off it, tossing them into the ocean where Elijah's brothers had poured out his ashes. I didn't want to look. I didn't want to see Elijah dissolve into the sea, the same sea where we'd swum with the stingrays, the same sea where his ancestors' ashes had also gone.

And then, just like that, Elijah was gone, and only the flowers remained, floating on the sea. I thought about the flowers floating there for days, wilting and sinking into the water to be eaten by turtles or whales. Nothing in the world made sense.

His grandma chanted as the boat motored back to shore. A soft rain fell out of what seemed like a clear sky.

Back on dry land, before Mom and I got into our car to drive home, Elijah's mom came up to us holding a small brown box.

“Elijah wanted you to have this,” his mom said.

I didn’t need to look inside. I knew what it was.

His last manuscript.

Chapter 40

You'd think I'd start reading the manuscript right away as soon as I got home, but I just put it on the nightstand next to my bed and left it there for weeks, just staring at it.

Instead, I read a book about how scientists had taken this woman's cancer cells to use for scientific research, and for years after she'd died, her cells lived on in petri dishes and test tubes. Her malignant growth had become immortal.

In one of our last conversations, Elijah and I had talked about the difference between malignant growth and normal growth. All growth requires destruction and repair, but malignant growth just grows without accepting death, without change. It is greed in cellular form. We like to live our lives thinking that our growth can be infinite. But things in nature don't just grow. They also die. Dying makes space for other things to grow.

The living are left behind to adapt, to recover, to repair.

There were many reasons why I didn't want to read Elijah's manuscript.

For one, what was the difference between his last words and those immortal cells in a petri dish? His words were no more *him* than a sample of his malignant cells would be *him*.

I didn't want to read Elijah's manuscript because I knew it would be Elijah's last words to me after his last-last words, and I didn't want us to run out of words. Whatever conversation I could have with those words would be a static conversation—a one way dialogue.

If I didn't read the manuscript, there were still words to be had. Imagined and intuited dialogues were best.

So, I slept in my room beside his last words, and when I had energy, I sometimes went out with Mom to buy groceries or go shopping or to see a movie and found myself relieved when I came home, and his last words were there waiting for me on my bedside table.

As sad as I was, as much as I just wanted to stay in bed and cry, I knew Elijah wouldn't want to see me die before I actually died, and so I'd drag myself out of bed and sit on the lanai with Mom, or I'd go downstairs to watch some television with Dad—sometimes more *Six Feet Under* or a game, and if I had energy, Mom and I would drive somewhere in town—the farmer's market, a thrift store, a coffee shop.

Without Elijah or Gabriel, the old questions crept back in.

I sometimes flipped through the pamphlet they'd given me at palliative care.

What are my goals and priorities for my remaining time?

Is there anything important you'd like to tell your loved ones?

I didn't have answers. Sometimes, all you can do is just keep living the questions.

Little things became very big things.

I helped Dad in the garden until I physically couldn't do it. Mom helped me walk to the ocean, and I soaked my feet in the water, then my whole body. Only the ocean felt big enough to hold my pain.

I developed a limp.

They did a scan. The metastatic cancer was compressing my spinal cord.

The aches in my joints and bones made it difficult to walk.

Even so, one the palliative care doctors told me that I was doing well, *living one day at a time.*

But no one could give me a clear sense of how many of those days I had. If I had several years, I might consider returning to school and trying to do my senior year, maybe even consider thinking about colleges. If I only had a few good months left, I'd focus on the things right in front of me. Time with family, days at the beach, trips to the mall, and movies. And if I only had a few weeks, well... then, maybe I'd start reading Elijah's manuscript.

But the doctors had no clear answers.

And so, every morning I woke up, checked in with my body to see how it felt, read a little, eyed Elijah's manuscript, and then, deciding that today wasn't the day—got out of bed.

Chapter 41

I wish I could say I died stoically and heroically like Elijah did.

But I did not.

I raged against it.

The last time I went out shopping with Mom in Hilo, we got to the parking lot, and I'd hardly taken three steps before I fell to my knees, not to pray, but to vomit, my body heaving.

That fall, as school resumed without me, I often smelled of vomit.

Mom would make elaborate meals—beautiful meals—lemon-crusted salmon, brioche French toast, grilled steak pulsing and pink in the middle, delicate rice puddings—and I'd take two bites and puke them up.

Mom tried to be stoic about it all, but sometimes I could see her turn her head away from me, so I couldn't see her crying from the exhaustion and grief.

When I lost the strength to walk myself to the shower, Dad carried me there, and Mom washed me. It was embarrassing, but what choice did I have? I shut my eyes and focused on the warmth of the water on my skin.

Mom tried to fix me for as long as she could, but eventually she realized she was fighting something larger than her love for me could fix, so she hired a nurse to come help in the evenings and during the day.

Some mornings I woke up with strength and felt like I could walk my way to my own dying like Elijah had, with courage, humor, and grace. I thought about what it would mean to have a project of my own that gave my life meaning, but eventually my strength would wane, and I'd lie on the couch with the television blaring, realizing that the only project I had the strength left to do was die.

It would have to be enough.

But some days it wasn't enough.

I woke up crying, my body poisoned by its own blood, the cancer asphyxiating me with its excess of malignant cells, which, like me, just wanted to survive. Who doesn't want more? More money? More time? More life?

Sickness isolates you. It transforms you. It steals your future, and it changes how you view your past. Had I wasted my life? I had always thought there would be more time.

You tell yourself you have more time, but you're so tired, hurting, scared, and confused that it feels like there isn't much you can do with it anyway.

One day, while sitting in the palliative care office, on a particularly shitty-feeling day, made extra shitty by the fact that this was where Elijah and I had met when we were both healthier (although if you'd asked us if we felt healthy when we met we'd have both told you *no*), I turned my head to one of the magazine tables, and saw a little card with a Zen circle on it, and a picture of a bald Zen nun beside it.

It was an advertisement for a Zen sitting that took place at a little monastery by the sea. Normally, I'd ignore all the cards left by chaplains and death doulas in the palliative care office, but something drew me to that little nun with the bald head and a wry smile. I asked Mom if we could go. Without hesitation, she said *yes.*

The room was made entirely out of Koa wood, and it could have been mistaken for a ski lodge if it weren't for the resplendent golden Buddha that sat in enlightenment at the front of the room. I wasn't fooling myself. I knew I hadn't come here to receive enlightenment, or peace, or comfort, or faith. I had come here to pass the time, because grief and dying were too heavy a load to carry alone and too heavy a load to give my parents to carry for me.

The bald nun sat at the front of the room, right in front of the Buddha, and she took the same posture of the Buddha, before ringing a bell, and asking us all to take a deep breath with her.

She told us about when she had been a young woman, she'd wanted to be an artist, but somehow found herself traveling through Tibet, meditating in Zen caves.

"I spent many days in those caves, lost to time. How does one know when it is time to leave the cave?" she asked. The question was rhetorical, but she looked right at me as she asked it. "How does one know when it is time to leave the cave?"

She paused for a long time, shut her eyes, and exhaled very slowly. When she opened her eyes, she stared at me for a while, my sick body in the room a kind of silent statement that she could not avoid nor turn away from. She glanced at Mom, who sat beside me. I could tell Mom wasn't entirely comfortable in this space. She had been raised Christian, and even though she didn't go to church, she still wore a delicate cross around her neck.

The nun finally started speaking again, "This life with its host of sorrows brings us so many gifts we do not want and wouldn't think to ask for. Nevertheless, if we can take the invitation life has given us, and see the gift for what it is, we might see it as an invitation to awaken."

I found myself getting angry again. I hated when people talked about my terminal illness as a gift, or a blessing, or anything but what it was—a nightmare, and the thief of my good life.

Everything in this life wants to live. It doesn't want to die. Even people who kill themselves don't really want to die—they just want to shut off the pain of living. There's a clock in every cell in our bodies that tells the cell when it's time to die. Some cells in my body managed to shut off those clocks. And those cells that had successfully evolved to ensure their longer life had created the conditions ripe for my own dying.

The nun took a deep, long breath, inviting us to breathe with her.

"Do it with me. Breathe in deeply. Let your exhale be longer than your inhale ever was."

We sat and breathed.

Doing the thing that Elijah, in the end, couldn't.

I felt the warm tears fall slowly down my cheek.

"People ask me, *what is the way?"* she said. "What is the way? What is the way? The way is very simple. Breathe. Pay attention, be kind. This life is precious, and time is fleeting."

The meditation broke open something within me.

I went up to her afterward.

"The idea of meditating in a cave in Tibet sounds very appealing to me, but I don't think that is something I have time to do. Can you tell me a little about what you learned in the cave?"

She paused and then smiled.

"In the cave, everything is dark. And at night, when you leave the cave, everything is also dark. The outside is no different than the inside."

I nodded. Embarrassed that I had asked her anything, I turned away to leave.

"I know you can't go to Tibet, but there is a cave I can take you to—on this island. Do you want to go?"

She didn't need to ask me twice.

Mom and I met her after dark in an empty parking lot.

"By day, the cave is illuminated, and there are many people here. But at night, it is dark and quiet," she said.

She turned on a flashlight and led us down a trail.

And she was right. When we got the opening of the cave, she turned off her light, and it was so dark outside, and so dark in there, that it was impossible to tell where the dark within began, and the dark outside ended.

Inside the cave, I could meditate with my eyes open, and everything remained dark. At first, this brought on a feeling of panic, like I'd suddenly gone blind. But when I finally settled into the strangeness of my own senses failing me, I felt the silence expand around me, palpable.

My pain felt as large as the world. My awareness as big as the sky. My heart as wide as the cave.

There was no difference between inside and outside.

There is a time to leave the cave.

I meditated until I felt it.

I made my way out blindly, guided by a blue light in the distance that grew brighter the closer I got to it.

I looked up and saw nothing.

I looked up and saw nothing.

I looked up and saw the whole universe—the Milky Way, the moon, and the other stars. It was so fucking beautiful.

It had been a good day. It was a good night.

Chapter 42

But there are only so many good days. And eventually, one day, I woke to searing pain all over my body.

Mom rushed me to the hospital.

I didn't need the doctors to tell me what I already knew. The medicines weren't working.

The cancer had literally broken through my bones, sending the fragments shattering through my body like shrapnel.

They let me out of the hospital that night with a range of new medications to take to manage my pain.

Back in my bed, covered in warm blankets, I reached for Elijah's manuscript.

It was time.

I read quietly for hours, the last words he had written. Sometimes I didn't always understand what he meant. It was hard to tell if this was because the writing was just bad, or if the ideas were too complicated, or if it was the brain fog from the medicine, or because I was just so damn sad that these were his last words, and these my last thoughts.

But maybe it didn't matter if it was good or bad.

What mattered was what it had done to him—for him.

It had given him meaning and solace in an impossible time, and now it was giving me some solace and meaning in my own impossible time.

Perhaps that would have to be enough.

I don't really know how I feel about the idea of there being an omnipotent God that gives a shit about each of us in our specificity. I think if such a thing existed, the world would be a far less terrible place.

But maybe I'm wrong.

What if humans are all just like the little kid who wants to touch the burner of the stove, crying hysterically because their parent just pulled them away from the burner? What if all this stuff we call suffering is just God pulling us away from the burner of the stove, and we, in our limited view of the greater Good, just see God being mean and terrible for not giving us what we want?

Maybe when we look at suffering, all we see is the suffering, but we don't really know what we're looking at?

Maybe while we're all here, focused on trying to preserve our specificity, God is up there laughing about how stubborn we are all being.

Maybe this is what it is to be a human, stuck in my own specificity—from my limited perspective, it appears that love doesn't always win, when in fact, from a wider perspective, one beyond my understanding or comprehension, it does.

I didn't want to keep reading. I only had a few pages left, and I didn't want to read Elijah's last last words.

The nice Zen nun came to visit me.

She brought me books that she and I both knew I didn't have time to read, but I accepted them graciously, because maybe Dad would find them, and find solace in them after I was dead.

She often just sat with me. Our sitting together a kind of meditation. It didn't make the hurt hurt less, but it made me feel sometimes like the person observing the hurt was somehow distinct from the person feeling the hurt. It felt nice to be watched over by someone not invested in my living.

Sometimes I drifted in and out of sleep, my breath so slow that I couldn't tell the difference between the air everywhere and the air in my lungs, the living air that became breath and the air everywhere else that connected us to the trees, and other animals, and ocean, and earth.

Sometimes I felt a glimmer of that peace, a sense that I could touch the peace Elijah had, the peace we all always had, the peace we had all always been.

One day, she brought big sheets of paper and paintbrushes, and together we made Zen Enso, which are those big, perfect circles. My circles were always messier and more ragged than hers, but I made one she found so beautiful it made her cry, and she asked me if she could keep it.

She told me that though we didn't have much time, but she could take me through the process of becoming a lay practitioner-teacher, and by the end of our training, I could be a Zen teacher if I wanted to, which made me laugh, because I'd be dead soon, and how did a dead person make for a good Zen teacher? When I told her this, she laughed and then got very serious and said that the dead make for the best Zen teachers.

One afternoon, Mom came in to check on me while I was reading the last pages of Elijah's manuscript, the pages I didn't want to finish reading.

Mom didn't ask me what I was reading. From my swollen eyes, she knew.

"Mom," I said, taking her hand. "I wrote to Brother John not so long ago."

"Who is Brother John?"

"He's this monk who lives in a monastery. Anyway, I asked him for spiritual guidance, but one of the secretaries wrote back letting me know that Brother John was busy and spiritual guidance was for people at the monastery."

"Oh," Mom said, her face growing sad.

"I don't care, Mom. I don't want to see Brother John. I know we don't like to talk about what's going to happen when I die, but can we talk about it for a minute?"

Mom looked away and physically pulled away. Over the last few months of my decline, she had somehow been able to endure it all. I realized that she probably could endure it because it was all happening right now, and now, and now, and she had no choice but to endure it, and when we have no choice but to endure, we can endure anything.

The one thing Mom couldn't endure was the future—the prospect of me being gone.

But I realized that Mom would endure that, too, just like she had endured this. She would endure one moment of me being gone, and then the next, and then the next.

I knew that if I didn't say what needed to be said right now, it would never get said.

"I don't want you to be angry about Brother John. That church stuff doesn't work for me, but I know it works for you."

Mom opened her mouth to say something, but she stopped when she realized I wasn't finished.

"Brother John said I could come to the monastery if I wanted. But I don't want to go there. My monastery is right here, with my tea, and my Zen circles, and books, and bed. But when I die, I want you to go see Brother John."

Mom opened her mouth to protest. I knew what she was going to say. She was going to say that I wasn't going to die for a very long time, and that she had no intention of seeing Brother John any time soon.

"Promise me you'll go see Brother John."

Mom nodded. She promised. She didn't wipe the tears away as they fell down her cheek. They landed in a big puddle on my blanket. I wanted to jump into her tears and drown there.

Chapter 43

In his last conscious day on the planet, Elijah spent a long time struggling to get one good breath in. When I meditated now, I thought about that a lot, how each breath came, like it was an inevitability–how we take each breath for granted, when someday, we won't be able to breathe.

The average human takes 600 million breaths in a lifetime.

When we breathe, we do something that has been done a million times before and that, if we are lucky, we will do a million times more.

While meditating one afternoon, I realized that death was no different.

A billion people have died, and a billion more will die.

When Elijah died, he did something that had been done a billion times before and will be done a billion more.

He did what I would do soon.

If he had been able to do it, I could too.

Chapter 44

Mom carried me downstairs to watch the news. People were protesting a war happening on the other side of the world. Children were starving to death. A man had been shot in one of the protests. There had been a scuffle between the police and the protestors. And in the chaos, someone started shooting. It wasn't clear who. Maybe it was the police. Maybe it was one of the protestors. But the man didn't care who was shooting. He put his body between the shooter and the protestors and the police officers, and he got shot himself.

He died, trying to protect everyone.

The president was vilifying him for being a protester.

The protestors had made him into a martyr, carrying his image in the street as they wept.

No one seemed to be able to agree.

"Don't resist arrest, and don't get shot," one person told a reporter.

"He shouldn't have been there."

"He was a hero."

"I don't want to live in a society where radical altruism is punished by death," another said.

It was all so horrible and senseless. I asked Mom to turn off the T.V.

The nun came to my bedside for the last time. I was a mess. Crying. I didn't really want to be seen, but she was adamant.

I asked her what she made of the shooting, and she nodded.

"There is this line in the Sallekha Sutta that I like that gives me some solace. Others will cause harm. We will not cause harm. Others will kill. We will not kill. Others will take what has not been freely given. We will not take. Others will be angry. We will not be angry."

"Okay, but a kind man is dead. And there are people out there saying horrible things about him."

"In life, we have a choice. We can choose to see ourselves as separate from everything or connected to everything. It is easier to live with your own hate and malice if you see yourself as fundamentally separate from everything. But that's a very lonely way to live. That sweet, kind man died knowing that there was no difference between himself and the police and the protestors. I like to think he died knowing he was connected to everything and knowing that there was no difference between the protestors and the police, and himself. He wasn't saving someone else. He was saving himself."

"It's so hard sometimes. The pain. It hurts so much. I feel so alone in it, sometimes. It has this quality of cutting me off from everything and everyone."

"True awareness is larger than even your ability to be aware of it. We are connected to everything, even when we don't feel it. It's good that you are showing up completely to this experience. You have the medicine within you already."

"What is the medicine?"

"In Auschwitz, years after the Holocaust, they held a memorial where the names of the victims were read aloud. Among the people in the audience were the grandchildren of the survivors and the grandchildren of the S.S. officers who had committed the atrocities. The end of every story is peace. The medicine is everywhere. The medicine is compassion and forgiveness. The medicine is surrender and peace. The medicine is acceptance. The medicine is presence."

Chapter 45

But what if I didn't want to forgive? What if I didn't want peace? What if I didn't want to accept it?

I didn't want to forgive the fucked-up universe for taking Elijah away from me, and for taking me away from me. I didn't want to forgive the shooter, whoever he was.

I didn't want peace. I wanted to *live.*

Anger was an energy that moved through my body like a wildfire. It made me feel strong and protected, but in the end, it just hurt me more.

I finally opened to the last page Elijah wrote. I read it, and I cried. It wasn't anything special or important.

In the end, he was not just a writer.

And I am not just a reader.

Why would the universe go through all this trouble to create consciousness just for consciousness to end up being such a pain? Like, what's the fucking point? The utter senselessness of it all is what really gets me. It's not just the kids starving to death on the other side of the world, or the senseless shooting of a kind man.

And it's not just that, either. It's all the kids younger than me who die of cancer. What about them? What kind of loving, kind, reasonable, or good God would allow such atrocities to happen?

I realize I do not know what I am looking at. When I look at my pain and suffering, I realize that I don't really know what I'm looking at.

And yet, between the anger and between the pain, I always found myself somehow somewhere else. When Elijah had died, he had done something a billion people before him had done and had done something a billion people after him had done. But his consciousness was specifically his. When he lost the world and his body and his memories, it was his to lose—not mine and not someone else's.

His.

So that when I die, it will be my body and my memories and my world to lose.

Like how it sometimes feels when you finish a good book, half wishing it could keep going, but knowing that its perfection is contingent on the book ending somewhere. A good book knows when it's said enough. It knows when it's time to end. A good book is the product of an author who knows her gift, and knows when her gift has reached its limits, when she's said all that can be said.

If we could go on forever, what would that be?

It would be like cancer.

I put Elijah's manuscript on my bedside table, next to a little stack of Zen circles I had painted. Most of them were ragged and raw, barely even circles.

It's easy to ask what's the point of all this art in the face of our mortality, but maybe we should ask the opposite question. Would this life mean anything at all without mortality to punctuate it? And if art is a conversation, would life mean anything without the dialogue?

There's a reason why brain surgeons won't operate on tumors that could take away a person's ability to speak or to understand language. It's what makes us meaningfully human.

"It's okay to let go if you want to," Mom said one afternoon, when not even the pain medicine could settle me.

To let go. To accept it.

What would that look like?

To let it all move through me, and then to release it. So, I let myself get angry. Though I told myself that my intention was to let go, rage and anger bubbled up.

What if acceptance was just a story I was telling myself?

What if I would die with all this anger in my heart?

It wasn't just going to go away.

I was mad at God, mad at life.

But what if that was okay?

Something loosened in me.

Acceptance.

"Maybe it would help if you said goodbye?" a voice said.

And so, I did.

I said goodbye to my perfectionism and my people-pleasing. I said goodbye to overthinking and procrastination. I said goodbye to my stubbornness, my insecurity, my self-loathing.

I said goodbye to my legs, to my hands, to my eyes, to perceptions, to bias, to feelings, to fear.

Goodbye body.

Goodbye self.

I could hear a nurse's voice through the static of my mind.

"Sometimes it helps to let them know that they are dying. This can be a confusing time for them. Having a loved one there to help them understand what's happening can be helpful."

I could hear Mom's voice. Quiet, pleading.

"You're dying, Maya. But it's okay. It's okay to let go."

What was she talking about? Was this really happening to me? Right now?

I slipped away from the room and woke in the middle of a forest on fire. In front of me, there was a fawn lit aflame, dying inside the conflagration.

And I was also on fire, also dying in the same conflagration.

Our burned bodies writhed in the fire. I waited for something to come and relieve our suffering, but nothing came.

My eyes met the fawn's eyes. Without a word, we had an understanding.

What's the point of all this pointless suffering?

I opened my eyes, and Gabriel was sitting on my bed.

"What the..."

He smiled.

"Go away," I said.

"I can't," he said. "It's time for our appointment."

"Go away," I repeated.

"I can't," he repeated.

"When I needed you, where were you?"

"Here," he said, solemnly.

"No, you weren't."

“Where were you when Elijah was dying, and I was crying on his bed?”

“I was there.”

“No, you weren’t.”

He didn’t try to convince me otherwise. I told him again to go away. I didn’t stop to think why he had come to my room to see me now of all times, or why he had left my life like he did, and why he had come back. He was as beautiful as he had always been, with those big green eyes that might have scared me if they had not been so beautiful.

“You don’t give a shit about me,” I said, finally.

“That’s not true.”

“Then why did you just disappear like that?” I asked, angrily.

“I had to.”

“Why?”

“It wasn’t time for our appointment.”

“What are you talking about?”

“I had to give you a chance to live your life, Maya,” he said, his green eyes penetrating mine. My heart skipped a beat, and I found myself taking longer than I usually would to exhale.

“You’re doing it again,” I said.

“Doing what?

"Charming me," I said, trying to focus on my breathing as our eyes locked.

"You know what they say...if you love someone, let them go. And if they come back, they are truly yours?"

"But I didn't come back," I said. It wasn't like I'd had a chance to, though.

"But *I* did," he said, his emerald-green eyes pleading.

My mind spun trying to make sense of what that meant.

"Every time I see you, it's like you're trying to say goodbye to me or something," I said.

"I'm here to *help* you say goodbye," he said, taking my hand.

I pulled my hand away.

"I don't need your help, and I don't want to say goodbye."

He nodded.

I didn't want this. I wanted to run away, but there was nowhere to run to.

"I just want Elijah. I want to die. I want to live. I want the pain to go away. I want you to go away."

He nodded. He stroked my cheek, and my body felt warm and loved.

Somehow, Mom was there, and Dad was there, and they were saying all kinds of things that made no sense at all.

Mom said, "It's okay to go now, Maya. We are okay. We will be okay."

In the corner of the room, I saw Elijah, his crooked smile.

"Why don't you just get up out of the bed and leave?" he said.

And I stood up to leave but Gabriel, held me down, and Elijah ran up beside me and held me down, their hands on my chest like two thousand-pound weights, and I said, "They won't let me leave the room."

"Who is they?" Mom asked.

"Is it us? Or something else that isn't letting you leave?" Dad whispered, his voice worried and sad.

I nodded. It was both. It was neither.

And then, Gabriel turned around and unfurled his wings, which were as dark as nothingness itself, but somehow were as wide as everything—as wide as Gabriel, but also as wide as Elijah, and my living, and my dying, and my pain.

Whatever Gabriel had been, he was gone, replaced with nothing.

And for a long time before I too, was gone, absorbed by that nothing, I held on to something.

It hurt to be something rather than nothing, especially now, at the end of being something.

But I couldn't let it go, not just yet. My world. My specific world, my body, my memories. Mine.

I lay there in awe of my specificity, of the sheer improbability of my life. Not just the fact that of the millions of eggs in my mother's body, my egg had been chosen, but that among all the possible lives I could have lived—that of a kid starving in the other side of the world, or that of a man who had died trying to save the police and the protestors, or the million other kids who barely lived because they died younger than I had, or those who lived, and died old—that I had been able, for a brief while, to be me.

For 18 years, I had been me, and no one else.

And that was the essence of what Elijah had written, even though he hadn't lived to be a good enough writer to form those exact words. Of all the things he could have been or not been, he had just been him. Not a writer, nor an artist, not even my husband.

Just a kid trying to make sense of it all, to find meaning in a situation that was meaningless.

What a brief, fleeting, almost impossible gift.

Thank you for reading!

If you enjoyed this book, please consider leaving an honest review on Amazon or Goodreads.

It truly helps independent authors like me reach more readers.

www.ingramcontent.com/pod-product-compliance
Lightning Source LLC
LaVergne TN
LVHW041108080826
845145LV00007B/1728

* 9 7 8 1 7 3 5 7 8 3 2 3 9 *